Tumulus

Andrew Murray Scott was educated at Dundee High School and Dundee University. After numerous jobs he became a full-time writer in 1987. *Tumulus* is his first published novel.

Tumulus

Andrew Murray Scott

Polygon

Polygon
An imprint of Edinburgh University Press Ltd
22 George Square, Edinburgh

Typeset in Galliard
by Hewer Text Limited, Edinburgh, and
printed and bound in Great Britain by
Bell & Bain Ltd, Glasgow

A CIP record for this book is available
from the British Library.

ISBN 0 7486 6269 3 (paperback)

The Publisher acknowledges subsidy from

THE SCOTTISH ARTS COUNCIL

towards the publication of this volume.

tumulus:
'unexplained antiquities of non-Roman period'
legend on Ordnance Survey maps

'repositories of the dead . . .'
OED 2nd edn, vol. XVIII (1989), p. 667

Dedication:

To Martin, whose book this really is,
and to the friendly ghosts of Dundee.

Prehistory Section
Dundee Museums
McManus Centre
Dundee

Dear Johnathan,

Anonymous Dundee Manuscript

I received the mysterious manuscript which you sent
me earlier this week. As you say, it certainly has gone
the rounds since it was found in Council property and
I absolutely agree with your comment that it seems
well outwith my usual field of study!

Although it seems rather unlikely at the outset that
it could be utilised in our new corporate PR campaign,
I don' t wish to pre-judge it, and hope to give you
my thoughts and ideas, *pro-tempore*, as soon as I have
time to look it over.

I' ve retained the original and enclose a photocopy
for your own use.

Yours sincerely,

Stella Auld
Documentary Resources Archivist

enc

1

RESTRAINED BY tar-stained rafters, pinned with ancient bolts, the pockmarked ceiling swells and rises upon flatulent waves of smoke and wassail of a hundred dedicated and distended and altogether useless boozers. Yet there are four tenement floors above, pressing down unseen. This is the lowest stratum. Only inches below our feet, in the founds, sweet mouldering soil frets and churns.

In this coffined interior, the boozers move slowly, ponderously, as if it is time itself which weighs heavily upon structures and membranes, slurring speech and dulling many an eye. Or if not time, words; explanations, justifications, excuses, the rubric of the failed, the marginal, the forgotten. It is words that bury us, words that smother, pin us down. And yet in words, at other times, we can push upwards against the inevitable, in words, fly free, wriggle out from under.

Lester Logan knows the strategic value of words. Trapping the yellowed pub light in two swirling inches of amber, he smote the stained oak with his hogshead glass.

I remember it alright. It was a great party, quoth he.

Ancient smoky shadows lingered across his sunbrowned face, in the cobwebbed spaces under his eyes, beneath a black mass of hair. Faded light picked out the rim of the star of David medallion at the open neck of his blue rugby shirt as he waited impatiently for Alec Stewart to offer him a Woodbine.

Eh mind ut ahriyt.

3

Stewart, in the corner, our friendly Viking in faded and patched denim, reluctantly handed round the almost-empty paper packet and placed a cigarette between his own hair-obscured lips. Self-consciously he fastened thick blond wings behind his ear. His voice was a low and reflective murmur.

Up thi Blackie. Tap flair. Eh mind thir wiz a bit a bahthir . . . sumhin t' dae wi Rab. Eh canna riyt mind.

As the smoke ascended to the black rafters of the wood-panelled snug of the Hawkhill Tavern, we quaffed ale from our perspex flagons, listening wide-eyed to their swollen tales. Reader, think of them as waking dreams or a voice in your head revealing secret histories.

There is a sudden hiatus behind us as the Iron Age ends and the Middle Ages become very elderly indeed and in the same prolonged flatulent sound, like a grinding of gears or off-note from some bashed bugle, someone somewhere else invents the wheel, Woodbines and contraceptives in that order, thus initiating the 1960s here in Dundee well before the second half of 1967.

Lester never needs encouragement to burgeon into story-telling mode.

1967? He burped. Ah. I remember it very well cause I'd just hitched back from the Smoke and got dropped off at the Angus Hotel by some high-ranking brabener. I went straight to Mennies, got there just before closing time and heard about the party.

He swirled, anti-clockwise, the frothy dregs of his beer. Yeah, Rab did cause the bother. See, he put a record on the turntable but he took off the one that was playing, that belonged to the guy, the guy whose pad it was, and threw it on the deck. But this guy this guy saw what Rab did and what's more this guy didn't like Rab's record and as soon as Rab's back was turned, he pulled it off so that it was, like, ruined, and stuck his own one back on.

Well . . . Logan shrugged, fag drooping below his moustache, well . . . Rab walks across the room and grabs the guy who's still holding the record player. I never saw Rab so angry. Grabs him by the throat. Carries him out the front door. Throws him and the record player off the plettie. And it's two floors up!

4

Yeah, man, Alec quietly concurred, fingering his dirty-blond goatee beard. His slender wrist encircled by strings of beads and a leather thong, his tattooed fingers ringed with heavy metal. Thi student's mates a jumped on Rab, like, an abdee got inta a rammy.

No me, boys, grunted big Bob, stolidly scratching at his unshaven chin. Eh wisna scrappin. Eh'd a grip o' a burd in thi loabby.

Your first time – eh, Bob? said one of the barmen, leaning in to remove the overflowing ashtrays.

At first it seemed old Bob hadn't picked up the comment in the general hullabulloo of a busy Friday night. Then his saturnine face darkened, the heavy eyebrows knotted and the big baw head turned slowly sideways. Ivins, yi cheeky get! he growled. Abidee kens eh've hud loadza burds.

Logan banged down his empty pint ostentatiously. Anyway – everybody's fighting except Mick Potter. *He's* sitting crosslegged on the deck in the middle of the room chatting up this babe, dead-serious-like, gazing into each other's eyes, moon in june, the whole bit. Wearing his tasselled fez, striped kaftan and his Manfred beard of course. And guys are stotting each other off walls but somehow Potter and this chick don't even notice. Then some guy comes in with a shooter!

A coors, Alec explained, naebdee bleevd ut wiz kosher. Then ee fehyurs ut inta thi ceilin an abdee jist keechs thirsels.

Logan grinned, teeth flashing white under his droopy moustache. Plaster coming down on everyone like snow. That kind of broke the party up. Potter and his babe still mooning into each other's eyes, fighting going on all up the Blackness Road, new guys joining in who didn't have a clue what the fight was about. Two miles away in Lochee there's fights breaking out. And everybody forgot about the record-player guy.

Stewart tipped his cigarette ash. Yeah. Ehd forgot um, Lester. Wut happened ti thi boy?

Logan put his face underneath his beerglass and loudly, irritatingly, drained the nonexistent dregs of his beer. Not discovered till dawn. Broken collar bone.

5

Ah, poor bastard, someone said, insincerely.

Logan delivered the coup-de-grâce. But the record player was alright after all. He belched.

That's all right then.

Athin wiz hunky-dory.

Stewart grinned ruefully. Brah ald days, eh? Thi sixties. Eh mind, Lester, Rab wiz that seek aboot eez recird. Eh think ehm riyt in sayin, Lester, ee tokd aboot suing thi boy when ee gor oot thi horspittul.

The cheeky get.

There was a loud crack and simultaneous cheering from the bar. A chair had given way, sprawling its luckless occupant and his drink to the sawdust floor, where he lay, stupefied, laughing, legs in the air.

Probably woodworm, someone said.

The channerin worm doth chide, Logan said jovially. There was a silence then, each of us wondering if our own ricketty chair was entirely secure.

Halcyon times though, Logan enthused after a while. Those bygone days of yore when we were beat and hip. Great parties. Not like now. Hey, do you remember Si Henderson?

Coors eh mind o um.

Remember he had the accident on his motorbike . . . got artificial clips put into his legs. Logan leaned back and demonstrated with both arms. See, he could move them alright, still had the use of his feet. There was a party, some other party, yeah, down off Perth Road, Strawberrybank? Or Eden Street? Some Art College boy showing off his yoga positions. Eowh I sey cheps . . . look-at-me-do-the half-lotus . . . aren't I fab!

Na, Lester. Eh wisna there.

No? Well, Hendo arrives at the party – god knows who invited him and sees this guy trying to impress the babes. Pushes through to the front and hears the guy boastin about being double-jointed. Oh yeah? Hendo says, call that yoga? Hendo says. See what I can do. He sits down on the floor and lifts his legs around him then suddenly he heaves them right up over his shoulders and around the back of his neck rocking side to side on his hands with that big stupid grin on his face. Blew everybody's minds. One girl actually fainted and everybody else is asking him how he does it. S'nuthin. S'Easy, he says. You know Hendo. Logan glanced at Alec and Bob and each of us. Modest he aint. Course what he'd done was whip the pins off first. So when no-one's looking he clips them back on.

Ee wis the only bam, Alec said lugubriously, thit cud git legless wi nae swally.

No-one laughed. We'd heard it too many times.

Waur iz ee these days? someone asked.

Hendo's in Perth, Logan told us contemptuously. He got four months for nicking some auld wifie's zimmerframe!

It is perfectly conceivable that my life will drift in the same desultory manner for a considerable period. There is no pressure upon me for dramatic change, or no pressure that I cannot resist. Like Lester, who has gone and been and now stays, he thinks, by his own whim, I, too, stay and remain and exist and live here, cowed, complaisant, bitter, resentful, impotent, dreaming of otherwheres.

Our winters are hard and cold, this city at night like a cathedral of stars under infinity's ceiling and perhaps a grudging god looks down, his view unimpaired, on frigid northern men straggling home trailed by blue breath. It was too cold for snow and there was none of the warmth and conviviality that snow usually brings upon this city. Once home from the pub, alone, always alone (at least that's how I remember it), I sat swaddled in blankets, facing down the snowy TV screen, which, with its inanities seemed somehow warmer than the one-bar electric fire. I had given up my painting and spent the days and nights merely trying to keep warm. The window in my tiny scullery was white with impenetrable ice and I did not linger in there. Similarly, the outside toilet, out on the plettie, was an arctic zone. I peed in the sink and had to shit on to newspaper which I parcelled up and deposited outside in the bin on infrequent forays. My life had shrunk to an existence within one room and I had to put two hot water bottles in the bed before I could tunnel under the mound of blankets. A hard life is the best education. According to some sod who'd always had it cushy. I found that I was always thinking about myself yet could not concentrate. If I started to read, a few pages would set me off into reverie. I could not focus. The only thing that seemed real were these bloated stories of other places and this place at other times. I was suffocating under mounds of smothering nostalgia for events I had experienced only vicariously through these drink-summoned eulogies. Dundee in the sixties and Swinging London through the eyes of Dundonians who'd been there were more real to me then than my own actual experience – which was minimal. It was ten and more years ago. It had happened while I was still at school. It was all over and done. I'd been born too late. The great moment had passed. All I could do was live in the hazy memories of others.

. . . we were supposed to meet Ginsberg, Lester shouted above the hubbub, as I ordered the drinks at the bar. He lighted a Woodbine and inhaled deeply, then exhaled through both nostrils. This is a true story, Gerry. Old fat Allen . . . and bring him back to Peddie Street. He delicately picked a loose strand of tobacco from his upper lip beneath the heavy moustache. See, there was a collection in some of the pubs and three of us – Eug, Charlie and me – we picked the short straws. But we got steaming in Edinburgh and spent all the shekels and got to the poetry reading late.

Hey, Logan! Big Bob roared from the far side of the gantry, yiz owe uz a pint ya bam. Mine's a Nooky Broon. When yuv feenished hayvrin.

In a minute.

Ya bam, Bob roared over the heads of other boozers. 'S half-nine. 'S'near last ordirs.

Ach, Boab, eh'll get thi roond in masel, ir wull a deh o thirst.

Yiz got thi last yin, Eck.

Nae mettir.

Anyway, where was I? Lester said, unperturbed. Before the rude interruption of neanderthals. He glared over at Bob and the others.

You got to the poetry reading late . . .

Oh, yeah. We climbed the Mound and found the venue. Pushed through the bow-tie and velvet jacket brigade to the front. There's old fat Al himself. Now, Charlie and me knew loads of his stuff so we start chanting along with 'Kral Majales', which did not go down well with the organisers. Especially when that eegit Charlie produces a stinking big joint and lights it up in full view. They tried to chuck us out . . .

Eh, they must have smelled Logan's feet, said the barman over my shoulder. That right, Bob?

Lester was indignant. MY feet? Never as bad as Raj's. Raj's feet – jeez, the honk – used to cause fights. You never smelt anything so rotten! We made him put his sannies out on the windae ledge at nights and made sure the windae was closed. And sometimes we even made him sleep with his feet out the windae. Some advice, Gerry, NEVER buy him dezzie boots!

Eh, Logan's riyt, Bob nodded sagely. Thi cunt's riyt. Thi wir bowfin. Yuv nae ehdea.

Raj was a bastard to live with, Lester said vehemently. He used to take the food money and disappear for days. One time, one time he came back drunk after he'd spent the gas money. This was in our pad in Annfield Street, Gerry. We turned his pockets inside out but no – he hadn't a single bean left. He got away from us and ran into the kitchen and did this almighty Errol Flynn leap on to the table – only he slipped off and fell against the open window.

Logan's no sayed this wiz on thi third flair.

Yeah. It was. That's right. For a split second it looked like he was going to go out. But you know what happened?

But ee didnae, sneered the barman. Wut a pi'y!

No, he didn't. It was a miracle. The window-frame fell out, but Raj didn't. Now, there was a young copper standing right below. Maybe he'd heard the ruckus. He was having a sly fag when the window fell on top of him. But it didn't touch him cause it was open at the time. There he was standing in the middle of it with us all looking down. He was in shock and he didn't even take our names. Lester drained his pint. Whose round is it?

YOURS! everybody yelled at once.

Reluctantly, Lester produced two crumpled pound notes out of his jeans pocket.

The barman held them up to inspect. Hey – these look real.

But Ginsberg? Did he come to Dundee?

Na. At the reading we nearly got thrown out without even speaking to him. But Ginsberg – give him his due – persuaded them to let us stay. So, when the reading's done, we hang around and Ginsberg comes out and we all go off to some place for a drink. We're, like, acting real mad cause it's summer and it's Ginsberg's first visit to Scotland. I'm doing cartwheels and Ginsberg's chatting up Eug and trying to kiss him. Anyway, in the pub we ask him about coming to Dundee. We tell him about the squatters' commune and Peddie Street and how hundreds are waiting for him to arrive and he agrees. He actually does agree to come but somehow . . . he paused to puff his fag, and made a wry face. Ach, I don't know . . . anyway, there's this babe . . . He stabbed the smoky ambience with the red end of his poised cigarette. Wish I could remember her name, and what I did with the fag packet that had her phone number on it.

So Ginsberg never came to Dundee, somebody said.

Na, Lester said. He didn't. You'd have to ask Charlie exactly why not. Then he broke out his usual wry smile. But what we didn't know was – Peddie Street's covered in red flags, hanging out of every window, and Annfield and Peddie Streets are roped off – barricaded in. See, Gerry, there was a shop at the junction of Corso Street, that was a sort-of social centre and it used to print a community free press news-sheet. Left-wing stuff, but they'd put the word out Ginsberg was coming. So everybody is waiting for the old King of the May to arrive to start the revolution. The polis don't want to provoke a riot so they're just waiting and watching. The whole area's roped off and hundreds of young people are inside singing and chanting and carrying on. Waiting for Ginsberg. Everybody was there. But there's no Ginsberg. Only us three. I had this fluorescent-painted tophat on, Gerry, and it was glowing cause we got back about midnight. We saw the crowds when we were driving up the Hawkhill. They were expecting something.

He paused for effect and he had us alright. He looked around and winked. So. I had to do something. Something had to be done. So. I take off all my clothes except the tophat as we turn into Peddie Street, it being a warm night, and I jump out and hop on to the roof of a car – a Humber Sunbeam I think it was – and at the top of my voice give them as much of 'Howl' as I can remember . . .

I saw the best mates of my generation destroyed by madness, starving hysterical naked, dragging themselves through Dundee streets at dawn looking for a fag machine that works, dandruff-heided hipsters burning for the ancient heavenly connection to the starry dynamo in the machinery of night . . .

He would have continued but Bob jabbed him in the ribs rather sharply. Ahriyt, Logan, dinna show aff. Eh ken yuv a photographic memory . . .

I can remember almost all of it even now . . .

. . . who poverty and tatters and hollow-eyed and high sat up smoking in the supernatural darkness of cold-water flats floating across the tops of cities contemplating jazz . . .

Yeah, okay, Lester, okay.

Logan, Bob grumbled ominously, yir stertin ti get oan meh tits!

But Lester, what happened at Peddie Street?

Ah, such a blast from the tortured soul. I could read it over and over.

Yeah, but . . . Peddie Street?

Oh, there was a riot! I didn't get my clothes back until the next day and I was done for breach of the peace. I couldn't pay the fine. My father disowned me again so I had to go to Perth prison for seven days, but we did old Allen G. proud. We put Dundee on the map. There was even a paragraph in the *Courier* about it. That's why everyone knows me as Looney Lester. People I've never even met come up to me in the street, even now, years later, and congratulate me.

For months after she left, her portrait remained on the easel in the corner. I could look at it in two ways: as a picture whose subject was a girl I'd known or as an unholy relic of a failed relationship. There was the painting of her and her as a painting. The her I'd known as an artist and the her I'd known as me. Looking at it, I see that the nose is painted too flat, needs more shadow to the left. Perhaps I paint what I want to see rather that what is actually there. Except she isn't. Not any more. Not since that embarrassing party when it all came out about her and Kenneth Syme. Settled since into a teaching job in Fife. Syme was her level anyway. Him and her dad should get on just great with the tunes of Victor Delgado and his wartime memories of Silesia under the Germans.

Since the day is clear and bright, I decide to take a walk and see what remains of the city, view the new advertisements on the billboard hoardings, watch workmen digging trenches, perhaps see an interesting demolition or fire, or a fight. There's always something.

The wifies of Pole Street converse, like a Greek chorus during an interval, leaning on their elbows, their top halves visible out of windows. Uniformed in grey cardigans, wiry hair pinned in buns, cigarettes dangling from carelessly lipglossed mouths beneath grizzled almost-moustaches, conversations audible halfway down the street.

Number 20	Number 22
See Aggie dehd Seh'irday.	Waur wur yiz last niyt? Wur yi oot?
Eh, low doon door tae.	Nut, Ella, eh wizna. Jim widna let iz oot.
Wiz ir hehrt thit took ir aff.	Eh dinna ken. Eez iy swallyin.
Eh dinna ken wut nixt, Rhoda.	Trehd ti git a sub aff iz.
Ehm shair eh dinna at a, Lizzie.	Ehd tell um tae awa'n keech.
S'affy, zit no?	Eh dinna bahthir wi'um, Ira. Rex, CUMMERE!

From the corner of Lochee Road, looking back, the washing of the whole street, billowing sails of an armada, steps up the hill. The street itself is flaking, pudding-stone dropping in wind and rain, lying in small mouldering heaps on the pavements. There's one or two wooden windows and others have cornflake cardboard sellotaped across broken glass. Someone somewhere is playing Bobby Goldsboro's 'Honey'. And Honey I miss you, and

I'm being goo-o-od . . . And I sing it to myself down the road and it kills me.

The pain is so real, so acute, so much aching sensibility packed into one short mood. For what? I don't know. The sixties? Wanda? It's like when I used to spend summer days, long, long days just longing for adulthood so that I could get beyond the horizon to goodness-knows where. I just wanted to be somewhere else. These sorts of moods I spent hours trying to phrase exactly into words. Unsuccessfully. I felt that I was wasting myself. I wanted to go and meet it whatever it was. And wherever it was it wasn't here. But I snap out of it and just as well for here are girls, in tank tops, flared jeans and platform soles. Long scarves and Afghan coats. Maybe this is why I stay; the feeling that what I want to happen can even happen here.

I'm really into clothes, yeah. My jeans are tight, faded – almost white. I've improved the crotch with silver buttons and I've sewed material around the pockets, red satin patches. The flared gussets are red velvet, they bell out above my cowboy boots, which, once brown, now have the red depths of mahogany and polish up like a dream. I love the clicking sound those high cuban heels make. I wear colourful shirts, my favourite is Carnaby Street blue with multi-coloured circles and blobs on it, and a reddish waistcoat, or a leather one. I wear leather wristbands and, around my neck, ceramic beads and a steel CND logo on a chain. Okay, my hair, which is dark brown, is a bit of a mess, too straight, hangs shaggily over the back of my neck and the sides of my face like headphones – and sometimes (I hate this) an ear pops out. So I'm always playing with my hair to make sure it's covering both my ears. I guess I'm obsessed with myself. Who isn't? These are hedonistic times. I don't kid myself I'm particularly good-looking but, for the record, I'm thin and quite tall and have a sharp chin, straight nose and grey-blue eyes. Obviously, I'm not actually ugly. You don't have to believe it.

Lochee Road is busy. A convoy of green Corpy buses struggling up the hill, tired nightshift workers, staring out blankly, heading for beds in Lochee, Charleston or Menzieshill. Passive people, accepting, with a few grumbles, their hard lot. Stoics.

13

Phlegmatic. Dour. Pragmatic. Practical. Oh, Dundee, the armpit of northern Britain, where real work is done, but not by me. Where the folks greet you with Y'ahriyt? Yi workin? – two crucial questions in the same stale breath. Work being of course entirely manual until early death.

'S Gerry. Eez a pentir.
Na. Nut a hoosepentir a nartist.
Oh eh, eez on thi broo, like . . .

That's life in the great industrial cul-de-sac. The billboard for today's *Advertiser* at the newsagents: 'London Detectives in Dundee'. Hard to believe but true. Yes, real London polismen all the weary way up from London. Big news! But see the trees how big they've grown. Dudhope Park now stripped of its summer luxuriance. Young workmen from the Parks Department are lopping off branches and raking dry leaves and feeding a roaring bonfire.

Lester Logan's eight years older than me but lives with his mother in a second-floor tenement flat at the bottom of the Hilltown, just down from the Mosque. There's a panoramic view of the river from the steps. Ring the bell. *Sonnez la cloche.* The Tay, the Tay, such a glorious sight, from Dundee to Perth and back tonight.

Sluggish, slow, glassy silver but slowly silting up, exposing sandstriped, seal-studded sandbars on the wide horizon of tidal waters. Probably walk across it in places. Creepy thought! But the flow strong – irresistible – hauling alluvial soil from Newburgh swamps and washing across the deepy, reeded graves of dug-out canoes at Errol and Longforgan and Invergowrie Bay. Ten thousand years ago it was here, deeper, wider, when nomads from Eastern Europe sailed around and across it in canoes and rafts. Tacitus must have observed yawning sealherds on miles of sandbank at Tentsmuir. Agricola, his uncle, a reasonable man, patiently wintered in Fife, planning his advance, observing the cruelty of the seasons, how hands froze on the spears, how the Caledonians vanished screaming into the vast forests. But early in the year he received the orders to return to Rome and the

Romans marched away, leaving behind their victory at Mons Graupius, abandoning the fortress of legions at Carpow, withdrawing from Inchtuthill, from Bertha in the west and from Kirkbuddo.

Who is it?

Me. Gerry.

The sounds of locks and chains but when the door finally opened, Lester, to my surprise, was fully dressed.

Didn't go to bed last night. The maw must have put the snib on when she went out. Anyway come in Gerry, I've some good news. Come into the kitchen.

The kitchen smelled of the wet laundry festooned from racks supported by pulleys. Through the small window the tenement behind, in whose shadow, a thin girl with black spectacles was playing alone with her skipping rope.

Read this, he said, handing me a typed letter on thick embossed paper.

Dear Mr Logan, I read, *Thank you for your enquiry concerning your ms 'Cramp In Strange Places', I have to inform you that this ms is still in the hands of our readers. We will let you know shortly our decision. Yours faithfully, John Spalding, Director, Spalding & Dougall, Publishers.*

What do you think?

Hopeful.

Bloody hopeful! Lester enthused, running his fingers through the mass of his hair. They've had it for four months, well not far off, and they're still reading it.

I wouldn't get too excited. What about a cup of tea?

But imagine if Spalding & Dougall take it. I'll be made!

The sound of keys in the lock indicated the return of Lester's mother. She was a little shrivelled-up woman, dark, with wiry grey hair. She'd recently retired after forty years in the stour of the jutemills.

Lester, y'in thi hoose? she called from the lobby.

Moarnin, she said, entering the kitchen. Lester treated her superciliously to the point of extreme rudeness and she retaliated, he believed, by behaving ignorantly in front of his friends. If

15

Lester talked about antiques, which he did particularly to annoy her, she'd mutter filthy old rubbish, or eh like brah-new furniture mehsel. Logan, without two shillings to rub together, was a snob.

Yiz workin yit, Gerry?

No.

Ach, sumhin wull turn up fir yiz, a young laddie lik yirsel.

Lester came back in the kitchen, having put on his shabby Harris Tweed jacket over his denim shirt. Ready? We're going out, Ma.

See yiz eftir. Mind an be back fir yir tea!

The sky had clouded over as we walked down the steps and on to the Hilltown. The river was dull grey, grey like the grey of slates and weary faces. Everything in the city lacked colour and, like slow-motion yellowed flesh easing itself on unworthy bones, shuffled through the shadow of history as its hostage.

Let's go and get drunk, Lester suddenly suggested as we passed the Central Bar huddling on its shabby corner. Blootered. Snottered. Bladdered. Pissed to the eyeballs. It's all this place is bloody well fit for.

We crossed the Hilltown and turned up the hill slightly, across the rolling camber, into Dudhope Street.

Have you any money? Of course not. Silly question.

I could borrow some, he mused. There'll be someone I know in the 3J's.

We passed the modernistic facade of the Terra Nova. I felt the need to deflate his monstrous ego.

Look, Lester, I've only ten bob.

We won't need it. Trust me. Any fags?

I don't smoke. Remember.

Sorry. Forgot. We can get some on the way. He broke into a Jagger strut, capering on to the road, hands windmilling in the air. Ahm gonna tell you how it's gonna be, Rangers nil and Celtic three . . .

We turned down Constitution Road, heading for Bell Street. Past the clap clinic. Lester sang: Do wah diddy diddy diddy diddy do . . . I said there she was just awalkin down the street . . .

He stepped back on to the pavement to avoid a car and

suddenly laughed. If you're in there, he said, pointing, you can ask them to give you a big buff envelope marked X-RAY in huge black letters. True. It is. It's kind of an alibi in case anyone you know sees you come out. Or so I've been told. Not that I've been there myself. He grinned. Well, between you and me, just the once but it was only NSU. Not such a stigma now of course, nearly everyone I know's been in there at some time.

Not me, Lester, I don't fancy getting that long spike rammed up my honourable member by some white-coated sadist with an MB ChB.

Yeah, it doesn't actually hurt but it's terrifying if you look down. Least that's what I've heard. Let's change the subject. He began another of his funny walks. Fav four three two one! he mouthed. Fav-four-threetowon!

Now, I have told you I've only got ten bob and that it's got to last me till Tuesday. You did hear me say that, didn't you?

Ach, don't be a schlemiel. I'll see you right when Spalding & Dougall cough up the dosh for my book. Lester smiled wryly at some High School senior girls and smoothed the sides of his moustache with his left hand without breaking stride. We'll be alright then. After all, they've had the script for five months. Five bleeding months and still reading it. You don't mean to say that after five months it's got no chance? He stopped to look wistfully after the girls. Absolute honeys! He turned back to me. Hey, when the advance comes through we could go to Paris. Fancy it?

Well, I do, but . . .

We could visit old Sammy Beckett. He lives there.

We traversed Albert Square, stepping around the obstacle of workmen digging a hole. They were always digging up Dundee for some reason or other. Was it simply job-creation, or were they secretly burying the unemployed?

As we crossed Ward Road, Lester's hands were working as his excitement grew. Old Jack Kerouac kicked around the Montmartre bars. Did you see the Tony Hancock film? He's a terrible sculptor, goes to Paris, meets the beatniks and they think his stuff is fantabydozy. Those petite chicks dressed in black. Man, we've gotta go! When do you get your giro? We could hitch . . .

17

Friday. As usual. For the last two years, as Logan had for the last eight. I half-wanted to let go and enjoy his euphoria, but the Calvinist in me enjoyed the denial, the negation, the misery of pessimism.

Right. He snapped his fingers. Friday. That's it. Come up for me early and we'll get passports at the post office – the one-year ones. We'll get wir photties took . . .

We entered the narrow portals of the 3J's and descended the stone stairs.

That portrait, I should remove it. Sitting there malignantly. It's not bad, but maybe any picture of a pretty girl like Wanda could never be . . . I've got the hair right. Masses of dark reddish, but it's not red, more like mahogany-purple. Silky fine, warm and scented. The skin tones an even tan and that teasing scornful smile almost like ·a sneer. The head itself tilted coquettishly. Wanda. How long is it now? A year? And of course, the vaginismus which made it impossible for me to penetrate. Funny how I put up with that so long. Wonder how Syme's managing? Maybe he isn't. Maybe he's built like a corkscrew.

2

P ARIS WAS REFERRED to a few times in the next week or so, with diminishing conviction on each occasion and soon we had lapsed into our previous routine. I'd spend the mornings moping around in the flat in Pole Street, thinking about myself, wondering why I persisted in the attempt to convince myself I was an artist, the scunner of all my friends, my mother, stepfather and society at large. Sometimes I'd see Lester, Alec, big Bob and the others. Our crowd was a hundred or several hundred friends or friends of friends or people whose faces were familiar from a dozen pubs. Most I knew by nicknames and some not even by that. It was a constantly expanding and more or less nocturnal demi-monde of party people, ex-flatmates, fellow artists, would-be writers, musicians, their friends, acquaintances and hangers-on. It included what you could call Dundee's actual bohemians but also young professionals, workers, apprentices, dole dossers, and the politically active.

I spent some of my dead time working on an eight-foot mural on a piece of red silk I'd found in a charity shop. It covered the entire wall of my 'boudoir', the curtained and mirrored alcove in the living room where I had my double mattress. Actually, it wasn't real silk, more a kind of Terylene and it was dominated by a vast silvery domed skull with psychedelic images rushing out of its vacant eye sockets and, in the background, what I intended as symbolic images of capitalism rotten to the core, such as wads of burning money, nuclear explosions, military hardware and mounds of skulls. It was pretty dramatic and some people refused to open the curtains and look into the alcove. Big Bob said he believed that he was followed around the room by 'thi ehs'. I worked on 'Psychomutant – Product of the Holocaust' only when I was in a deep Hendrix mood with the volume up high and bold as love. Then I could journey to far distant galaxies with Hawkwind, full volume. And I could only do that when all the neighbours were out at work, or were over on the dark side of the moon.

Jim Carroll says Liz Valentine's heading out to California next week, Lester said, one afternoon. That's another place we gotta see. Fantastic. Imagine it, San Fran, Haight Ashbury, Golden Gate, Fisherman's Wharf. No, honestly, he countered, perplexed by my contemptuous snort, with a hundred quid each we'd do it easy. Greyhound bus tickets, Kerouac-style, like Dean Moriarty, or hitch part of the way. Get wir kicks on route 66. We could get jobs and save and do it next summer.

But Lester, keen to live in dreams, and the concept of a hundred quid, existed in different universes, the latter where they'd never even heard of Dundee.

Money, schmoney? Why does everything come down to money? Okay, Gerry, we'll definitely get to San Fran and Paris too, when I hear from Spalding's. I know – we could apply for a clothing grant. They give you a fair whack.

Lester, the maximum's sixteen quid and no-one ever gets that much. Takes weeks anyway.

Must be some way to raise the shekels. His eyes gleamed. I could sell my typewriter. He clapped his forehead. *Mea culpa* – it's still in Hugh Dickson's.

What? The pawnshop in the Hilltown? Bloody hell! I gave you a fiver last week to get it out of there, you bastard!

He made a wry face and shrugged his shoulders, arms out-stretched, palms uppermost. Had to, man – like, what gives? You'll get your pearl diver when Spalding & Dougall's cough up what they owe me. Hey, let's breeze around the bookshops before they close.

He could always get the better of me that way. Paris and San Fran were carried with us like enormous, gaily-coloured dream balloons up Reform Street, which, sepia-tinged like a postcard, was stuck in an unchangingly monochromatic tenure of a more prosperous century. Into the 3J's and downstairs to the stone-flagged basement for coffee and more optimistic patter. Hardly anybody in. Rab Stewart, looking like a Leon Trotsky he'd barely heard of, Stewart Mouncey, Billy Bennett, Alec Robinson with some new blonde schoolgirl in tow. All skint. When we came out, drizzle had started out of the overcast grey sky. Seagulls carried on a war with dingy, oil-stained pigeons for scraps from bins in sidestreets. Some of them were bigger than the bairns of Beechie. I felt dizzy and nervous. I hadn't eaten for hours. I felt I was on the verge of something different, something new and exciting. And all it was, of course, was regurgitation of the past, and not even my past, a kind of essence of the past that owed nothing specific to any particular epoch or historical period. We were slowly eating ourselves, here in our own declining city because there was nothing else substantial to feed on. Weaving dreams out of an impossible future and an impossibly distant past, in a place where little remained to show us what we had been. The city fathers had wilfully destroyed all traces of the energetic and enterprising grandparents to cover their own sloth and their kids were scrawling over what was left with shimmy pens.

Sorry Shug, Lester was saying to a big bearded guy in a brown leather jacket. We're skint ourselves till giro day. Soon he was telling him about the idea of going to California.

That's cool. You guys uv, like, really got it together. We're still gigging at the weekends wi the band.

Toadface something?

Yeah, Toadface McGurkie.

Folk rock, I explained for Lester's benefit. Electric, like the JSD Band.

Not a lot a dosh in it, Shug said. Fun though. Loadz a chicks.

Shug's been paid off at Dayco Rubber, Lester told me as we walked on. Funny place to work. People always getting the wrong idea that you're a rubber johnny-maker.

Only you would, I said. Everyone else's normal. Last time I saw Shug he was on strike.

That's right. The yanks that own the place came over and sacked everyone. Masters of negotiation. I told you about the demo at the American Embassy, in Grosvenor Square, didn't I? The time I nearly got arrested?

Lester, you've told me at least a million times!

We went into Frank Russell's basement bookshop in the Nethergate. But soon this depressed him; all the glossy new paperbacks, published new authors, some even younger than him. Even the reminder of Spalding & Dougall's prolonged consideration of his manuscript couldn't lift him.

Ach, so much crap. Publishers don't know their arses from their kneecaps these days.

But as usual he became absorbed in the books nevertheless. Gerry, here's the new Saul Bellow novel. Now *this* is an author! Nearly as good as me! He's coming to Dundee next month, to do a reading at the Univoisity. You must remind me. Yeah? Promise?

He continued to rave in like manner until we had negotiated the heaps of packaged books, climbed the steep spiral stairs and emerged into the open air. He'd forgotten to nick anything.

Bastards! I wanted to get Mordechai Richler's *Duddy Kravitz*. I wore this jacket specially. It has a large inside pocket just the right size. You should have reminded me. Ach, ye tongue-tied sons of bastard's ghosts! At least that if no more . . .

Out of the corner of my eye I saw a bent-over and slow-moving elderly couple stop to give us reproving looks and tut-tut as we crossed the road. Sheer jealousy. Just because they'd almost no hair!

I caught up with him. If you're going to shoplift, Lester, it's up to you. Don't involve me.

Ach, knowing my luck I'd probably have been nabbed anyway.

My mother, stepfather and older brother live in Craigiebank, a well laid-out scheme which climbs the hill in the winter sunshine away from the cranes, the scaffolding, arc-lights and the busy clang of hammers of the Robb Caledon shipyards. The houses all have the same colour of doors and window-frames and stand in symmetrical lines. Each tenant pays the same rent from the day they move in to the day they are moved out in a box, yet Strips of Craigie Road is near the private houses of West Ferry and the affluence seems to be oozing westwards. Each tiny rectangle of garden behind each savagely tailored hedge proclaims its privacy. Behind these hedges sentry sunflowers and rosebushes vie with those of their neighbours for a place in the sun. The geraniums in windows are temporarily obscured at election time by election posters, dayglo yellow, of the sitting Member of Parliament. We're no Labour, the houses seem to say. Labour is for poor Cooncil tenants wha dinna ken better but uz wi gairdins in this nice area, wuv heh aspirations, ken.

Our house, number 2, Strips of Craigie Road, brand-new since the pre-fabs, has recently been converted, as a consequence of the area being declared a smokeless zone, to all-electric. Workmen tore out the mahogany fireplace, the old-fashioned grate, into which as a teenager I'd stared for hours at glowing coals. In its place they clipped a cheap-looking wooden surround, actually some kind of plastic-wood, with a tin-alloy electric heater of three kilowatt bars. Yet the sofa and the armchairs still face this monstrosity rather than the real ruler of family life, the TV.

So I switched on the telly and sprawled on the sofa and watched cartoons while my mother in the kitchen made the evening meal. My stepfather, Ronald Bennet, a time-and-motion inspector at the NCR plant, had not yet arrived home. My brother Phil, who's two years older than me won't be home till 7pm. Thursday is the late night at Brown's Department Store in the High Street. Phil's done well with no O-grades to get the job and keep it. He's been a suit salesman in Menswear for six years and he actually enjoys it. He's the wild, reckless type, is Phil. Only joking. He's good-natured, obliging, effortlessly optimistic. My mother is fiercely proud of Phil. He's her boy. Sits in every night. Rarely goes out and only then on works' nights out. Doesn't mind spending his life in front of TV or reading comics. I'm glad he's happy.

Bennet (can never think of him as Ronald) arrives. I see his green Vauxhall Viva pulling up opposite the window. Mother comes bustling in just as the pips start for BBC's six o'clock *News*.

Get your feet off of the sofa! Tea's nearly ready.

My mother the automaton bustles back into the world of steam and the sound of bubbling potatoes.

Oh, so you're here? Bennet said sourly, slinging his piece-bag on to a chair. He was nearly always ill-tempered when he came home from work, now the honeymoon period was over. It's lasted for almost a year. Bennet first started to get his boots under the table with my mother about four years ago, two years after dad died in an industrial accident.

Hard day of work was it? he asked sarcastically.

I didn't reply. I avoid antagonising him until he's had his tea. It just upsets my mother.

She came in just then, carrying a fold-up formica-topped coffee table which was placed in front of the sofa, then she set three places with knives, forks and a tomato-sauce bottle. Then three plates of mince, potatoes and peas. It was like the TV was so crucially important we couldn't bear to drag ourselves away from it to eat on a proper table. My dad would never have allowed it. Bennet shook the ketchup, bending low over his plate, shook it, and splodged the red goo on to his mince, then, lifting his plate, began shovelling it down using his fork. His eyes never left the TV screen. Mum brought in three mugs of tea and soon we were all gawping and eating, eating and gawping at the predictions of doom for the NHS.

Nothing new, grunted Bennet, sopping his mince with bread.

Is that electric fire working alright, Gerry? mum asked.

Yes, it's fine, I lied, having sold it weeks before.

Remember we only loaned it to you. We might need it back sometime.

Yes, mum, I know.

It's really quite a good one. I was lucky to get it.

Get what? Bennet asked, looking up and blinking bemusedly.

That electric fire dear, I lent to Gerry.

Oh, that, Bennet said, losing interest and making slight, sucking noises with his teeth. What did you want to give him that for? He doesn't need electric heaters. He needs a job. Probably sell it anyway.

24

Mother dropped the subject. Busy today, was it? she asked her husband.

Aye, always is.

Are you eating properly again?

What?

Are you having proper meals?

Of course. I'd tried vegetarianism a few years back and she was never going to let me forget it. It was all down to a girl called Susan I'd had a brief, almost nonexistent thing with. I hadn't seen her since.

The political correspondent was considering the chances of a February General Election and pictures of Wilson and Thatcher the party leaders loomed on to the screen. Bennet was grumbling.

Should have Margo up there! They're talking about bloody England again. No use telling us the Tories are going to win, they haven't a ghost of a chance here in Scotland. Aw, get on with it, ya eegit! He'd found the ideal scapegoat for his accumulated frustrations in the bespectacled, scrawny figure of Richard Fairfax, who was obsequiously interviewing Margaret Thatcher – Bennet's actual and only bête noire.

Bennet is a nationalist, though purely on grounds of economics. It's his only sally towards any sort of idealism but he detests 'erty fowk' and for me life without Art is merely an existence. Just as work that's not of the mind, that's not creative, is mere exercise.

I sipped my tea, absurdly sweet. My mother keeps forgetting I gave up sugar years ago. No point in reminding her. She believes tea is sugar with hot milk plus teabag dangled briefly in it. I'm already wondering how soon I can leave. The ghastly Clarence Dean, all teeth and insincerity in a spangly blazer is introducing, in prepackaged blare, the *Opportunity Game* and his hostess with the mostest, Sylvia, legs, arse and bosoms – ample of each – for the nation's males to salivate over. Dean introduced, with knowing sidelong glances and back-of-hand innuendo, the ten-year-old twins, Trudy and Judy, in pink velvet, who raced tunelessly through some god-awful rubbish before taking their awkward bows amid thunderous taped handclapping and whistling as the scoremeter rocketed them into the eighties.

And now . . . will Trudy and Judy still be in the lead after tonight's other acts? And remember if you the viewers want to vote . . .

Is there *nothing* on the other channel?

The *Two-Billion Dollar Man*, said mum, peering at the evening newspaper, already folded down with the TV guide outwards.

American rubbish! Bennet snorted, roused briefly from sleep. Sunk in an attitude of abject torpor in his armchair. But we can rebuild him.

Oh, there's Phil now, mother said, jumping up to open the doors for her boy. Not that I'm jealous. Phil often has trouble with locks. Mother is already fussing over him in the hall.

I'll get your tea. Your brother's here. Fussing over him and arranging his priorities, like she probably will all his life.

Hallo Gerry, Phil says, coming in and leaving the door open. The thick green kipper tie was hanging out over the wide lapels of his chocolate-brown polyester suit and there was a stain on his orange shirt collar.

Shut the door, Phil, there's a lad, Bennet ventured without turning round. Bennet was winding down for the evening. Usually he fell asleep early and went off to bed during a period of wakefulness about nine.

Neither smoked but here now I saw for the first time nicotine stains on old Phil's fingers. Puzzling. Maybe he has a secret life after all? I must say I find his eating habits interesting, if rather loathsome. He sullenly chews each large mouthful for ages, his eyes staring at some point on the wall as if he forgets that he's to swallow it. His moustache is still immature, little more than a heavy shadow on his thick upper lip. Not that I need to shave every day either. But this weak mouser elongated rythmically as he ate, while his red irritated-looking neck strained at his shirt-collar. Even food like mince and mashed tatties seemed to need to be ground under his molars for an interminable time. He eats very slowly. I'm sorry to say it's really the only time he looks capable of sustained deep thought.

What're you lookin at? he suddenly asked, mouth open, in mid-grind.

Nothing. Just thinking.

Thinking about what?

Just a painting. Uh-oh. That word wakes demons in Strips of Craigie. Here it comes.

Huh, Bennet grunted. The starvin artist.

About time you got a job, Phil said, dutifully repeating his stepfather word-for-word.

There was a good job you could try for, mother said. I've got the paper somewhere. She began looking under the sofa and in the sofa and around the sofa.

I've always said you could get a start at the Cash, Bennet said. In the lab. A good clean office job. But that's not good enough for you. You want to be knocking about with those art student tarts. They've got the money for it but you haven't. He had been embarrassed when Wanda had come to the house, hadn't understood what she was talking about. I had planned never again to bring a girl back here. If I had a girl that is.

. . . living off other people's money, Bennet said, ending a sentence I hadn't heard. It was the best way, just keep silent and switch off.

Phil laid his plate on top of the others and a splodge of tomato sauce oozed between them onto the carpet. I kept my eyes fixed on it, watching its surfaces reflect the TV's blue light. There had been a murder in Glasgow on the news all week. An ordinary man had killed his wife, cut her up and packaged her up in the stair cupboard. One drop of blood had given the game away.

Are you listening, Gerry? my mother was saying, lifting the plates and treading on the bloodstain with her fluffy carpet slippers, or 'baffies' as they're called around here. It's nice as a hobby of course, but you can't make a living out of it. I've been telling you that since you were at the school.

Phil was steadily masticating his way through peaches and semolina, both of which had come out of tins. One of the packages had contained his wife's head, her legs were found in a ditch and her arms in the Clyde. The advert with the sycophantic Englishman saying . . . but your beer *is* good! came on. A blob of semolina remained on Phil's chin and probably will all night. He bounced to his feet and thundered up the stairs. I heard him clump across the linoleum of his bedroom floor, floorboards creaking, then silence as he plunged down on to his bed.

In a lull between bouts, I went up to the toilet. From the upstairs lobby at the top of the stairs, I looked out at next door's garden, nondescript grass and the remains of a broken TV on the gravel path. I suppose I was thinking about Margaret. She lives in Aberdeen now, married an oil worker. I grew up with her and never did have sex with her, although she let me feel her breasts once. She had become quite a stunner, last time I saw her. Used to wear white thigh-length pvc boots with four-inch heels.

Back in the living room, I announced my departure.

Cheerio, Bennet said, without turning around.

Okay, Gerry, now mind about that fire. When will we see you?

Don't know, I'll phone.

It's one of those bitter cold north-east of Scotland winter nights with a raging torrent of billions upon billions of stars glittering like diamante black velvet. Made me want to walk and walk underneath it. I was feeling hopeful again and romantic. Until I heard the shouting of a knot of youths a few hundred yards along the deserted Arbroath Road. With the Cemetery wall on one side and no houses near, I had no option but to keep going. I lost my courage though and just before they would have spotted me, if they'd not been so keen on pushing and shoving at each other, I climbed up on to the wall and got over the railings and jumped into the breathing, misty, moist graveyard, the damp, mushy soil muffling my footsteps. I walked in a little into the mumbling darkness. With the moon almost full, I could see where I was going, I could even see the frost on the grass and feel it falling stunned and frozen out of the air. The fresh clean smell of earth was all around me. I stood behind a big stone and peed, watching the steam rise, inhaling the strong goatish urine-smell, leaning my forehead on to the rough granite, enjoying the soft cool dampness there. I heard the youths pass by. They hadn't seen me. There were seven of them, probably younger than me, but tougher, rough from regular manual work. Coming back from the TA Centre at Rodd Road. Spoiling for a fight against whoever, whenever and wherever; common gallowglasses, the muck and scum of all armies, hired killers for pay, for the flag, boys, these dross of maleness the backbone of empire, were what I was probably meant to have turned out like. Bennet would have been proud of each of them. Worked like cumberlachs to earn a handful of coins to piss against a wall four nights a week. Where was the honour in that?

3

THESE PICARESQUE but not-quite apocryphal tales of not-quite-so auld Dundee. In a dingy two-room flat where the wallpaper shudders off the walls and the sticky brown carpet is deep in detritus which it clasps to its own in the manner peculiar to cheap polypropylene. The scullery, yellow-painted, smells of chip-oil. The black iron legs of the cooker, visible because the kitchen door has been removed, are coated with living yellow grease. The smell of incense almost masks the mustiness of a living room shaded in deep purple since strong sunlight fails to penetrate the thick velveteen curtains. Six of us lounged deep in bean bags on the floor around a low wooden table in the centre of which flared the thin blue smokelines of a joss-stick, caught in a stray beam of light, leaning sideways in its brass holder. Six of us, killing time, watching our lives go by, waiting for the pubs to open.

Coke's no been riyt since thi days o Peddie Street, Alec Swan mused, fingering his sharp beard. Swallied 42 acid tabs during a polis raid. Leastwez, that's wut eh heard.

I heard that, agreed Jim Carroll, tearing off the flap of a fag packet to use as a roach, but he was never right as far back as I can remember . . .

. . . which is at least ten minutes . . .

. . . which is at least ten minutes. Funny how your brain loses the detail.

Jim finished rolling and lit the joint, inhaling harshly. He passed it on and there was silence for a moment or two.

Alec sucked the smoke deep into his lungs and held it.

Brah dope, he croaked.

Eh, Paki black. Thi best, said Billy.

Na, man. Thai sticks are unbeatable.

Gold Leb is mellower.

Na, yiz canna beat thi Paki black, man, Alec insisted. Huz embdee trehd opium?

Ehd a blast o ut in thi Smoke.

Smoked it?

Eh, in a wattir pipe, man, ken, a bong. Wiz riyt brah an a.

We inhaled in turn, red injun ceremony, Alec, Jim, big Bob, wee Billy Forbes, Shake and me. My knees were up on a level with my head and one dezzie boot was planted firmly in the middle of the Bardot sex-kitten poster. You know the one. Masses of blonde hair and naked shoulders garlanded with flowers. Six feet by five, this poster, scrawled-over with girls' phone numbers and obscene and fascinating graffiti, covers half of the wall behind the bed. My neck chains slid around the open neck of my denim shirt with a fine tinkling sibillance as I reached over my forearm to pass on the smoke. Somewhere from beyond Pere Lachaise, in the scented halfdark of his mausoleum, Jim Morrison lost vocal control amidst the spiral of Manzarek's electric organ. Music. Is his. Only friend.

The silky words of conversation drifted slowly in the laden air.

Now he only gets oot at thi weekend.

Makes the most o it, mind. Drinks a his money in Mennies, then goes for a curry which ee canna pay fir. Ends up being taken home to the bin beh thi polis. Ee's barred fae every curry-hoose in thi toon.

Hey, yiz bogartin bastard – z meh shottie! Gies ut!

Alright, stay cool, man.

Poor Coke. I first kent him when he shared a squat with Phinny in Peddie Street. Hey – mind the time Phinny got took out on a stretcher? Thrombosis. Talk about sufferin fur yir art!

I don't remember hearin about that, I said.

Na? See, Phinny was that daft about playing eez guitar. Night and day. Never came out except at night to go to the chipper.

That's how he's a pasty-faced gowk, is it?

Mind he had that sign on his door: 'Nae Tits, Bams, Houlets or Arseholes. Genius at Work'.

31

Still does.

Ee bides i thi Cleggie noo.

Eh. He was in that band that near made it – wut wur they crehd? Crimson something. Na. King Crimson. Yeah. Phinny played bass in King Crimson. He done the Hamburg bit too in the early sixties. Kent the Beatles.

I'd no idea he waş that famous.

Oh, eh. Chucked it in for thi classical, said Billy, with a grin. Ee micht duneh noo ee wiz ever inta rock an roll. But eh ken better. Crehs it monkey music noo. Eez riyt inta eez concerto orangutan . . . orange ears . . . wutever its crehd, ken. If yuv heard um yull ken hoo brah ee iz. 'Z how ee got thi thrombosis. See, pressure o eez guitar on eez theh caused a blood clot. Leastwez that's wut eh heard.

And big Bob had to have the last word. Ach ee refuses to gie concerts. Hides awa in his room, jist goin bald. Eez a recluse. A genius, but a recluse.

I drew deep and held the smoke inside and felt the tingling buzz in my brain as my eyelids crumpled. It was strong. The words of the others intercepted each other pleasantly in the fragrant mellow semi-dark.

I heard he gives guitar lessons.

Bob begged to differ. No seriously. No as a business. Eez no oarganezd. Ach, ee'll never mak it here, no in Dundee. Naebdee maks it here. Ee should uv stopped doon in London.

He's got some great Merch stories though.

Phinny was in the Merch?

Oh, eh. Been around the world dozens of times, has Phinny. Been everywhere.

Hard to believe he's goin wi that High School babe. The ane with the lang rid hair.

Rachel she's crehd.

Rachel? Billy gaped. Eh dinna bleev ut, lads.

Her folks are loaded an all.

Anybody *seen* Rachel recently?

Still in London. Studying acting.

Eh'd love ti git a hud o ur. Billy rubbed his hands. Ehm riyt inta thi shaggin, boys, cause meh lassies left uz. 'Z been moren a week since ehd a lassie in thi sack. Ehm feart o lossin meh touch, boys, ken wut eh mean?

Better see Phinny then – find out how!

Yir huvn uz on! She's no goin wi Phinny?

Aw, no now, ya dope!

Ach, loads a guys huv been oot wi Rachel, Bob said. Mind, Lester Logan wiz thi first thit eh ken.

Eh, then Eddie Lambert went oot w'ur.

That lazy bastard! You been in his pad in Pole Street? I swear its ninety-five degrees in both rooms. He has the cooker full on with its door open – the meter's turned round of course – and there's tropical, like, banana plants all round the place. In the winter his pad is the only one with no snow on the slates.

That's true. Yeah, I've seen him come out of there with three sweaters on under a full-length black greatcoat and those woollen gloves he wears, and leave all the heat on while he goes off for a weekend at Rachel's.

Mind that time the Gas Board inspectors turned up in Pole Street?

Oh, eh. Eh bliddy mind o it, ahriyt, Billy said. Cause oor meter wiz bliddy turnt roond an a, ken. Eh wiz bathird thi wir daen Black Street nixt and boys eh dinna mind telln yiz, eh wiz bliddy keechin mehsel.

No wonder I mean, Jim said. Everybody in the street was using gas like millionaires and all the meters were fiddled. If some people had used a little more restraint, everybody would have got away with it.

Awa an pish yirsel! Bob grunted. Daft cunt.

They had the ladders up against the walls. Lookin for a gas leak.

An that Stephen Walsh was shitting himself an a. Cause it was his name on the rent book. He fuckin ran a the way doon to Rab's . . .

. . . that's about a mile . . .

Just to get a monkey wrench. Ran a the way back and elbowed his way past the inspectors standing around the van. Didn't say nothin. Got up those stairs, kicked in the door, barricaded it with a sack o lead pipin he'd been rippin aff derries an wis taakin tae the

Kelbie's and got the meter turned round in the time it took the
Gas Board nazi to climb the ladder and lever up the window and
take a look inside. The whole thing was a miracle. He got away
with it cause the meter must have been so far forward, ken, that it
had run backward to just about its previous level. So the Gas
Board couldn't prove a fuckin thing. Stephen blamed the broken
meter seals on the tenant that wis there afore.

Rab's wrench came in handy a few times.

Billy showed his awful yellow teeth in a grin. He could have
hired it oot, man.

Remember that party at Rab's folks' place in Windsor Street?

No me, boys. Yiz fergit ehm only seevinteen, Billy grinned,
patting his straggly blond hair. Short, skinny and undernour-
ished, Billy was an orphan, who'd escaped his foster-parents and
the orphanage to live in a squat at the age of twelve. He barely
knew the meaning of school. He was kind of our mascot and
everybody liked him because he was always cheery. Girls liked
him most of all. Mothered him until he fucked them.

Rab's parents left him in charge for a week while they went off
to Butlins at Ayr.

Some party. Parents must have been daft to leave him.

Eh, the place was wrecked. Party lasted a week.

Na. More than a week. It was still going when his folks came back.

Yeah, but Rab wisna there, man. He beat it the day afore cause
of the grandfather clock. Mind o the grandfather clock?

I mind he done a bunk with Scott Walker on a boat.

Eh, see, Scott was in the Merch and they were a man short on a
trip, so he got Rab on even though he'd no papers. But Rab was seek
a the way to Cadiz and didna – couldna – do a stroke of work. But
Scott'd bullshitted him on to the boat ken, put his own reputation
on the line – so he got a right kicking for it by these Puerto Ricans.
A hell of a rammy. So Rab takes the hint. Jumps ship at Cadiz and
hitches tae Madrid. Starvin and livin off rotten fruit from the gutters.
Gives himself up to the Embassy and gets shipped home.

In some comfort, I heard.

Eh. Meanwhile . . . Scott's interrogated by the *Guardia
Civiles* for hours on end. Gave him a hard time.

I wondered why Scott hates Rab's guts.

Ach, Rab is an erse, admit it.

Great party though. Loadz a babes. Seemingly there was this valuable antique Grandather Clock at the top of the stairs. Family heirloom. God knows how it got up there. Anyway some buggers started using it as a sledge down the stairs. Someone else – and it wisna me, honest – cut a painting, an S.J. Peploe, believe it or not, right out of the frame, right while everybody was there – and flogged it to some dealers in London for a hundred quid.

That wiz Piggy. Craig Trotter. Nothin's safe with him around.

Eh, but Piggy got riyt sortit, eh heard, Billy said, grinning. Mind eez eh on thi mooch? Lads, seemingly Piggy wiz steyin doon in Chelsea last year, man, wi some boys thit wir ehwez snortin thi charlie, ken. But ee got riyt up thir noses . . .

Ho, that's a good one, Billy. No pun intended?

Billy rubbed an eye and blinked rapidly. Wut? Oh eh. Eh git ya. Eh. Well, wut eh heard ee wiz ehwez moochin, see. Hud ti huv it. Jist cudna lave it alane or that. But thi boys fixed um. See they hud a pairty. This is riyt brah charlie, man, sais ane o thum. Eh, it's pure fab, sais thi ither ane, huddin up a sheet a broon pipper. Ee winks ti thi ither boay. Ehm awa ti huv mehsel a wee snort. Piggy jist cudna hud hissel back, ken wut eh mean? Dehves riyt in an snorts the lot in a oner. Billy's grin widened. But abdees pishin thirsels, man, cause it's fucking Harpic. Harpic, man! Blasted his nostrils tae buggiry, man. Hud tae get took t'thi horspittul.

Harpic's a bleaching agent, y'see. Corrodes flesh.

Ooyah bugger!

Serve him right, the daft cunt.

Billy's enthusiasm increased. He rubbed his hands together in mirth. Lads, did yiz no hear a thi time yiz musta heard o the time – Piggy wiz in America? Yiz didna? Seems he got in wi an affy wealthy wumman, ken. A real cracker an a, eh heard. Eftir they'd been going oot fir a few weeks, she waants um ti meet ur folks . . .

Jeez, naw, poor bastards.

. . . but ee's got some . . . some business t' dae so ee goes – eh'll meet yiz at yir folks' place, honey. A long time passes. Ee's awfy late. They're a sittin there. Ee's no exactly Mr Popular afore they even meet um. But the door opens and in comes Piggy. On eez hands an knees, ken. Yeah. Crawls inta thi room wi thon glaikit grin on eez pus. Crawls riyt across thi room in front o them a . . . owir tae eez fiancee's mother, ken . . . and shoves eez heid riyt up ur fuckin skirt!

Na? Really man?

Daft bastard. Hey, who's rollin?

Eh. Skin iz anither wee number, man.

Ahriyt, gies yir Rizlas.

Yes, Piggy is weird, Jim said. His philosophy is simple. He believes if you go up to one hundred women and ask for a shag, ninety-nine will slap your face but always one will say okay you talked me into it.

No wonder his pus is so scarred. A they beltins.

Eh aince heard um, Bob – this is no leh – go up tae a lassie and say: Fancy catchin a dose a herpes thi niyt? God's truth.

Yeah, that sounds like Piggy!

There were muffled sounds from the hallway and in walked a lanky long-haired guy I didn't know with legs like matchsticks in pink loons. He was angular and bony all over, but his weak chin reverberated above his teeshirt into a sequence of smaller chins. Mostly what you noticed about him were his hands, limp and ineffectual flippers, and his myopic eyes, blinking frequently as if he was always on the verge of an attack of nerves. But walked is wrong, he sort of bounced when he moved, or vibrated vertically as if he had springs in his sannies.

Hi, Dangerous, what's cookin? Jim said.

He stood above us, wobbling. That's like, uncool, man, yeah? Un-c-o-o-l.

What is?

He was in the grip of barely-suppressed rage. Like, man, uncool, he repeated, flipping his hands upwards nervously.

I was, like, coming up here, man, up to your pad, man, and I was crossing the road, man, like, just at the . . . like, the traffic lights and I was . . . like . . . just waiting, man . . . the lights to change, yenaw. They were red man, lights were red . . . and this woman, like, this old lady, man, seevn'ay if she's a day, man, like, know what I mean, she, man, like, yeah, just starts, like, man, yeah, starts . . . hitting us, man, you know, hey, like, man, I was doin nothin man like nothin but she, man, she was just hittin us man with this . . . like bloody big umbarella man, all over meh bonce like, man, yeah, know what I mean? For nothin man, I swear and, like, that's uncool, man, like. That is uncool. Yeah?

It is. Have a toke, Danj.

He looked sideways at it and his hands came up. Like yeah, riyt on, man. Yeah, like, eh'll huv a wee toke, man, yeah. Cool.

Later I asked Jim, why's he called Dangerous? What's his real name?

Jim frowned. No idea. He's just Dangerous – always has been. Still is.

Like something out of the Furry Freak Brothers.

Maybe it's cause he drives peaceful little old ladies into extreme violence for no reason. Put that guy into a quiet pub and he'll end up getting barred and everybody'll be at each other's throats before the night's out.

Anybody fancy a cup of tea?

Christ, man, I could do with a real drink.

It's only four o'clock.

So. Prohibition's been repealed yiz ken.

Well, there's *nane!*

During the lull in the conversation we heard the sounds of schoolkids coming along the street below. Alec and Jim drew the curtains and let the strong sunlight dazzle us and set a million dust motes dancing in the thick smoky air. The joss-sticks flared and spluttered.

Time for the schoolies, boys. Whoah! Here they come.

Nice babes!

I couldn't be bothered climbing up to look. I felt heavy and relaxed, some of my muscles were asleep. I was glad to be out of school, away, and grown up, even if my life wasn't exactly racing ahead in high gear. I knew that much. *Steppin out of school across the graveyard gates an educated fool . . .* The sound of a tinny mandolin vibrato in my ear. Gallagher & Lyle.

Yur a riyt babysnatcher!

37

Na, no me Billy protested – look they twa are almost sixteen. If thir ald enough ti bleed, man . . . he grinned, thir ald enough fir thi deed, man.

I clambered to my feet and joined the others crammed on the window ledge. The light was powerful. I shaded my eyes in the backrow.

Aw, eh ken thae lasses. 'Z Sally and Angela. Billy loudly wolf-whistled and, with his fist and forearm, made the universal sign of sexual intercourse.

Two Harris Academy girls – women – in maroon blazers and pleated short grey skirts smiled demurely up at us.

Eh took Angela ti *Guns o Navarone* at thi Plaza last Frehday, Billy explained. She tellt uz ehd nae chans. Fillum wiz shite an a. Bogin.

Knockbacks are nothin new for you, Billy boy.

Speak fur yirsel, yi cunt! Ehv never hud ane afore.

They babes, Dangerous stuttered, flippering, they babes are, like, brbrbrah, man.

Eh. Sally's in fir thi Dundee heats a the Miss UK contest, ken. In thi Playhoose in Juleh.

But we'd been up all night and the daylight was too strong for me. I slumped back on to the bean bag.

Wha's skinnin?

Top a thi Pops thi niyt, Billy.

Eh, they Pan's People lassies ehwiz git uz riyt horny.

'Za loada crap! Better wi thi *Ald Grey Whistle Test* an whisperin Boab. Leastwez yiz dinna get thi bliddy Wombles on that!

Eh, then later its thi *Liver Birds*.

Aw gee. When's yir penshun day?

Gie it a rest, lads, yir shaakin the table. See, Mac's in the nick again.

Best place for him.

Eh, eez a bliddy womble an a!

Done for fighting outside the Three Barrels.

Outside? What was wrong with the fight inside?

Aw. It wis wummen only inside.

Polis gave him a doing this time. You ken what he's like when's he's blootered. I mean he's no sensible. No like us, no moral code. Sells athin ti abdee, even schoolies.

Eh nivir liked thi bam, big Bob grumbled. Yased ti be merriet on Dave Stewart's sister, Susan. Did ur a riyt bad turn. Evil cunt.

She still in Dundee?

Na. Merriet again eftir thi divorce. Some Canadian. Lives in Moosejaw Creek ir someplace last eh heard.

Living in Dundee is a game of senses, requiring anaesthesia on a regular basis. Don't get me wrong, I love the dear old place and I feel I own it or it owns me, otherwise I would have described it under some pseudonym, Duntaw perhaps or Tayburgh, or, like Sir Walter Scott, Fairport. I love its honesty, its lack of pretensions, its familiarity, friendliness, but these can also be its worst points. I suppose it's the same everywhere else but somehow I feel convinced it's more so here.

I was trying to remember, as I sit here in my dusty cold room in front of the painting I haven't put a brush to for a week, about the time when I first met Wanda. How did it happen that we came to have a relationship? And how come I'm still thinking about her when there've been scores of girls in my life, though mostly brief encounters. So why am I so hung up on Wanda? It's not even as if I was entirely monogamous when I was with her. Not entirely? Okay, the truth, there were four, okay, five women in the two years I'd been with her. Seven maybe. Who cares? I can barely remember these encounters. I must have enjoyed them at the time or why bother. Seems so pointless now. They were mainly one-offs. That French girl, Blondine, in the long grass on the side of the Law after a party, seeing the dawn coming up over St Andrews. A girl called Ann I met at an Art College disco. There were the two Donnas. Funny, in French that means give. A weird fact they both worked in Brown's and I met them separately on the same day when I went in to see Phil. One was a window display assistant and the other worked in Berkertex Bride and was a part-time model. I ended up seeing them night about, taking them to the cinema to see the same film so that I wouldn't get confused. Two showings of *The Tango of Perversion* at the

Tivoli. Almost fell asleep both times. Actually, this was before I met Wanda. Donna Berkertex was a virgin and I didn't know till she burst into tears in the Scout. Ended up taking me to meet her folks. Expected me to propose. Saw her in the coffee bar in Littlewoods not so long ago, looking like shit, really bedraggled, with some pluky eegit in tow. What a come-down. She was gorgeous when I knew her. There was another girl after a party in a flat in the Blackness Road. I think I proposed to her twice in the same night. Blew me out. Later, I learned she was only sixteen. Never saw her again and I can't remember her name so she doesn't really count. I think I was pretty pissed that night.

But what I want to do is paint. So get out some other painting and mix some colour, y'waistir!

But I ended up in the Scout as usual. Now while the Tav and Willie Frew's are working-men's pubs that've been taken over by the bohemian crowd if you could dignify it with that name, the Scout is a rocker's pub and always has been. Scruffy old posters for rock groups that never had and never will come to Dundee hang off its walls. It is crammed most nights with the leather-jacketed, the denim-clad, the long-haired. There are campaigns on the part of the bar-staff against dope but sometimes laxity extends to the bar-staff sharing joints in the toilets. Speaker cabinets mounted in the cobwebbed rafters bang out progressive rock with lengthy guitar solos and bass beat so loud that no-one can hear anyone else, except in the interval between album tracks. It is the place to go to escape from chart sounds, pop singles and the dreaded Radio One.

Wattie is the bar manager and also bass guitarist for the Sleaz Band, local R'n'B veterans. He is in his early forties I guess, the oldest man I know. Above the bar on a hook, he displays the Viking helmet he wears on stage. Like at the Caird Hall when the Sleaz backed any touring artistes who made it this far north. Deep Purple, Led Zeppelin, Hawkwind even the teenyboppers' delight, Slade. According to Wattie, the Sleaz are the loudest band bar none in the Western Hemisphere. Built like a wrestler, low to the ground, with enormous shoulders and pectorals, he sports a tiny pair of pebble-rimmed glasses that look odd on a guy so muscular.

Now and then he takes it into his head to throw someone out just to be unpredictable. Just to show he still can – by picking them up bodily and throwing them out on to the pavement.

See you, yi cunt – *yir barred*!

After a pint in the Scout, I ambled up the Hawkhill and located Lester in Willie Frew's. We greeted each other like heroes returning from the Trojan Wars. After the pub shut we joined up with Eddie Lambert and tried unsuccessfully to get into the Students' Union. But old Pete wasn't on that night and we were not welcomed with open arms.

Laings? Art College? Eddie suggested. I've got a coupla quid.

Na. Let's walk out by the Ferry, Lester said, doing the Jagger-strut and playing imaginary maracas.

There was a glorious midsummer full moon, to which he declaimed some lines of gibberoon, à la McGonagall, as we straggled down the hill to the city centre. There was the usual grim rammy outside the chipper in the Nethergate. A punch-up or two at the taxi rank in the High Street. The fag machine in Crichton Street that sold packets of 8's was bust so we had to make a lengthy detour up the Conchie to the all-night bakery in Kinghorne Road. The summer air was warm as we sauntered back down the Hilltown, moonlight silvering the Tay beneath the pale lights of the Road Bridge. There weren't many people about, the occasional stationary taxi-cab, it being a Tuesday. Everyone else was in bed, workers all, not like us leisured scoundrels. More fool them. What they were missing.

No lights on, Lester said, peering up at his mother's flat, the maw must be in bed. Wait, listen. No, I can't hear any snoring.

Bloody hell! I should think not! Eddie exclaimed. Not from the street. I could murder a curry and a pancake roll, he said, as we continued up Victoria Road into Victoria Street. We should have gone to the Universal Garden for a chinky. Or the Bangla-desh for a vindaloo.

Or the Bangladesh for a punch-up, said Lester.

Same thing!

Eddie's always hungry yet he's built like a whippet. His shoulder-length black hair hanging straight down the sides of

41

his face gives him the expression of a startled ghoul. So we called in past the Park chipshop opposite Baxter Park and our chips lasted us to the Strips of Craigie circle. But that was too near my maw's place so, on Lester's suggestion, and after peeing into someone's hedge, we doubled back to the docks to visit Atholl Graham in Patullo's Seed Potato warehouse. The Robb Caledon lights were on and welders worked high up in the rigs on a steel hull of a new ship. You could see the incandescent sparkle of their welding torches.

Athers is a good mate of Johnny Bett – the actor – Lester told us. 7:84 and all that. A Dundonian by the way. We'll be sure of a cup of tea there, maybe even a sannie. Athers used to be a dock gateman, Lester said, as we found the steep steps down off the main road. But he was sacked after one week. You wouldn't believe. He only had one job to do all night. The only thing he had to do was check the tide level on the dock gates at high tide. It was the cushiest number anyone's ever had. But Athers blew it.

How?

How indeed. Believe or not, lads, Athers fell *asleep* while he was bending over the dock gates checking the tide. Stoned out of his brain of course. They had to fish him out with the boathook. Sacked on the spot. I could've done with that job. Good money for nothing, but Athers blew it for all of us. He has an allergy of course . . .

To work?

You got it! He makes more effort to avoid working than he would just working.

The warehouse, one of a long row, backed on to the gloomy Camperdown dock. Banging on the door inset in the massive double doors failed at first to rouse Atholl. Eddie found a large wooden batten and swung it at the door.

Ooyah bastard! He dropped the batten as the vibrations ran up his arms. Ow.

We heard Atholl's faint voice inside just as we saw a police car in East Dock Street coming our way.

Let-us-in-man. It's the pigs! Lester shouted urgently through cupped hands pressed around the keyhole.

The door opened slowly. Atholl stood inside and languidly rubbed his eyes. I guess I must have dozed off a bit.

We dived in on top of him. Safely in, and the door locked, we picked him up and he preceded us in the musty-smelling dark, carefully picking our way across the concrete floor of the vast empty warehouse to the wooden shed in the far corner. When the shack door was opened the radio and electric fire – both bars – blasted out noise and heat.

It's bloody roasting in there! Lester shouted, recoiling. The place is almost on fire!

Like I said, Atholl mumbled. Must've dozed off.

With this racket? Eddie dived inside to switch off the trannie. What a relief. The heat washed over my face as I followed him in and we all saw the smoking joint in the ashtray.

Stoned as a fart.

You're actually paid to work here?

I do get paid, he said gently, smoothing his long blond hair. But work is nothing to do with it. Thirty notes a week to sit here. He smiled melancholy. I mean, dear boy, who'd want to nick seed potatoes? I enter at ten and depart at seven. I never see anyone, except perhaps the occasional policeman checking up, when he's nothing better to do.

So what do you do all that time – apart from sleep?

Atholl made an expansive and unmistakably aristocratic gesture. Read, write. There's plenty to do. His tone was reasonable, his voice confidential, pleasant, slightly mesmeric. With his white shirt extravagantly unbuttoned to reveal his hairy chest, he looked somewhat Byronic.

Two of Atholl's poems, Lester informed us, were published in *Aquarius* magazine last year. Tenner each. Now that's good pay for a poem.

My dear boy, one tries.

And at least you're in no immediate danger of drowning in here, Lester said sarcastically.

There was a sheet of onionskin sticking out of a portable Smith-Corona on the desk with a lot of Xs on it. It looked like he was a two-finger typist. He saw the direction of my glance.

43

Poems about my time in Greece. And about my wife, Elena.

You were married, Lester queried. An actual ceremony?

Atholl made a deprecating gesture with his hand. Like, does it matter, Lester? Actually we did go through a sort-of civil ceremony in Lerissos.

Which part of Greece is that?

The Halkidiki peninsula. I was there for four years.

I always thought it was funny, Logan said, helping himself to a cup of cold tea from the pot, how you got out of Greece. At least if the story I heard is true.

Ah, everybody exaggerates, Atholl complained, smoothing the hairs on his chest. But I would still be there if I hadn't fallen out with Elena. And her folks.

They threw Athers out, Lester grinned. Bam wouldn't work. As you can imagine Athers was playing up the Byron country connection for all he was worth.

Simply not true, dear boy, Atholl protested. Anyway, I didn't need to work. You can live quite happily there on the wages of one and Elena had a good job.

So what went wrong?

I've absolutely no idea, old chap. The first I knew something was wrong was when she started to fling the pots and pans at me. I couldn't really make out what she was complaining about. We had a right ding-dong in the middle of the street. Rather undignified. Couldn't really say whether she threw me out or whether I walked out. It was rather too hot for fine explanations at the time. I moved in with a couple of friends, but their place was unsuitable for me and after a couple of months they asked me to leave. The next time I saw Elena she was with her brothers and I didn't get the chance to speak privately. They were not too keen on me. I don't know what she'd told the six of them. Trust not Greeks bearing cudgels seemed like good advice. So I got the next flight out. And that was that.

And that was Switzerland, Lester said. Yeah? Lucerne? Middle of the Alps. Middle of December. Snow up to his arse and Athers is still wearing shorts, teeshirt and sandals. All his other possessions in a brown paper bag mainly consist of his unpublished poems. He hasn't a bean.

44

I looked from Lester to Atholl, who grimaced.

Well, that part of it is right. I only had a few drachmae.

Not much good in Switzerland.

I won't deny it.

What'd you do?

Went to the Embassy. Explained the situation and asked them, politely, to kindly fly me home immediately. They refused. Got rather shirty about it. It was a holiday weekend, y'see. I think they had some urgent ski-ing planned, or some scheduled social-climbing elsewhere.

Lester interrupted, Athers didn't help the situation by trying to sell his poetry to them.

You can understand how that might not help.

Thank you, Edward. No, they were rather stiff English types and seemed to dislike the sight of me, a suntanned Dundonian vagrant, hanging around their nice clean modern efficient English Embassy. Everytime I took out my tobacco tin to roll a cigarette, they were watching me like hawks. I thought they would confiscate it.

Athers was chatting up their daughters in the library after they'd told him to go, I heard, said Lester.

Very pleasant young ladies, Atholl smiled in pleasant reminis-cence, impeccably-educated, don't y'know, well-finished, nicely-rounded characters. As it happened, one of the girls – called Sophia (the most nicely rounded of all) – knew somebody who might have been able to put me up. But the officials came in and, rather rudely I thought, ordered me off the premises. So I did the only thing I could in the circumstances.

Which was?

Athers hasn't said, Lester explained, that the Embassy had these huge plate glass windows . . .

Yes, well, I gave them an ultimatum. I said fly me home now or . . . I had hold of a large marble ashtray in both hands . . . this goes through those. Needless to say, I was on the next plane. Me and my rather frozen arse. Although I regret to say it was only standard class accommodation, I felt in the circumstances, a complaint would have been pushing it a bit, dear boy.

45

4

COMPLETELY OVERWHELMED by the past, the dumbing weight of dead years pressing down on me, yearning for something I seem to have lost, that I never had. I get back to the flat ringing wet from a night in the Tav standing in the crammed and sweaty snug listening to Diamond Lil playing in a space so small the drummer has to sit on the speaker cabinets and the guitarist, big John Coutts, perches on the mantlepiece above the blocked-off grate, bushy black hair hanging down to his fretboard. Everyone except me knows all the words to all the cover versions and has more tales than Sheherazade. They all seem to be able to converse in the noise, which deafens me beyond the ability to communicate. Made me feel insignificant, left out. I was passive, callow, an observer, and they lived in the company of each other. It was like a closed order and somehow I couldn't get in. It got so that I was trying to pretend I *did* know the magic passwords to the songs of the Loving Spoonful, miming along to 'Brown Eyed Girl', 'Sweet Baby James' and 'Out of Time'. But I couldn't mime the tears or fake the nostalgia. They knew I'd never hopped out the window of a Chelsea pad in the early morning when my girl's husband came home. They knew I hadn't been at the Stones' free concert in Hyde Park in June 69 to see Jagger, in white minidress, read from Shelley's *Adonais* as a thousand white butterflies held aloft in twig-like hands fluttered above the forests of heads, in memory of Brian Jones. To me, Woodstock was a film, Dylan was already well over the hill and I would never go Into The Mystic.

For the others those were the dear dead days of fond recall. In place of Logan's generational melancholy I could only substitute my personal grief over Wanda. So I might as well tell you how it began.

She simply came up to me in Laing's one Saturday night. Blobs of light folded across the walls of the dark, thundering cavern in the basement. I'd not noticed her before but it turned out that I half-knew her friend, Jean. Next thing she was *there*, beside me in the noise, long shiny dark hair and suede jacket, jeans and leather chokers and a loose white cheesecloth blouse with colourful beads sewed onto it. I thought she was fantastic, delicate, pretty. I couldn't believe what she was saying. Anyway, I could hardly hear her in the din. Skeets Boliver were blasting into their single (the one that had to be renamed) 'Brickhouse Door' . . . *ma baby bangs like a shithouse door* . . . Pete McGlone's saxophone blaring around the vocals of Gus Foy and Mike Marra. Platform soles and cuban heels stomped on the wooden floor, arms and heads waving, a mêlée of hair and faces and chanting.

I had to read her lips. Take me home please, I've had too much . . .

She almost fell into my arms. She was awfy unsteady. Then I was walking her up the road, ears buzzing. From noise to no noise. She was clinging to me, tottering carefully, not saying anything.

I got her up the hill to Pole Street, eventually, and she threw up in the toilet. I lay her on the bed, took off her red sneakers, threw a blanket over her and turned out the light. I didn't even kiss her and I slept on the sofa in the living room, feeling honourable.

Next morning, I went into the bedroom and her hair clung darkly about her face. She was sleepy and none the worse for last night's drinking. I felt . . . well, proprietorial . . . We chatted and shared a cigarette and soon we kissed. She was sleepily coquettish. It didn't take long for me to get very keen on her. It didn't take long for me to become rabidly possessive about her, paranoid. There were some grounds for it, men did gravitate towards her and she was rather flighty. I felt I could never trust her absolutely . . .

47

This, almost two years later, was where it ended: the party in Arthurstone Terrace. I regretted agreeing to go the moment we arrived. There was an obvious shortage of girls and some frustrated mock-violence among the guys because of it. It was all Wanda's friends. I was sprayed in the face when someone opened a can and someone else fell against a window laughing and broke it. Wanda drifted off, chatting to some guy who began to give me ugly looks from across the room. A fight started and someone was thrown out. I tried speaking to the girl beside me – just ordinary chat – but the guy on the other side of her didn't look too happy. I could overhear his conversation with his mates. All about fights and sticking the head on. I tried to talk to the other person who didn't seem to fit in, hovering in front of the drinks stash in the kitchen – there's two at every party – but we had nothing in common once we'd found the clean glasses. There was a loud bang we even heard in the kitchen and everybody jumped in the air and the record stuck. It turned out that an idiot who was a part-time soldier in the TA had tossed a thunderflash into the room. I went back to the kitchen and sat on the sink drainer, in the cool open window breeze. A couple were screwing in the airing cupboard. I could hear his arse slapping the inside of the door.

By the time I went back into the main room, Wanda and the guy were gone. I looked into the farther room, bedroom, but someone had removed the lightbulb. All I could see was fluorescent globs of magic stuff swarming on the ceiling, on faces and clothing. It was an inchoate heaving sweating mound of inarticulate bodies tripping out. I somehow knew she wasn't in there. I gave her a few more minutes then I sneaked out, pretending to be going to the toilet. As I closed the outer door behind me, stepping over necking couples on the stairs, I got a blast of *Emily tries but misunderstands . . . ha-ooohm . . .* I felt sick and very very jealous and weary.

I walked the wet streets for hours, directionless, thinking only of her and him together, and what they might be doing. Imagining the worst, trembling with jealousy and fear and self-pity.

48

Is it chinks in the ceilings of the past that allow us glimpses of daylight? Knowing the past is not the same as having it always with you. What lies beneath? Reach out and touch what is forever gone. We are so limited. Fleeting. Peripheral. Marginal. Stones and bones. Dem dry bones.

> *a rickle o sticks*
> *a mickle o bones*
> *a muckle o stones*
> *the wind saws the gap in the rock*
> *like toothache in the jawbone*
> *of a mythical sea-creature*
> *trapped in an estuary like ours*
> *in a dream we have almost forgotten.*

Kept behind in school for some misdemeanour. Fifteen. Imprisoned in a room I'd never been in before. In the Girls' School. Musty room with high windows, clanking radiators, oak desk and blackboard. Victorian. Third floor. Rows of desks carved and written upon. Hundreds of names and dates and comments. A history in wood. Some date back to the early 1930s. Owners perhaps killed in the war or now achieving the high seriousness of early middle age and responsibility. Losing hair, teeth and sense of humour. Prostate trouble. Perhaps their own sons and daughters have also carved their names upon these same desks. For posterity. We were here.

An austere-looking teacher I didn't know looks in and goes. Snow falls thickly outside upon every part of the school playground and all over Dundee, Scotland, Britain, Europe, the World. Muffling, deadening, softly falling, killing all sound. Unable to resist the ingress of light and drawn by a mysterious tropism, I climb on to the radiator resisting the burning heat upon my knees and palms. The city's dense shadows are surrendering to the weight of light. In a distant classroom a choir is singing. I can hear the piano, tiny voices. *Once in Royal David's City.* Almost the words. Sometimes it seems to end. But somewhere a door opened then closed and it begins again or perhaps it had never stopped, perhaps the pauses were gaps in my own breathing. A louder burst, a fade. It stops. A welling-up sob chokes me into breathlessness. I climb down off the radiator to hide my tears from the world. I feel immeasurably deep and warmly intense. Love for the school, those tiny voices, all teachers, my classmates everyone everywhere a part of me. A deep regret that it cannot last. For sooner or later the snow would melt and I would be revealed as an adult. I would leave the school and the world was so wide, so vast, so open. I would, one day, walk through those iron gates and never come back. Those gates, these stones, this snow, those voices would no longer be a part of me. I wanted that bright prospect to be always alluringly in the future but never to actually arrive. I wanted to suspend my future, its inevitability, slow down time. I was irrational, a prisoner to vast cosmic emotions. Tears that I did not understand streamed down my cheeks.

For weeks I forgot about routines though this in itself was a routine, or soon becomes one. Washing dishes or laundry, shaving or tidying-up got the go-by. I climbed into the same clothes each morning, didn't wear socks, ate out of the chipshop on old newsprint, barely washed my face. My skin began to flake from the rough treatment, began to drop in clouds of skin-scales and flow about in the sea-breezes. By afternoon, Pole Street itself was caked in a fine dust – the disintegration of the sandstone walls, flaking in the heat – which blew in clouds and gusted into the eyes. Window glass was caked with it. There was no solidity. Everything and empires would meisle awa, crumble to dust. Buildings and people were mirages of floating motes.

Mornings were clearer, brighter. Then, it was easier to breathe. Each day began with coffee, a banana roll and a joint, in that order, consumed in the humped, legless armchair on Eddie's plettie, looking out to the river. By mid-afternoon, as the haar rose in a vast cloud from the estuary, I'd be ready to walk over to Lester's house.

Frequently, my knocking would wake him. I'd sit on his bed while he dressed, washed and shaved. His small untidy room always smelled of feet, stale tobacco and cigarette ash. Cobwebs attracted dust in the corners of the ceiling. He'd shuffle through to the kitchen, bleary-eyed, and I'd pick up whatever was near to

50

hand, a manuscript he'd been working on late or a long letter to some High School girl who'd probably long forgotten him. The room was crammed with dusty books in bookshelves, on bookshelves, on the floor, under the bed and on the writing table, under ashtrays, in cardboard boxes and even on the bed. On the back of the door hung his busted tweed jacket and an expensive, second-hand pure new wool blue-black Crombie coat. Even the paintwork was faded, nondescript, formerly magnolia. Light filtered in from the sky between the Hilltown multis, through the orange unlined curtains and limned the dusty disorder of the table. Rusty dip pens, a pile of letters, *The Pocket Book of Heraldry* and *My Fight For Irish Freedom* by Dan Breen, a cup and saucer with cigarette stubs in both, a plastic wallet of dog-eared photos from the sixties, a cassette tape of The Corries. Lester doesn't have a tape recorder of course. Actually, he doesn't need one. Give him any first line and he'll sing you the rest of the song, but his musical tastes end where they began – in the sixties.

I began to read a manuscript typed on onionskin paper and discovered it was *Memoirs of a Bicycle-Seat Sniffer*. It soon made me laugh. This is great. Why don't you try sending it out again?

What is it? He peered over my shoulder and I smelled the stale sweat from his open shirt. Oh, that? No point, he said gruffly. No-one'd publish it. It's too damn *good*. Mum, where's my shoes? he asked, moving into the hall.

His mother from the living room: Eh dinna ken. Waur didya lave um?

That's what I'm asking. Here they are. There's no laces. Have we any spare laces?

'Z in thi press. Zi lisses ur in thi press.

Well, there's none.

Ur thir no lisses?

That's what I'm saying. None. And what's all this for? And this? Lester began turfing out the drawers. His mother sprang from her seat in anger.

Yi waistir! Yir no owir big t'belt i' thi lug! Aw see, thers meh weddin photies. You – get!

Alright, I hear you, Mother. He came back into the bedroom,

put on his brogues then returned to the living room. I'll need money for laces.

Yull huv ti wahnt.

A teabag floated in a perspex mug of hot water on the formica-topped kitchen table. Washing hung from the pulley and Hain bleakly fingered the wool of a pair of socks.

My socks, he grunted. I've no bloody socks. Mum . . .

Dinna bahthir iz. Yull jist huv ti wahnt. His mother was down on her knees collecting up the contents of the drawers. Lester reappeared.

Lend us a pound then, till Friday.

His mother looked up at him in distaste. Ji hink ehm made o money ur sumhin? Yuv no peyed iz fae thi last time.

Just a quid.

Nut. Eh canna. Ehv meh mulk ti pey . . .

Alright, alright. Just gese a fag.

Eh canna ffoard to keep yi in fags. Yiz uv nae money yiz shouldna smoke.

What about laces?

Eh fund um. Sowir thair. Yull be late fir thi broo.

Yeah, yeah, keep yer wig on. Coming, Gerry?

Dinna be late fir yir tea!

After Lester had signed on in Gellatly Street, we ambled around the town centre. We would tread the same weary circuit around the bookshops, coffee shops, then pubs, sauntering hopefully, Joyce and St John Gogarty, waiting for something to happen, looking for anyone we knew, and with each circuit we reinscribed the limits of our failure and concealed it beneath successful patter and the nonsense of companionship. If one was lost, then we all were. And that made us feel better.

Hey – there's Tony Woods, Lester said. He's looking even glummer than I feel.

He did too. Staring at his feet through his thick spectacles, a thickset squat figure in a dirty sweater and sneakers and a thick thatch of heavy hair.

Hi, Tony. Like, what gives, man?

He looked up blearily and scratched his red neck. Lester. Ach, I'm that fed up, yi ken. Eh've been turned doon fir the Foreign Legion cause o meh ehs. See, eh hitched t' Marseilles last week but they wouldna tak us. Failed thi eh test.

The eh test?

Eh, the eh test. Meh een ir buggird, ken. Uv wore glehsiz since eh wiz a nipper.

And I thought the Legion took anybody, Lester said, *sotto voce*. Still, things can only get better for you, Tone.

We managed to get round the corner. It was the lugubriousness of his face. Turned down by the Legion that admitted the scum of the earth. You couldn't get lower.

What kills me is the depth of his disappointment, Lester said. Other guys couldn't give a toss but Tone's really really down about it. Do you know Mike Ward? Lives in Byron Street.

Can't say I do.

Aw you must. Mike's parents split up when he was a kid. You probably have met him. He had what you'd call an unsettled childhood. Went to school at Blairs College, Catholic Seminary. A step up from the Johnnies. Well, his maw wanted him to be a priest. But he was always running away from home. When he was eighteeen he disappeared for days. His maw was frantic. The polis were scouring the town and it was on all the news. He turned up one week later in France. Guess what? He'd joined the Foreign Legion. Yeah. Served two years in Algeria and various other places. Trained as a sniper. After two years though he got bored with it.

Pretty brutal. The discipline and that, I imagine?

Tellin me. Tough. Anyway he was on Corsica and he and another bloke, a Yugoslav, deserted, with the help of some American girls and got smuggled over to Rome, where they hid for a few weeks then Mike made it back to Dundee. That's why he can never go back to France. There's a warrant out for him. If he's caught, they'll hang him. He hardly speaks about it though. I told him to write a book: Dundee Man In The Legion. Mind you, he hardly looks the type. He's kinda short and academic. But he did it, I don't know how, at the age of only

53

eighteen, and you've got to give him credit. Don't fancy it myself at all.

Did you ever read . . .?

Yeah, yeah, P.C. Wren . . . *Beau Geste, Beau Sabreur*, etc. When I was a kid. Seen the films too, the Doug McLure and Telly Savalas one in 1966 and the much better earlier version with Gary Cooper and Ray Milland. Never fancied the Legion, Gerry, because I imagine it'd be like an international version of the Lochee Fleet. In fact most of the Legion guys are probably only there to forget that they used to be in the Lochee Fleet.

That's almost funny, Lester. Almost. Trouble is, most Lochee Fleet guys are Arabs.

I'd baffled him for a split-second, then he was clicking his fingers. Ah, ah, I get you. Football. Dundee United fans . . . Arabs . . . so . . . they'd be in the desert anyway?

Yeah, but the Legion wear *blue* so no self-respecting Arab . . .

Yeah, yeah, very funny!

I knew another Dundee man who'd been in the Legion. Belair Billy. You wouldn't have got odds on Billy making it through the year. The Casualty Officers at the DRI lost money each time Billy turned up, out of an ambulance, in their antiseptic pale-blue curtained cubicles, pickled on shoe-polish and coughing blood and teeth. He'd moved into the flat above mine when Eddie left and while most of the gadgies in the area were far from respect-able and respected, Billy retained a fragmentary dignity even when he was drunk beyond all blindness. What it came down to was that he never stole. Actually, he couldn't, he was incapable, his hands shook that badly. His place was in a state of constant siege by shuffling hordes of gadger men and women, black-faced, stumbling, swearing and every time a window or door was busted in at night you could be sure Billy was entertaining. All of Billy's gear had been removed bit by bit: his lighter, the electric heater, blankets, clock (though it had never worked), even his shoes. To set the seal on his misfortunes, some unidentified bastards tore out the lead piping in the second-floor flat and the water brought down his ceiling on top of him. For days, he went around with an eerie covering of white plaster dust on his hair and shoulders that was like a rusted halo. The factors ignored the problem; Billy was a non-tenant to them, not human, he owed them three months' rent, but they couldn't get him out. They'd tried every method in the book and some that weren't. Billy was as impervious to hints, threats, court letters as he was to the weather that came in his broken windows. Even sending round the heavies on Sunday mornings at 6am didn't work. Billy couldn't be any more beat up than he already was.

His giro came on Wednesdays. Sometimes, he'd ambush the postman in the close but if he was incapacitated, which was almost always, the postman flung it through the open doorway (Billy's door had no lock fitting, not even a doorhandle). Even in the midst of the deepest stupor, Billy could somehow always detect the landing of that flimsy brown envelope among the clumps of plaster and turned-over furniture and bottles. First, one burst eyeball would appear and then the rest of him would spring into action. Before the postman had even come back down the stairs, Billy'd be skipping off down the street to the off-licence for his weekly treat, a bottle of Four Crown fortified wine, a half-bottle of rum and a can of coke. With these, and an ounce of Black Bell in his tin, Billy was a happy man. Later in the week, he'd be scrounging pennies for a plastic bottle of Belair hair lacquer.

'Z how yiz dae it, son. He squeezed the tube out into the neck of an empty milkbottle. When the tube was empty, he took the bottle over to the tap and as carefully as his juddering hands would allow, filled it to the brim.

Yiz huv ti get a thi lumps oot wi yir thumb. See, boy.

I watched lumpy pieces overflow the top of the bottle until, satisfied, Billy lifted the milky-white fluid aloft like a connoisseur. Five parts water to one of lacquer.

Huv a wee shottie. It'll pit hairs on yir chist!

It smelt like hot perfume, cheap and pungent and the metallic taste remained in my mouth for hours.

Yiz huv ti keep shaakin it ti stop it fae goin solid, ken.

The gadgies call this drink the White Goddess, god knows why.

In a way, Billy was my gadgie. Lester and the others would have nothing to do with him – he wasn't cool – but I had chats with him and then he used to come downstairs on the scrounge for food. He was profusely grateful for anything I'd give him which gave me the daft idea that I was helping him when what I should have done was push him off the plettie when he was least expecting it. I never let him in till I'd hidden my paintings. For some reason, I felt it would be obscene for him to share a room with my art, as if Wanda would be tainted by the air he breathed. Or maybe I thought he'd take umbrage at being mocked by the falsity of it when he was on death row. He was dying, there was no doubt of that at all.

When I'd first seen him, he was tanned like a man in his fifties, a sort of Dundee's Anthony Quinn, but his face had taken on a green sallow glow as though his skin was made of luminous rubber. His hair was falling out and lay untouched on his shoulders for days. Stubble refused to grow on his meagre chin. As the weeks went on, he got thinner. But there was no point in giving him money. He was living on supplies of pep pills and uppers and Black Bell, but often his hands shook so much he couldn't make roll-ups. He didn't sleep. I could hear him moving about on the floor above at all hours. Sometimes he'd tap on my window and I'd give him some bread. He was a scrawny bird alright.

Some mornings I'd be awoken by the sounds of him leaning over the plettie hawking and vomiting and spitting mucus into the backgreen. Once I saw his dog – a gap-toothed mongrel with a shambling slouch that had attached itself to him – lap up this thin gruel. Next thing I heard was Billy's wheezing, mirthless laugh through parched white lips as the dog choked and regurgitated in its turn.

But on giro days, with his Four Crown, Billy'd tell stories which may or may not be true. I had no way of knowing. He'd gained a thousand tales of life, of mice, and men. He told me bits of his life story in between satisfying swigs, like a Monterey wino from the pages of Steinbeck. Except Billy wasn't fictional, he lived in Dundee. He was all too real. He had spent eight years in the Foreign Legion, spoke Legion French, a curious argot, swore in it when he was high. Knew a little Arabic and some Spanish. He'd worked on the docks at Marseilles, had worked his passage on many boats in the Far East, claimed to have been a hitman for a gang in French Quebec, had fallen foul of the Mafia in Naples because of some woman. Fantastic tales. He proudly showed me the badly-healed scar of a large letter S on his back. He talked about the men he'd killed. His total was nine, though he remained convinced that a few more lurked, ready to spring in his memory. Stooped and pale, he looked incapable of killing but I found myself coming up in goosepimples all over my body and quickly changed the subject.

Ehv no dehd yit! he used to shout sometimes in the middle of the street if people looked at him in a funny way. But things weren't going well. He was banned from chemists' shops, the police used to harass him at all hours of the night, the Social Security withheld his payments for no reason. When he couldn't get Belair anymore, he used to pay boys to buy surgical spirit for him. It wasn't his preference. It was all he could get and it made him spit. The postman found him. Half-in and half-out of his doorway, stone-cold. The plasterers took almost a week to restore the ceiling, but the factors couldn't relet the flat for almost a year. There was a sort of stink about the place. And of course, the hordes of gadger men still visited occasionally at night, like the undead, forgetting that Billy was gone. I'd hear the muffled sounds of their bafflement as they found the new door locked. After they'd each tried the handle and cursed a bit they'd shuffle off somewhere else.

A long ago summer's day, Bumper and me, we'd walked the long way out to the country. To the burn beside Murroes kirkyard, dodging evil-looking bulls and curious cows that frolicked after us. We skinny-dipped in three feet of emerald water beside a small wooden footbridge in a tiny glen then dressed and worked our way upstream. We fought with swords and machetes and tommy-guns through impenetrable thickets and came to steep banks at a dark place where the burn was wide and deep, a mill lade hemmed in by ancient sluice-gates and rusting iron levers inside thick bushes and brambles. First, we tiptoed precariously across the top of the dam walls climbing over the jutting branches and then we lay on the beam and lowered ourselves to the swirling black surface of the water so that our faces were cooled in its sullen reflections. Holding on tight, in that mysterious place half afraid, I half-closed my eyes and let myself be dazzled by the glissade of light on the dancing water molecules. Where the sunbeams struck the water I could see in! It was a tunnel to somewhere else. There was something mystic, ancient and holy about this swirling deep water hidden in bushes. I saw my eyes reflected as they probed the depths, my face a pink blur. I slowly became aware of objects under the surface, of objects briefly swirling up from the depths for my inspection. An eel appeared, close to the surface and its dead eye regarded me as it slid slowly past and past and passed and in its wake, I saw a rotten cabbage, a piece of torn tartan ribbon, a used condom grotesquely expanded, a piece of twig, a sheet of printed paper from a book. Half in a sunstruck trance, I reached out an unsteady childish hand and grabbed at the page but before I had time to yell, fell face first into the water, right under.

5

T HE WHOLE OF perception in just that one wee movement of the retina. I saw upon that sodden page the regurgitated underwater history of our nation, the distaff disorder of society, its meaninglessness, its squashed spectacles, dentures, hair, blood, faeces, dead cats, lacerated tyres, rind of bacon, brown skins of onions, used tampons, flattened tubes of toothpaste, mushy seed potatoes, rusty baby-carriage filled with sodden papers in which weeds are freely sprouting, cracked pots, dead goldfish wrapped in oily cloths, mucus white of chicken skin slopped into sticky tins of peas, jam-jars with trapped wasps feebly struggling against the screwed-down lid, seven-week abortion in a half-empty milkbottle, greenish wizened carrots, mouse stretched stiffly with its neck severed almost completely, leather boot without laces, pornographic magazine with all the pages stuck together, bottle of wine with rose trapped behind green glass, poetry books of unknown poets printed by unknown presses, ripped tights, matchbox of nail parings, smashed light-bulbs, cardboard box of fascist newspapers, dried human turd inside a seemingly new three waveband radio, combs stuck with human hair, swimming trunks, chlorine-rotted, wrapped around an artificial limb, fish inside a knotted pair of baggy trousers, battered and slashed plastic dolls, newspapers with crosswords half done, broken scissors, worn-out toothbrushes, newspaper reviews of films whose actors long since dead, leaky batteries for cheap hairdryers, pocket calculators, multi-speed vibrators, pocket torches, broken milkbottles, rusty electric heaters, disreputable carpets, broken digital watches, mouldy coats, useless umbrellas, suitcases so beat up the cardboard was flaking out, inside-out socks shiny with flaky scabs, tubs of rancid margarine, dried flowers, cracked bathroom tiles, broken plates with foodstains, carryout cartons, tinfoil and polystyrene, used disposable razors, *Oor Wullie Annual*, pvc belt with broken buckle, wardrobe door, perspex shower attachment, broken WC pedestal, complete white toenail, preserved and brittle grass-snake, toy machine gun with red plastic bit that shoots out and in of the barrel, china horse much repaired, polythene bags stuck together with hardened glue inside, *A–Z of London* all scribbled over in a childish hand, hypodermic syringe with blood in the end, handbag with credit cards and small change inside, mascara bottle, splintered cricket bat, unopened packet of digestive biscuits, warped record *This Is Soul* – Atlantic/Stax, blunt chisel, bent screwdriver, Armistice Day paper poppy, envelope with a lipstick kiss below the address (East Acton), yellow y-fronts filled with diarrhoea, melted purple candle, nylon Union Jack with bloodstain in one corner, sleeve of a leather jacket, cardboard box full of last-year's calendars, used growbag, lump of putty on the lens of a pair of sunglasses, lady's wig covered in blue ink, live rat inside a brown paperbag, pages of a cheap paperback, frilly pink knickers browned at the crotch, framed mirror smashed into splinters, flick-knife with half a blade, pack of greasy cards in a bucket of solidified cement filled up with dusty water, part of a human ear, red tin teapot, dog collar, bale of twine, tin of undercoat paint, hundreds of greenish mouldy bread rolls . . .

From that childhood day to this, immersed and gagging in that stale stagnant water, I've felt sickened to my soul with what Sartre called noumenal angst. I climbed out then, and hauled myself up the bank and retched and retched. But you can't retch up your facticity. You're stuck with that. With all of it. Each of us owns it. It sums us up. It's what we are. It's all we are.

I look out of a window that has never been clean on to a backgreen in deep shadow, a huddle of overflowing aluminium dustbins, ramshackle sheds, damp and grimy with missing slates, cracked paving stones fringed with fecund and dusty weeds. Dundee. I'm still only in Dundee. Damned dreary old Dundee doldrum day. In the window directly across the street a bare electric lightbulb silhouettes a pair of socks hanging from a string beneath the snib and the top of the window. Actually, they are not a pair: one being longer than the other and a different colour. Not that I've been that close to examine them in any detail. I can't think what this means. Is it some kind of allegory? And if so, who is the alligator?

You're my one and only she said. My bestest friend ever she said. If you were a rubber plant I'd water you every night and give you cold tea and tell you stories about jungles every weekend she said.

Painting
Eating
Sleeping
Listening to music
Walking around town
Talking to friends
Hoping for better things
Escape.

There are many modes of escape. You can escape into your work, into a daydream or into a song, you can tranquilise yourself, spend the entire day in bed – but all of these are means of avoiding physical escape. If you can't change your circumstances, relocate. That was finally it. That's what it amounted to. I told Lester what I intended and he said great idea. I'll come too. But I knew he never would. Secretly, I planned a solo escape. I did not need a destination, or at least, did not need to know a destination before I set out. I needed a motive and I think that all those stories I'd been hearing for years finally convinced me that what I wanted was to be the subject of stories of my own rather than an eavesdropper on the doings of others in the past. Stories. The avoidance of deeds. Talking rather than doing. I had to break out of the dunghill.

61

Yeah, in London, you see, Atholl told us, Lester had got himself a sort of temporary clerical job at the War Office. Must have lied through his false teeth. So he's wearing a brand-new pinstripe suit and tie. He's had his hair trimmed. He's strolling down Horseguards' Parade feeling on top of the world, particularly since he's chatting to two nice girls from the orifice, and has asked for a date with the prettiest one, who hasn't yet said no. All is going well for our man Logan and he's giving out with the usual big-shot – pater's an aristo, large estate up the glen – type of boloney. But big Bob's working the fruit and veg barrow opposite the barracks and his best-selling line is apples.

Aipuls! Beh yir aipuls here! he's bawling. He sees Lester and waves. But Lester totally ignores him.

Disna wahnt ti be brung doon in front o thi posh babes.

Yes. Well. Lester! Lester Logan! Bob shouts. But Lester keeps on walking.

I sey, do you kneow thet chep? one of the babes inquires.

Of course not. On second thoughts, Lester says, perhaps he's related to my dad's butler.

Big Bob gets irate and starts to fling apples at him from the other side of the street.

Logan! Yi snoaby cunt! His language was choice. Apples flying all around, a few hit bystanders, none hit Lester. But a van-load of polis on door duty at Downing Street belt up the road and capture big Bob. Gets done for Breach of the Peace. So Lester has to quit the job at lunchtime and sneak out the side door, cause he knows big Bob will be out and looking for revenge.

It wasn't because I ignored him, said Lester, from the corner, it was pure jealousy. Bob's never had a girl, least not a decent girl of the kind that he's not had to pay. It was typical Bob. If he can't get a girl he stops anyone else getting one.

Later, Lester had recovered some of his *sang froid* and was holding forth and fifth about paintings.

Used to make money forging paintings, he boasted. Modern art. Piece of cake. Those Bernard Kleg's were dead easy. One red square and a blue triangle. Used to flog them to these dealers on the Kings Road. Put on the good tweed suit . . .

. . . Get it out of the pawn . . .

. . . polish up the posh Scots' accent and give them some dirge about having to get back to the estates and being a bit embarrassed of the readies due to crippling death duties: two uncles and a maternal aunt. I didn't know that when they took it into the backshop, you see, they tested the carbon of the pencil that'd been used to sign the painting. But by pure coincidence, I'd used exactly the right kind of pencil. So they were all set to give me fifty quid. But that bastard Toshy, Brian MacIntosh, you know, comes past pushing his Westlers' Hot Dog stall. Sees me in the shop. You can just imagine his brain cell working overtime. Lester Logan! Lester Logan wi a suit on! Lester'll be ahriyt fir thi loan o a quid! So he comes barging in and starts pestering me. The gallery owner immediately smells a doctored rat, needless to say, begins fiddling with his bow tie.

Is this 'person' an acquaintance of yours, Lord Kiltravock?

Toshy bursts out laughing while I'm trying to kick him on the shins. Wut dodge ur yiz trehin thi noo, Lester, an wha's thi pooftir?

I have never seen this uncouth person before in my life. He is obviously under the drunken delusion that I am someone else.

I see, sir . . .

Logan! Yi snoaby cunt. 'S me, Toshy! Gies a quid, man. Eh need a fehvir t'beh this brah lime-green suit eh just seen doon thi merkit.

That blows it completely. Toshy and his lime-green suits! I was lucky to get out before the polis arrived. Which reminds me.

There was a general groan from the assembled boozers. Not another Toshy story! We want to forget the guy!

Wait till you hear this. See – we were in the Chelsea Antiques Market and he suddenly decides he's gonna steal a painting. I think it was a disease with him. Sees something and he has to steal it. Even if he's got a pocketful of dough and a brand-new lime-green suit on at the time.

Eh. Toshy's an opportunist ahriyt.

Eh've heard this story a hunder times, Alec complained. And each time it's different. Carlo minds it wiz you done thi pinching.

Lester went ballistic. Me! Flaming cheek. I wouldn't mind only it wasn't even a good picture. Toshy hasn't a clue about art. Typical that he'd try to steal one of those Tretchikov-type Spanish women portraits, all tits and black hair with a matador doing his mascara in the background. It was ghastly! I don't want my reputation besmirched by association with trash like that. Anyway there we were and Toshy suddenly whispers, when I say run – RUN! Oh no, what's he gonna do now? I'm thinking. Suddenly he grabs this painting that's on the wall and yells. So I beat it pretty quick. But the painting's fixed to the wall and so he brings down the entire partition on top of himself. Meanwhile I'm off down the Fulham Road with two security guards hard on my heels. They think I nicked something. All the way to Victoria bloody bus station. Three miles! Finally, they give up and later I meet up with Toshy. The bastard's only been helped to his feet and taken into the backshop for a cup of tea and a choccy biccy while I've been legging it all over London. Free fags, the full VIP treatment and are you sure you're alright son? Bastard!

Mind o the time . . .

There was general outrage. No! Not another Toshy story.

All tosh if you ask me.

You should know, Lester roared, jumping up on to his seat, pointing. You were there. When he nicked the shooting brake and drove it to London?

How could I forget.

You, me, Carlo and Toshy.

Yeah, see, Lester said, sitting on the ledge of the mantelpiece above us, I was blootered – stocious – and ended up outside Mennies one night with Carlo and Johnny Haggart and . . . Willie Jacuzk. Remember Willie Jacuzk? Anyway, flipping Toshy was coming along the street. Lester mimed the familiar actions of Toshy's head swinging from side to side and his hands pushing out to each side (so cool! I'm so *cool*!). So we wandered up some street. Anyway he nicked somebody's car – an old shooting brake. I got into the backseat and fell asleep. I must have reckoned they'd drive around Dundee for a bit but when I woke up . . . Hendon! Course we'd no money and we were starving so a few hours later, Carlo disappears and it turns out he's gone into Cannon Row polis station and given himself up. Tells the polis who we are. Well, by next day, we are absolutely ravenous so there's nothing for it but to go to the polis and ask for help. As luck would have it, of course wouldn't you know – the polis station we go into is only Cannon Row. Course we don't tell them anything about the stolen car, just that we've run out of money on a holiday.

How did you get here, boys?

We came down by coach, officer.

When was that?

Last week, last Friday. We've been here a week but we had some money stolen . . .

Last week? Funny I had a Dundee lad in here yesterday with the same story. He said he got separated from three friends. He your friend?

Eh, yes, officer, that sounds like Michael.

Michael? No he said his name was Carlo. And he said that the names of his three friends were, let me see, Lester Logan, Brian McIntosh and William Jacuzk, not the names you've given me.

Well maybe it's not Michael then, Hamish, says Willie.

You could be right, Angus.

So what bus was it you came down on, lads?

Oh, a big blue one, says stupid Toshy, with four wheels.

The copper was annoyed. More like a shooting brake registration KY4 2EX. I've had enough of your games. You're nicked.

But Toshy suddenly jumps up on to the desk where there's a ton of paperwork it's taken the sergeant all week to sort out. He shouts *You won't take me alive, copper!* and he kicks the files all over the place. It took four cops to hold him down and when we saw Toshy again he was covered in bruises. So we were all in dead schtuck. Got flown back to Edinburgh with a police escort. First time I'd ever been on a plane. We're handcuffed in the back row. So Toshy says . . .

Big Bob came in. Still bullshittin, Logan, he grumbled, 's your roond an ehm wahntin a Guinness. He reached up and pulled Lester off the mantelpiece.

Eh, Boab, says wee Billy, ee blabs awa so naebdee sees ee disna git a roond in.

I got a round . . .

Eh. In 1965. Sees yir dosh. Bob pushed Lester against the fireplace. They glared at each other but Lester's hand was already diving down to his hipper. It came out green.

Look, a quid. It's all I've got. Take it, clean me out, why don't you? Food? I don't need it. I can live on air for a week.

Yi lehin mink! wee Billy jeered. We a ken yir maw gies yi fuhll board!

Yeah, but she makes me pay for the privilege. Like, with real money. But take it, Lester held the pound note aloft and let it flutter. Enjoy. He turned back to us. Pardon that rude interruption. Anyway, let's pretend we're terrorists, Toshy says. Terrorists. He had the long beard at the time and we all had long hair. So just as we're touching down at Edinburgh we start with the clenched fist salutes and long live the revolution. And believe it or not, Gerry, the passengers on the plane gave us a round of applause as we were hauled off, thinking we're brave idealists with the courage of our convictions . . .

Would you believe it?

All those bourgeois Edinburghers. Toshy did look a bit like Che.

No in the lime-green suit he didna. He looked like a poof.

Ach, in they days, fowk used to creh uz a poofs. Jist cause o wir lang hair and the wey we wiz dressed. Abdee thit looked a wee bittie different wiz . . . a poof. White sand-shoes . . . poof! Hat o any description that wisna a flet bunnet . . . poof! Dezzie bits . . . poof! See in the mid sixties, like, yiz wid git chased if yiz werena a teddy boay. See the looks yi yased to get in thi street jist fir huvn lang hair.

If they liked you, Lester said, they'd let you live.

I lay in bed in the dusty, itchy black, listening to the sounds of the tenements around and above me. Directly above, in Belair Billy's old place, the new tenant, Mrs Grimes' bed – Mrs Grimes who sported large white sunglasses, dyed blonde hair, a beerbelly, and different men every night of the week – creaked in rythmic unison

66

of its rusty springs, faster and faster, then silence. A few minutes later, another creak, padding of feet to the window, tap turned on and water flowing. Someone was peeing in the sink. Then the feet went back across the room to the bed, another creak, a lull, then it would start again. Across the backgreens, there was an argument. Someone screamed, plates smashed, maniac laughter indescribably ugly in the glass night air. Now singing in the distance, scuffling of feet on my stair. Once I'd to listen to a fight just outside my window, someone being beaten up, wordlessly, and too drunk to fight back. I wish that woman would stop screaming. A pair of cats explode into noisy violence nearby. Another morning I found knickers in the toilet and yards of unravelled toilet roll. My thoughts trouble me towards sleep. Somewhere a door slams, a bed creaks, a clock ticks, a distant siren wails, a dog barks, an old man dies, a newspaper is printed, a baby wakes and cries, a record player switches itself off, a cat arches in self-defence, a policeman walks a rainy beat, gods look down. Time to go.

I went through a period of planning, taking all my paintings and materials to my mother's house and acquiring a rucksack and camping materials. They stood in the corner of the living room for several weeks reminding me of my obligation to leave. Friends donated advice and stories of travel. I told them I was going so often that it almost became a joke. On some days, Lester seemed to be coming with me, and those were the days we'd end up drunk. Days after I said I'd go, I was still in Dundee and then, when nobody expected me to go, I went.

I got up at 6am and walked over to Lester's mother's and put my keys in an envelope through the door. I'd promised him that he could sell my bed and furniture and anything else he could find. It was great being up so early and being of no fixed abode, walking down the Hilltown with the sun barely up and the wide river ahead.

I stood on the verge of the Road Bridge approach for an hour before I got a lift and then everything was in free flow. By lunchtime I was on a roadside in East Lothian, then I was on the slip road for Dumfries and then, in a low-slung red MG sportscar, we were tearing down the M6.

6

I TRAMPED AROUND Piccadilly, Leicester Square and Soho for hours gawping like a glaikit provincial at the carnival of lights, the colourful gear, the gorgeous women. With my rucksack, tattered bell-bottoms, dusty boots and hair falling in front of my face I must have seemed like the archetypal village idiot on the make but it didn't bother me because, through the tall tales of Lester, Alec Swan, big Bob, Carlo and Toshy, I felt I knew and belonged in these metropolitan streets. I felt no fear of the dark and homelessness I would face. I could find love here and plenty of sex and adventure in the meantime.

I bought a burger off a stall outside Raymond's Revuebar and took a slow schmooze past Rabin's Kosher Nosher, looking at those swell Israeli chicks in tight cheesecloth tucking into their borscht and gefilta fish. There was a whole different class of superbabe in the darkened neon-streaked doorways of peepshows who summed me up in a glance and then ignored me.

I settled down on the stone steps of Eros in the Dilly. For some reason I began to remember an unflattering story about Lester Logan. Apparently when Lester got off with a girl at a party, he was entirely selfish, excluded all his pals and made off quietly and in a rather sneaky manner. This is hardly surprising given the nature of his pals. On one particular occasion at a party a number of said acquaintances had remarked his singular absence and someone revealed that he'd been seen with . . . a particular female . . . in the bedroom area. All the latent jealousies of

Lester's womanless 'friends' had been brought to the surface and they began to hunt. It didn't take long. They detected Lester in a small attic bedroom and he could be seen through the keyhole going at it. I've never seen anyone going at it so fast, Atholl had said. His arse was thundering up and down. No technique except speed. But, given that this was a casual sexual encounter, Lester had wisely taken precautions. He had barricaded the door as well as locked it from the inside. There was a chair against it. This soon became apparent as more and more 'friends' attempted to peer through the keyhole while Lester, from inside, told them to get lost. But the sheer pressure of the thrusting bodies against the door put such pressure on the flimsy wooden structure that it began to shiver. It didn't collapse inwards though. What happened instead was that a small brass doorknob on the inside of the door was propelled into the room at speed and struck Lester on the extremely tender part of his anatomy between buttocks and genitals, causing instant temporary paralysis. He was, to put it crudely, as Atholl said, frozen in the doggy position. His terrific howls as a dozen males burst their way into the room to 'give medical aid' to the girl trapped under him remained a talking point for years.

It was while I was thinking of Lester in this way that a girl sidled over to me and, not for the first time in my life, I was picked up. Julia wasn't exactly hip and trendy – she wore a knee-length denim skirt and she was broader in the beam than I usually go for. Her hair was short and curly and she was even a couple of years older than me, but she was friendly and it was good to talk to someone after hours of loneliness. She was from somewhere I've already forgotten in south Wales. We went for a coffee in Leicester Square (she paid) and she took me home on the bus to her brother's place in Stockwell across the Thames. The brother and his wife and family were out when we arrived.

My first London morning. I looked out the window at dull grey streets and city noise just like Dundee writ large. The brother wasn't too bad about me being there although his wife wasn't too keen after he'd gone off to work. There was a lot of malarkey then about my rucksack. It was a question of whether I should take it with me or leave it in the flat. What it came to was were we going to be an item (which she hoped) or was it just a one-night stand? I left it at the flat and we set off for a bus. She looked a helluva lot fresher and sexier in the daytime in jeans and a tight teeshirt which she was rather busting out of. We wandered around in the parks, did the tourist bit, peeked through the railings at Buck House but Sweaty Betty and Phil the Greek werenae in, so we had a sandwich in Green Park and fed the ducks then lay on the grass in a lush shady bit and had a bit of a grope. Lots of people were sunbathing on the grass and I guess none of them were Dundonians. There was a brass band playing 'The Floral Dance' at three different speeds simultaneously behind the trees.

I went about with Julia for almost a week but it wasn't really me. It was too normal, not the kind of wild adventure I'd promised myself. I didn't have much in common with her. She liked pop. 'Una Paloma Blanca' and 'Lady Marmalade' and she had tapes of Lace and the Bay City Rollers, who had just hit number one in the States with 'Saturday Night'. She liked Rod Stewart's 'Sailing', which I didn't mind too much though all the rest was crap. We saw a good new film though, *One Flew over the Cuckoo's Nest*. She didn't really like it but it blew my mind. It summed-up everything I believed in. I was the very reincarnation of ole kick-ass R.P. McMurphy. Next day I bought the paperback and devoured it cover to cover when I was supposed to be going with her to do some brass rubbing in some cathedral or other. She wasn't pleased. But there seemed to be some kind of direct psychological link in my mind between Kesey, Kerouac and Lester Logan's Dundee Beats. The romantic failures, international hobos, restless dharma bums fae the Hulltoon, cross-country hip travellers heading west up the Hawkie. Which is why I sneaked my rucksack out a few days later and deposited it in Victoria bus station. I was thinking, as I turned the token in the lock, of Logan's flight from Chelsea. I was thinking a lot about Lester and the others as it happens and remembered the play he had written in Notting Hill, *Game of Senses*, which I had seen, on onionskin, in his drawer. While waiting for him one morning, I had read a few pages of it. It was only a matter of time I'd reckoned till Lester was a successful published author. His stuff was that good. But his light was still well hidden under bushells of rejection letters. Was it that the Dundee postmark on his manuscripts gave the game away that he lived too far north of Watford? And why am I still thinking about Dundee?

I slept in Hyde Park, dodging the park police by climbing into a tree near the central toilet block. It was a long, cold night and I didn't get much sleep. Funny being alone in the vast surging black park, like an alien from the end of the universe, with the bright lights all around in the distance. There were noises too, odd sounds I couldn't work out, which spooked me. Long before dawn, I'd abandoned the park and was patrolling Knightsbridge. All I could think about was how alone I was. It was a nice area, white stucco, wide steps, terracotta planter pots with bushes growing out of them and neat iron railings. But there were lone women in the shadows on streetcorners, mostly in their thirties but elegant and I saw a streetsign, Shepherd's Market. They didn't even glance in my direction. It was as if they could see through my pockets, my small wad of four fivers and three pound notes and loose change and felt it was hardly worth the bother. I just kept walking and found an all-night coffee bar. I sat in there until well past dawn and London was already up and thrumming when I emerged. I'd found it an interesting three hours, listening in to the desultory conversations of several pairs of men whom I assumed to be homosexuals, to a few elderly Greek men, some taxi drivers and a couple of likely prostitutes. Hunched in the corner, collar up, over a coffee, making like Jack K. Scribbling occasional notes in the school jotter that went with me everywhere. In the warmth and joy of my beat-ness.

Later, I bought a newspaper and read it drowsily on a park bench in the full sunshine. It meant nothing to me. Carter, Callaghan and a demo in Edinburgh against Giscard D'Estaing. My eyes kept closing in the warmth and glare. Then I began a repetitive circuit, ever widening, around central London. I had a roll and pint in a busy Soho pub frequented by loud-talking blue-jeaned PR-types talking hyperbollocks about some record deal. I checked out Carnaby Street, sad and seedy and tacky, now only frequented by Japanese Kodak-clickers. By mid-afternoon, I was beginning to get a bit bored with London so I sought out an employment office but discovered that, without an address I could not sign on. I didn't have enough money to pay a month's rent and a deposit on a flat.

It was later that afternoon that I met Ronnie, in a pub in Kensington called the Elephant and Castle. He must have been watching me and sent his huge old English sheepdog over to make the introductions. The dog was called Boogie and it was a friendly mutt. Ronnie was from Maybole, Ayrshire, about ten years older than me, a typical aging hippy, long lank hair, rugby shirt tight over his bulging belly and floppy flares. Most noticeable about him was the bouncing gait that seemed to emanate upwards from his busted tennis shoes, which he referred to archaicly as plimsolls. He had a cherubic face and one of the first things he told me was that he'd been a member of the Blue Angels, a Glasgow gang. But that was before he'd rolled joints at various literary bashes with Hugh MacDiarmid, whom he called wee Shuggie. He was full of bullshit but somehow I didn't mind. In fact, he reminded me a bit of Lester Logan and that's why I tolerated him. And Boogie was a decent sort, bounding ahead optimistically.

I stayed for ten days in Ronnie's squat in Clapham. To say it was grotty was an understatement. Even the floors had been removed. When you entered the place you had to climb down on to bare earth. I never did find out why Ronnie was disliked so much by the other inhabitants. He was so crassly insensitive that he ignored all their barbed remarks. He was the kind that would take a slap in the face as not entirely discouraging. Ronnie called himself a writer and a poet and regarded the Scots as ethnically superior in terms of creative imagination. To him the English were a race of plumbers and sewage inspectors. He preferred the West Indians, Portuguese, Spanish, Irish, anyone who could claim non-English ancestry.

And Ronnie got us jobs, in the kitchen of a large bank headquarters in a tower block overlooking St Paul's. You turned up at a tiny agency office off Fleet Street at 6am and queued. We were sent to the bank because Ronnie said we'd loads of kitchen porter experience. The rest of the staff were black but the banking staff who ate in the restaurant were the snobbiest I've ever met. They treated us kitchen coolies like *shit*, didn't deign to look or speak to us and some of the prettiest babes were the worst. In retaliation we stole everything that wasn't nailed down and stuffed ourselves silly all day. I was on a ham and egg roll kick and ham and egg rolls I was pleased to see came in catering size logs about two feet long. I could just about get one down my trouser leg and get past the security men on the door without being detected but sitting down in the Tube was impossible. But the snottiness of the bank staff got to us and we lost the job. Basically, it was a bum rap. Desperate to get a reaction from the babes we advanced rearwards into the dining area and dropped our kecks. Not even one of them cracked a smile. We had trouble with the agency after that so we had to change our names to get day shifts. James Joyce and Brendan Behan were fully employed for another week. But Ronnie was getting beyond a joke.

He insisted on playing up to the Scots stereotype of drunkenness and it didn't suit him. One night we were on a bender and when closing time came we were in the Elephant and Castle in Holland Street.

Come on, I'll show you the flat which I shared with Jimi Hendrix and Kathy Etchingham, he said, taking me up Hornton Street, just around the corner from the pub.

I wasn't really in the mood for his bullshit but allowed myself to be persuaded.

We stood on the steps in front of a terrace of imposing houses developed into flats and Ronnie knocked. 23. I'm sure it was this one.

You mean you're not even sure?

It was about eight years ago, man. He broke wind noisily and grunted with satisfaction. Yeah, I think it was here. Looks the same.

A Chinese man opened the door, meek and polite but Ronnie just barged past up to the first floor. Somehow or other we gained access to a flat where about five or six Chinese men and girls were sitting around on a bed. Ronnie spotted a guitar on the bed and picked it up and began belting out a 12-bar blues and singing a bit like Joe Cocker. All the time bullshitting about Hendrix and him and this flat and the sixties. And the Chinese people were agog and even interested and started asking him questions. I heard them repeat 'Jimi Hendrix' incredulously to each other as if Ronnie was the authentic voice of the past. Unfortunately, I'd not had anything to eat and six or was it eight pints on an empty stomach will have consequences. I heaved up on the carpet and Ronnie apologised for me and then I was outside. I waited for him for almost an hour and I didn't feel well. But Ronnie turned nasty then and started talking about fights and violence as we walked into Oxford Street. He started a fight with two English guys he thought were looking at him and he was still simmering as we got into the Tube. Suddenly he'd become a Proddie and a racist and I realised I hated the guy. I suppose it was fear really. I waited till the train doors were already closing and I leaped out on to the platform. He tried to come after me and the last thing I saw as the train pulled away was his contorted murderous face pressed up against the glass and his shout that he would get me.

I spent another week in London, though. I'd got a job in a bar at Euston Station and a cheap room in the Wellcome Inn in Sussex Gardens in Paddington, which I shared with a builders' labourer who drank an entire bottle of whisky neat each evening then fell asleep in his clothes. Stone me. His name was Jeff and his claim to fame was that he'd driven for the Krays. It was a shitty room whose whitewashed walls were scrawled in graffiti in several languages. The sink hung off the wall by its water pipe and there were rusty nails in the walls for washing lines. To get into the room you had to climb down a wooden ladder from the poly-propylene door, which was fifteen feet higher up. The toilets were like little cabins in a spiralling construction which ran around and up the sides of the building.

One day I was schmoozing about over Waterloo Bridge and I heard someone shouting my name. Eventually I detected where it was coming from. Jeff. Standing on a girder above the railway track, in a yellow plastic hardhat, holding on nonchalantly with one hand and hammering at some beam with a sledge hammer in the other. He wasn't bothering to wear his safety harness. Well, stone me, me old bugger. I felt that if I looked away, he'd fall off. He was absolutely and completely and utterly mad.

On the Sunday, I was reading when he woke and blinked awake. The whisky bottle rolled on to the wooden floor and all the way across to the bottom of the ladder. He heched and spat. Go get us some scran, Gerry boy. Bacon and eggs.

I've no money.

Money? Stone me, he growled. I'll get it meself.

I trooped out after him into the bright daylight of Sussex Gardens and over to Spring Street. I followed him into an Asian-run minimart. He billowed out a plastic bag that had miraculously appeared from his sleeve and began filling it with provisions. But he had no intention of paying and put his face unpleasantly close to the face of the startled Indian woman, swathed in colourful rayon who sat patiently at the check-out, and he snarled.

Grrr!

Then he stomped out like the psychopath he undoubtedly was. I had no option but to hurry after him.

Don't worry, kid, there's no film in them cameras. We're gonna have us a fryup, Gerry me old mate, stone me!

But I'd seen an advert for kitchen staff at Pontin's Holiday Camp in Weston Super-Mare. I had phoned the number, expanding on my kitchen porter experience with the bank, making it sound like a vocation, and a career. So, early on Monday after Jeff'd gone off to work, I was spending my last few pounds buying a rail ticket from Euston to Weston.

7

LESTER HAD ONCE pointed out to me in the pub one of his old mates, Innes Thompson, a quiet, bookish type with straggly thin fair hair and cracked pebble-rimmed glasses. I was surprised when he told me Innes was Dundee's most determined revolutionary hero. He didn't look the type but he'd done five years for a politically-motivated crime.

Mind you, Gerry, Lester said, pulling at his moustache, I don't think Innes can spell revolution. And actually, I believe this to be a fact, the only Marx he ever had a passing acquaintance with was skidmarks. The skidmarks in his own knickers.

Yuch!

You think I jest? Apparently old Innes became converted to the cause by something unpalatable he read in an Enid Blyton story. Seriously! Anyway, he became motivated by this extreme class-hate. Down with this and down with that and brothers we must stand together. He wanted to make a bold revolutionary gesture but robbing a stately home was all he could think of. So he found out by lengthy research . . . he grinned . . . looking in the *Courier* or perhaps somebody might have told him . . . that one of the leading aristos in the area was the Earl of Airlie, who lived at Cortachy Castle near Kirriemuir. So he was badmouthing the Earl for a few weeks. Then he roped in a few other Che Guevara types and they made their move. They'd found out that the Earl and family were on holiday. It took them two days to find the place. First they went up Glen Prosen, all the way up, mountains towering above them and came to a wee cottage at the far end. Even Innes could see that Cortachy Castle it aint. So back down and up the next glen. Glen Clova . . . and so on. Eventually they ask this old guy, who only turns out to be the local policeman, off duty, and he gives them directions. Luckily the man's spent his whole police career in darkest Angus so he doesn't know what those long fat cigarettes are. Or the funny smell.

Anyway. They case the stately pile for a bit, blowing another joint or two and then they make their move. Get in by breaking a window. They successfully steal loads of gear. Yeah, in fact they steal everything in sight including furniture, paintings, carpet, plates, knives, forks, tablecloths, tables all of which they laboriously load into the furniture van they'd hired under a false name. Finally they make their getaway. Oh, I think one of them desecrated the family shrine first. Anyway, they're off, whistling the 'Internationale'. Unfortunately half the neighbourhood had spotted their bright-yellow furniture van during the previous three hours. In fact, it had become quite a topic of conversation in the village. Nothing else happens there, you see. No TV. Entertainment highlight of the week is watching the grass grow! Lester rubbed his eye and blinked rapidly. Where was I?

The policeman.

Yes. Our off-duty polisman, now in uniform, had phoned the Removal Company and elicited the name of the hirer. J. Givera. Lester grinned hugely. J. Givera. Honestly, Innes' spelling was atrocious. Anyway, the Removal Company had listed the van as missing since it was two days overdue. So the police were already looking for it as stolen. Innes and his comrades found that they couldn't even get up to thirty miles an hour in it, what with all the junk they're carrying, as they tried to outrun several police cars. They didn't even get one mile from the Castle. Within another hour, they had put everything back in its place and been carted off to clink. Even that wasn't the end of Innes' burgeoning career as a revolutionary. No, what really finished off his credibility, Gerry, was the humble letter of apology he wrote to the Earl, thinking this would help him get off. Unfortunately, the letter was read out in court and it was so appalling and the spelling so atrocious that the trial had to be adjourned and the courtroom cleared. The judge was furious. He suspected that Innes was taking the mick. Anyway, five years he got. Of course, there is the other version.

What's that?

Lester grinned as he raised his pint. That Innes is just a born-in-the-bone, tealeafin bastard!

The Pontin's camp at Sand Bay was exclusively for elderly holidaymakers. Being on a level plain, being flat and thus accessible by wheelchair and no strain on the varicose veins or wobbly knees. So it was bingo, bingo and bingo with the kind of entertainment that only blue-rinses enjoy, comics with gags about mothers-in-law and big tits and wobbly beer bellies. A few crap child singers and oldtyme dancing contests. No decent babes. But. Mainly we staff got bevvied-up every night and it was a scrumpy area. The first night I was there it was – Well, you're a Jock, you'll be able to hold your drink. There was a party and I thought great, I'm really in with the guys. They had a black plastic dustbin, filled with gin and vodka and god knows what else. Then someone suggested a contest and I was forced into it for the honour of the Scots. I didn't notice that their polystyrene cups had their bottoms removed while mine was intact. After about a dozen cupfuls, I collapsed and next thing I knew I was on my bed in the dark. I could still hear shouting and noise from the party but it was distant. I was gasping for breath and everything had that sweet melancholy exquisitely beautiful look as if it was the last look I was ever to have of it. I could smell my own blood and vomit and that's a weird thing, and I gagged for breath throughout the long night. Many times I thought I'd lose control over my breathing. I guess I nearly died that night.

The next day the under-chef was on the roof of chalet 26 in his underpants and refused to come down. They had to get the firebrigade.

The main work was 'on the plates', washing heaps of dishes, greasy mountains of pans and pots and utensils in scalding water.

Slopping out food remains in the stinking bin area. Crawling on all fours along the slippery, disgusting floortiles, hauling myself along by means of the bolted-down legs of iron kitchen cupboards to bring the laden trolleys of plates to the stillroom doors for the waitresses. All supervised by the brutal and humourless Commis Chef, known as Shep, a fat Elvis clone and number one psychopath.

Come on, ya Scotch bastard! Get yer back into it!

If I'd broken plates, and that was often, he'd launch a skilful kick at my behind. It was always me he selected to clean out the boilers, which were thick with the scummy sludge of jellied weeks-old chicken carcasses. The more I retched into the boiler the more I had to clean up. The boilers were of a size you had to get a stool to stand up on to lean into and what was in them had been in there for a good couple of weeks while the liquid stock had been drained out.

The kitchen was so damn hot – a warzone – that I often took my lunchbreaks at the Swimming Pool in an adjacent building. For some reason, it was always deserted except for this one sleepy lifeguard snoozing full length on a bench. The water was ultramarine, so blue, so green, gently wavy with brilliant patterns of sunlight reflected from the clear plastic roof panes. I sat on the edge of the shallow end and watched it for ages, letting my eyes go out of focus, eating my sandwich, listening to rock and roll clanking from the roof speakers, Cliff Richard and the Shadows, twangy guitars, a summer-holiday sound. I'd been scared of water since my childhood when I'd slipped on a cracked tile in a swimming pool and knocked myself unconscious and had to be pulled out. And there'd been the incident up at Murroes. Since then, I'd avoided water. But here there was no-one to see me, and the water looked so fresh, so inviting. I stripped myself to my underpants and climbed down the ladder. The water was cold. It billowed out my underpants and I peed myself. There was no-one to notice as I treaded the shallow end. Maybe I could . . . maybe . . . I began to hop with my arms in front of me. No-one was watching, the music was soothing, emboldening. The water came in little surges, lifting, buoyant, chlorinated. I got a mouthful.

After several days of visits to the pool, I got both legs off the bottom and floated, slowly, laboriously, then more vigorously, moving forward. I was swimming! Still nervous of getting it in my face, still rather stiff but now confident of making it across the pool. I experimented, lying on my back. I shut my eyes and half-opened them to watch parallelograms of light shimmy around the corrugated white roof. I was a swimmer. I began to luxuriate, submerging myself, drifting, eyes closed.

What is this mad bond with water, this trickling elation, this Yeatsian faery magic of ancient tarns? We Celts long not just to hear the rain or see it in the dark but to get absolutely, irredemiably wet by it; to run stumble and drink it and in it, to feel its mystic power, more than 'water'. More than simply 'wet' – pure and clean out of I know not what subterranean place. The Gaels have a word for this supernatural sense of water. They call it *eicse* meaning revelation at its brink. There is no comparative word in English. Perhaps the only approximation is the Japanese *satori* but you can have your *satori* entirely dry.

There was a football match one afternoon, Pontin's staff versus campers and I didn't get a game. Rather than sit with others on the touchline, I decided to go for a swim.

Good idea, I'll come too, said the receptionist, Ann. I was mildly surprised. She was five years older than me and she was Shep's girl. According to Shep, anyway. I went back to my chalet and when I got to the pool, she was already there. Had my bikini on underneath, she said. She was a powerful swimmer, did fast efficient lengths. I crossed and recrossed the middle depths. We swam for a bit and chatted at the edge and then I got out. And she simply followed me back to my chalet. We didn't say anything at all, just accepted the opportunity. My bed was too creaky so we did it on Steve's. Later, we went back to the football pitch as the match was ending.

Everything would have been okay if Steve hadn't discovered that we'd used his bed. He got very English about it. I laughed at him for his fastidiousness. He could always wash the sheets and surely he could see that my bed was too creaky? He got new sheets but his complaints soon reached the ears of Shep.

Everyone expected Shep to batter the hell out of me, it being a Saturday night, his night off and the night he bevvied up. Ann'd tried to placate him. We finally confronted each other in the entertainments hall, in front of several hundred incredulous campers and staff. But it wasn't me he hit. He battered the fruit machine I was leaning against so hard it literally fell to pieces. But he was looking me right in the eye at the time. Shep was summoned to the Manager's Office and blamed it on the drink. He didn't mention Ann or me and he was allowed to pay back the costs of the fruit machine from his wages over the next two summer seasons.

So I reckoned staying around wasn't a great idea. Anyway, clear blue skies and miles of flat summer sands called me. I was wasting the summer away. I handed in my cards and caught a bus to Weston.

The sea and the sand with the horizon low somewhere above Wales, crashing through dense green leaves, tree branches, rounding the headland. Leaving behind three weeks of cider parties, old-age pensioners glittering like Christmas trees in their blue rinses and sequins and pearls. Leaving on a whim, lighting out for parts unknown, the euphoria of complete freedom no destination, spitting over the open upper deck of the bus. I trail my hand along the side and wave at dragonflies. All the red-gold cider in the afternoon, the green tiled swimming pool, birds' feet somewhere on the glass roof, a radio playing a very echoey, tinny-sounding 'Be Bop A Lula'.

Miles of whitewashed hotels, Cinzano umbrellas, rosebeds of municipal gardens, a brass band, rows of fish and chipshops, arcades, funfairs, teashops and knickery-knackery nooshops. Candy-floss pink bites children's heads off. Victorian iron pier filigree, pavilions afar, the sea barely visible a mile or more out. Such a flat, featureless land.

On the road south, rucksack at my feet, thumb working, the blazing sun almost dissolving the oncoming cars. Sheer euphoria. Have cut all ties. I'm solid gone.

I camped behind the slip road on the north side of the M5 at Edithmead. Millions of red and black ants, but I couldn't discover their anthills. No clean water. Two boiled eggs for breakfast, coffee without milk, some bread. No trouble with tent. Legs still sore. Some ant bites. Got lift in RAC van to junction 25. Waited for hour and a half in torrential rain. Picked up in battered Triumph Herald by Bill and Bob, students of Italian and French at Bristol University. Bought them coffee and sausage rolls at roadside café. They want me to come surfing with them at Croyde but I get out at Barnstaple. Climbed a big rounded hill just to see the view. The first hill I've seen since the Law. Then I bought groceries and headed out on Bideford Road. Lifted by three guys in a Cortina to Bideford Bridge. Hiked for three-quarters of a mile until I found a good campsite in among some tussocks by the banks of a small stream. Asked farmer's permission. Built camp fire and ate rice and lentils, toast and cheese, pork pie and cup of tea. Laid some branches around tent to prevent cows invading at night.

Sunday warm and quiet. Two or three small lifts. Last one a Rolls Royce Silver Cloud. Tiny little ancient man driving. Deaf. First thing he asked me was, you're from Scotland, do you know Dr MacKenzie? Then he started to take me up the wrong road. I got him to stop and put my paper bag of groceries on the road but he'd driven off before I could get my rucksack out. Had to chase him for half a mile banging on the rear window before he stopped. Then I'd to walk back and when I reached my grocery bag all my eggs had smashed. A sort of allegory of capitalism – take you in the wrong direction, steal your possessions and leave you with egg all over your shoes.

The lush green wolds and clotted wealds of Devon and Cornwall. Bude, Wadebridge. Camped secretly in field behind hedge. These rambling roads are narrow and screened on either side by high thick hedgerows. It's very warm. Sent Lester a postcard from Wadebridge. Weather here. Wish you were beautiful. Spend the enclosed £1 note stapled to this card. I even made two little 'staple' holes with a needle. Such a merry jape!

We drove in to Penzance and I stayed a night in the Youth Hostel, a friendly place where I nearly got off with a bonzer Australian girl. Monday morning I counted my money and found

I'd four quid. I walked down the steep main street to the Employment Office, arriving just after it'd opened and spoke to a Mr Cameron, a Scot.

Holmans, the Ship Repairers need six labourers for a fortnight, he told me. I've sent five guys down there, are you interested, its eighty quid a week?

I was there before he could finish telling me how to get there.

Working in the burnt-out engine room of the mv *Supremity* (renamed – get this – *Celtic Crusader*). Confined space of bedlam, sirens, hooters, klaxons among the low-beamed soot smoke shouts ringing steel on steel feet on rungs of ladders. Like the Robb Caledon.

Trenoweth Trevarrack Trencom Towdenack Trendreath Trewynne Chyan-gweal Crowlas Zennor Sennen Cockfast Chyanmour Cliffs Redruth St Austell St Ives Trevithick Pendeen (Dick Quick) Marazion Market Jew Street. Dark almost gnomic, romany-gypsyish-hispanic types, old, gnarled, silent cadaverous scarecrows, mysterious lost Celtic peoples.

Like Davie, our diminutive and wiry foreman, never seen without his woollen hat pulled down low over his forehead, who'd never been out of Cornwall.

Oi aint got no right reason as I? Everything oi wants is right 'ere in Penzaance.

Who hated incomers and the outside world with rural fervour.

Them damned 'ippies used to camp on the beaches all along 'ere. That Donovan an his damned crowd. Faancy boogers. Out from the towns, they be, boy. We used to creep up on 'em like, and stone em. Give all on 'em a good 'iding. No, boy, we never did want no damned emmits down 'ere.

The green water smashed white smithereens in my face, here, at the absolute end of England; white horses of retreat. Motorlaunch, yellow and orange tilting up and down on twelve foot high breakers. Land's End.

Any port in a storm but she was really the worst. Green dress like a sack on her. Plump legs, red vinyl coat, protruding red lips and discoloured teeth. Margaret. I'd chatted up a pretty New-castle girl I'd seen walking past the boat yard but she'd stood me up and so I'd got tipsy on Devenish Keg Mild and Glenmorangie and this guy I was drinking with he looked and fancied her. I told him he'd no taste at all but it was me ended up with her. I pretended I was a merchant seaman, and when she asked my name, told her it was Phinny. She was twenty-seven but looked even older. I was embarrassed at being seen with her. We sat on a bench then she wanted to have a photograph taken and that was her bargain. Get a photograph together then go to the railway station and go in a carriage. I had to sit next to her in the photo booth and when the pictures came out, she put them into her purse and a large wad of other pictures fell on to the pavement. I was amazed to see the faces of half the guys I knew from the ship. Anyway, we got into the carriage in the dark and she lay back but I felt sick and had a sudden unexplained terror and ran out and left her there. I didn't stop running till I got back to my digs. And I had to climb in the window and that was when I ripped my Nico Spitfire leather jacket.

Just as the sun came out, I rounded the final bend, the harbour caught the light, the ship sounded her horn and gracefully, slowly, the sharp iron bow tilted off and turned, slowly, out into the bay. Inside were Hughie from Perth, Ian from Comrie, Bernie from Cardiff, Raymond from Galway, Dave from Liver-pool. I'd worked on the boat for two weeks and it felt kind of neat seeing it trim and beautiful, fixed up, sailing off to Lisbon. I could have been with them.

I got a lift from a wealthy hippy-type with a feather attachment in his hair and a fringed suede jacket. He looked like a stock-broker and drove so fast in his flash estate car that he passed everything on the road despite the angry flashing headlights of oncoming cars.

We turned off at Stonehenge to spend the night. The free festival was more or less over; this was its third week. The police almost outnumbered the festival goers and the toilet blocks were blocked beyond hope of repair, feet deep in urine and faeces. I pitched my tent near the outskirts and went on a wander. The platform had been disbanded and there was only a music tent and several other large marquees remaining. I'd just missed Hawkwind. There were a lot of stoned people around. I felt out of it.

Everything grows they sing nothing but light when money is rocks. Kids, dogs, mud, competing musics and cacophony. Hirise tepees. Bikers ride around without helmets. Kids like naked hamsters run inside huge steel wheels. The army parades by in distended tanks and bulbous troop carriers. Turgid bluebottle helicopters irritate the aqueous sky. I can smell the toilet blocks from here and hear the noise of the pumps. The whole of SW England is out and making noise. They're saying you can't even see the stones of England's greatest prehistoric monument. The police have been blocking it off to prevent Druids and other pagan worshippers getting anywhere near, as if it belongs to them. I return to my tent and try to read. Hemingway's *Moveable Feast*.

All night some stoned band or other drones the same mantra 'Take Me To Your Commander The End Is Near', and a deranged dog lies on its belly near the flap of my tent, staring evilly at me through the nylon and barks every few minutes. *All night*. At dawn a milk float clatters through the tent lines and I buy some milk, then pack up the tent and wearily trudge up through the mounds of dried rutted mud, picking my way around the tumescent earth pit latrines which, like the rampart defences of prehistoric peoples, line the exit road.

8

I 'VE LOST COUNT OF THE days and nights since I walked
through the ferry terminal at Calais around 4am to work my
way south. The heat in the daytime is terrific and I've thrown
away most of my clothes, except my teeshirt, jeans and my second
skin, the Nico Spitfire leather bomber jacket. I abandoned the
tent somewhere near Versailles in the mad race down the Auto-
route du Soleil. The ground was rock hard and I couldn't get the
tent pegs in anyway. Off the roadside in the dark was junglelike
and in daylight, revealed itself as rough mountainous country
traversed by dry dusty roads, pale-green washed-out bushes and
scrubland. I did 600km in one day with one lift, through Sens
and way past Lyon. A discharged national serviceman returning
to his fiancée, deliriously happy, driving like a maniac. Then it got
slower. It took me two days to get to Montelimar. I had to spend
a night on an exposed slip road. It was so hot, I abandoned my
cooking utensils, my camphor fuel tablets, the fold-out cooking
tin and mess tins. My sleeping bag was an encumbrance and I
didn't need it, so it too was folded neatly and left in a neat pile
under a stunted tree. It's probably still there. The ground was a
hard bed but I was always tired and I had the incredible clear
night sky and millions of happy stars to count. I felt strangely
secure even when cars passed slowly. The mornings were bright
and warm, the heat building up very quickly. The white of my
teeshirt got whiter as the skin of my forearms darkened.

I tried to calculate from my memory of maps, how far I was

from Dundee, but it was a pointless calculation, I was beyond cartography and I gave it up. I had no protection from the sun, the fashionable sunglasses proving useless. My face was sore from screwing up my eyes against the glare. My skin was gradually weathering to the colour of the dirty road. There were deep cracks around my eyes and when I had access to a mirror, I was amazed at the whiteness of my teeth and eyes.

At Avignon, a gaggle of international hippy-tramps huddled in the main street in the shade of the enormous Moorish walls. None spoke English. Some of them were gathering left-overs from a café table when two burly well-fed German tourists set upon them. I threw a plastic chair at the Germans from a safe distance and after the square had got back to normal, they beckoned me to follow them. We trooped out to a campsite at the end of an orchard across a footbridge from where you could see the famous, incomplete Pont d'Avignon. Funny to think of the old Lonesome Traveller himself, Jack K, being here fifteen years before me, criticising what he called a crumbling, dusty, dismal place, then dining at a posh restaurant and paying by Lonesome Traveller's cheque.

At the campsite, about fifty nomads, Ti-Jean's illegitimate offspring, clustered around homemade tents, playing flutes and battered guitars. All wear the black shapeless uniform of the long-term vagrant, and the girls were indistinguishable, though some could have been pretty if they'd washed once in a while. Most were French or Belgians. They had a beaten-down, whiny docility, and stank of defeatism. But they made me welcome and I shared some of their drink and dope. When darkness came though, I thought it safer to drift back towards town and slept on a tarpaulin hidden away at the corner of a sports field. I was feeling dirty and sticky. My neck, red with sunshine, prickled with suppressed heat and my chin was stiff with bristles. I had no trouble sleeping. My stomach had adjusted to less food, although I spent time hiding in the orchards stuffing myself on ripe peaches, plums and oranges. As a Northern European, a Calvinist Scot, I had to adjust my consciousness to the idea of free fruit by the roadside. Hiding wasn't necessary but I still did it. It was instinctive. Fruit, bread, cheese and lots of water. That was all I seemed to need.

I kept experiencing an intense exhilaration that lasted for minutes then dissipated. The next few nights I spent ecstatically at Montpellier, Beziers, Narbonne, Perpignan, talking to myself, singing. Then I was near the Spanish border. I hadn't thought of going to Spain, had planned to head down to Cannes or St Tropez. But what the hell. I let my direction be decided by the lifts I was getting – or not getting. I remember seeing a sign for 'Arles', but I'd got beyond curiosity and it was too hot anyway. I was getting nearer and nearer to the grim-looking mountains which bulked on the horizon.

I spent a full twelve hours outside a gas station somewhere trying to get over the Pyrenees and when I finally got a lift was only taken up as far as the border. I walked through Customs and had to bullshit about my lack of money.

Plenty money, plenty money! Cheques! American Express! I lied and luckily they didn't ask to see any of it. I don't think they got many walkers.

I sang my way along the dusty road between the mountains, watching a train high above pick its way through the spurs and ledges. *Freedom's just another word for nothin left to lose...* I sang all the songs I knew and sat down to consider my life from all angles with the sun full on my face. No-one I knew in the world knew where I was. I was completely, utterly and totally free. Yah – I was one real true bullgoose looney. I hadn't a care in the world. I kicked a stone over the edge and watched it plummet into the ravine, listening for the distant clack of rock on rock. For long stretches of time, I had the entire mountain pass to myself, winding around rocky inclines and bluffs with nothing living in sight. Except maybe snakes and sort of small lizards. But the landscape I was moving in was other than the actual. I was off my head in song. I was carrying in my head the entire Western world of rock. Springsteen's *The Wild, The Innocent and the E-Street Shuffle*, Blue Cheer's *The Hunter*, Rory Gallagher, Steve Gibbons, Loggins & Messina, loads of Neil Young, Van Morrison, Hendrix's *Bold As Love*, Dylan's *Desire*, Lennon's *Mind Games*, Led Zep *II,III & IV*, the Ozark Mountain Daredevils . . .

I'd stopped hitching in earnest and simply stuck my thumb out half-heartedly while continuing to walk towards Spain. It was such a religious experience that I was almost reluctant when I heard a heavy lorry behind me dropping gears to stop fifty yards further down.

I climbed up into the cab and the first thing the swarthy, grinning, Spanish driver did was offer me a bottle of whisky which was already half-finished. Then he let out the handbrake with a wild yelp of glee and began to career around those terrifying ravines, hitting the accelerator every time he approached a tight curve. He stank of sweat, frequently raised himself on one buttock to emit a noisy fart, and laughed uproariously every time he looked round at my white face. I swigged the whisky as fast as I dared and dreaded handing it back to him because then he'd take his eyes off the road to gulp down a mouthful. We went for miles but the drink must have had its effect despite my screaming nerves and when I awoke there was no sense of motion. We were parked tightly between stunted bushes in a vineyard. The driver was sleeping flat out on a bunk behind me. The whisky bottle on the dashboard was empty. Sunshine was barely reaching the cab through the dusty thick leafy screen. There was an alkaline smell of earth, of wet undergrowth and fruit blossom. I climbed down on to the track with my rucksack and found my way out on to the road. I walked towards the distant wash of the sea and some high-rise buildings. Quite suddenly I came upon a beach and there was my first-ever sight of the Mediterranean, playfully lapping the sands. Cerulean, peaceful and sleepy. The Med. I was enraptured.

This was a holiday resort. It was only about an hour after dawn, everything was still, deserted, a patchwork of muted pastel colours. The little twig-screen umbrellas planted in lines in the sands above the white plastic tables and chairs were empty and the Cinzano and Coca-Cola signs and the shuttered bar seemed somehow irrelevant in the cool, watery air.

I walked through the place and all the windows were shuttered heavily and there was no sign of life. I heard a slight sound and turned quickly round, tense. Down the road where I had come, a thousand rats were crossing the square in one huge, undulating, almost silent, brown pack, like a thick swarming carpet. They poured off down a sidestreet. I found that I was trembling and after a few seconds of rubbing my eyes began to doubt what I had actually seen.

I spent some time in Barcelona, finding a pension room right in the dock area, the crowded and colourful Barcelonetas, with a view of ships and the smell of the fishmarket. I washed my clothes in the sink and hung them on a string across the room then lay down on the bed, the first real bed for a long time and, in the delicious cool breeze and shade, I slept undisturbed for twelve hours. For 200 pesetas, it was the best sleep I'd had for weeks. Later, I went out to celebrate in a café in a narrow dimly-lit sidestreet where hams and strings of chorizo hung from the rafters and the floor was covered in dirty sawdust. I had a giant tortilla and coffee and a carafe of wine and smoked some Spanish cigarettes – Ducados – from a blue paper packet. I had great difficulty in finding my pension after that. I walked up and down silent cobbled, sourly-lit alleys for hours until my feet hurt, before I found the harbour again and from there it was easy.

How to get out of Barcelona: 500m W from Plaza Santa Lucia along Angel Guimera and Ave De Cid (N111) to join with Ave de Peres Galdos. Take side road up and round and well away from autopiste if it is crammed, as usually it is. This gives you a dusty, shimmering, heat-shattered vista of the city.

Somewhere on a road I was trudging later that day, I saw a boy selling watermelons from a streetside shed and bought one. Get this – he tried to cheat me three consecutive times with the change and I had to offer to sock him one. Hell – didn't he know I was a bullgoose looney? I took my melon over to a small copse of trees and hacked into it with my penknife. I ate as much of it as I could then, damn, I fell fast asleep while the sun shifted round. When I woke up, in burning heat, everything was magnified, hotter, whiter, redder. I felt sick, I *was* sick, had an evil headache, my eyes were hazy, sunblasted. I guessed I'd got sunstroke. I kept needing to shit and puked up a couple of times before I could even get into the shade. Then I bought aspirin and took two every couple of hours and drank plenty of water. I couldn't think straight for days. I remember seeing a tap in the middle of an astonishing patch of actual real green grass outside a car showroom somewhere. It was like a mirage. I slid myself underneath it and turned it on full. Cold, lovely cold. I manoeuvred my body back and forwards under it until I was sodden and cool. Surprisingly, no-one bothered me. Guess they knew a bullgoose looney when they saw one! Then I shook myself and lay back in the partial dusty shade of a stunted tree. The water evaporated in minutes of course and since I didn't have the energy to do it again, soon I was as hot as before.

I spent a night under the stars near Tarragona and drowsed through the next night in a slow truck south along the coast to Valencia. I was completely empty and the diarrhoea no longer held fears for me. I was shaky though, and weak. I got a room in a rather splendid pension, the Princess, in the shaded backstreet, Calle de Moro Zeit, where I spent two nights. I had a craving to stay indoors then in the cool shade but I was beating the sunstroke because my appetite was coming back.

All this time, I didn't have a clue where I was headed but had the idea I might get a job in the big city and so I turned inland and north to Madrid. The trip took two days and I broke the journey at Vallecellas, just 12km short of Madrid, where I spent an uneasy night in a bus shelter. On the way, between Valencia and Madrid, I counted, on the hilltop hoardings, eighteen black toros advertising Osborne's Sherry.

I became an expert on cheap accommodation in Madrid (*¿donde este agua corriente?*) and spent days hanging about the Puerto del Sol and the Plaza Mayor looking for English or Scots tourists I could latch on to. I'd lost my sense of shame and embarrassment. I learned how to enter cafés just as wealthy patrons were leaving, thus gleaning uneaten scraps of food from their tables before being required to order a coffee. There were places where free tapas were provided. I got to know all these hot spots. There was always bruised fruit at the market. Days merged into weeks.

All that was before and seems long ago. I'm not quite now as you would have known me. I've come a long way since crossing the

Tay Bridge. You have to adapt or die and there are things I've done here – had to do – which I know I'll regret. I try not to think too deeply about it and regard each day as a new opportunity. It's a long way home but I have no intention of travelling it today or in the conceivable future. I still don't know what I'm searching for.

I didn't find it in Madrid. There were no jobs and it was extraordinarily hot, reaching 95°F in the shade most days. There was a Saharan heatwave all across Europe. Too hot to work anyway. I did meet a girl, an art student, almost transcendentally beautiful, but I was no longer an artist, no longer able to paint or even think about painting. I'd been too transfixed by the getting here, by the journey itself, the escape, to look beyond the horizon. Eliza Craigie-Aitchison, last of Norfolk's Scottish broads, you may read this someday. Even two days in the Prado with you could not rekindle my desire to draw. After you'd returned to London, I sold several pints of my blood. I stole. I cheated. I fenced. I collected fallen fruit from the gutters. I slept in unsanitory hidie-holes beyond the torch-beams of the *Guardia Civiles*. I harvested tourists' coins from the fountains of the Retiro at midnight. I shucked off the heavy mantle of the city altogether and it was then I began to realise that what I'd thought to be lingering sunstroke was something more serious. But by then it was almost too late anyway.

I remember the apocryphal story about Lester's brother, Larry, passing along Landsdowne Place near Foggeley Gardens one day when he saw a suicide happen. The way he told Lester about it later, the main thing was his angry regret at not having had his camera with him. For, on the second top floor, a person had carefully planned to commit suicide by getting into a bath with a live electric heater in his hands. However instead of merely being electrocuted in the bath, there was an explosion which sent him, the heater and the bath smashing out of the wall and to the ground fifty feet below. Larry'd reckoned he could have made a mint if he'd had his Kodak. A snapshot of the incident would have been the scoop of the century. He was wrong of course. He would have needed to get a close-up snap of the expression on

92

the man's face, otherwise it would just have been an ordinary picture of a naked man, a bath and an electric heater with a background of a rather ordinary multi-storey building shooting skywards. You can never expect the unexpected. I feel like that every day here. The best-laid schemes . . .

Now I just have little details, tiny but accurate ones. Easier to get right. The light here is pure and dense and skims equably the distant flat horizon and the gentle evening waves. It pokes into the familiar corners, spreads its shadows under the corbelling and reveals the illogical mapping of veins in my eyelids. I'm no longer desultory, drifting, now I'm wrecked in the uncharted shallows or stranded perhaps beyond cartography but I no longer see it that way. I have no strong motivations, uncover no mysteries, merely get through each day as it comes and shade my eyes from the white, sand-blasted sunlight that drives us all mad, that makes us all ghosts in the end.

Sunday 25th: She's been here again and how I resent it. Always interfering and fussing when I just want to be left alone. Today I collected a large mound of sand at the high water mark and waited all day just to see if it would be undercut, surrounded and invaded by the sea. It took many hours and the tide at first merely swirled around it, pushing upwards, inwards and sucking underneath. Then the outer walls began to dissolve, slide slowly down, like Jericho all over again, and the defined shape slumped, mounded, shapeless, merged. By twilight, there was the merest shadow of a minor sandhill at my outstretched toes and tears rolling, rolling loose down my cheeks.

Don't know the date; this record seems increasingly pointless in the circumstances. Today I finally breached the outer ramparts and uncovered the pattern of what is beneath but could not find the way in. I can hear them in there, beneath, although they are all around me now and in my head at the very least. I feel as if I'm part of it though everything depends on my memory and there is always variance in that – process of recalling is different each time but no version necessarily false – merely raises problem of the evidence, which is why I linger here upon the brink of water and hope to be carried out of myself

Prehistory Section
Dundee Museums
McManus Centre
Dundee

Dear Johnathan,

Anonymous Dundee Manuscript

I have briefly read our enigmatic manuscript, an original
document of a most singular nature, if not exactly
first-rate literature. It relates stories of Dundee in
the 1960s, as reflected by a local artist, who apparently
lived in tenements in Pole Street in 1975.

As you know, it was found in a Council house (22 Dean
Avenue, Craigiebank), recovered from a binliner in the
attic by the tenants in 1992 who handed it in to the
library where it was rediscovered last year. Because
pages of the *Courier* dating from January 1980 were
also found in the binliner wrapped around
the manuscript, we must assume it had been placed in
the attic at that date, or later. Therefore presumably
the author must have returned to Dundee after his
travels in Spain. If indeed, he ever went to Spain.
That seems positive, at least.

It is unexpected that we have had no response as yet to
our appeal in the 'Craigie Column' of the *Courier*.
I did think something – or someone, would turn up and
I'm surprised that there has been absolutely no response.

I will need to obtain a complete list of tenants for
the property at 22 Dean Avenue and for the other address,

2 Strips of Craigie Road. Inquiries at the NCR factory
for a Time-and-Motion Inspector with the surname Bennet
will also have to be made. All I can say so far is that it
is an autobiographical manuscript which may be entirely
fictional, but which reveals some knowledge of the modern
city. It's a mystery, but of course there may be useful
clues inside the body of the manuscript itself. I will read
the entire text again more thoroughly as soon as
possible and list any possible lines of inquiry.

The two final paragraphs, jotted in pencil, might have
been added at a later date and I note that there is no
full stop at the end – if it is an end – which means we will
simply have to presume that other pages have not been
mislaid.

I'm sorry if this is vague and inconclusive at the
moment.

Yours sincerely,

Stella
Stella Auld
Documentary Resources Archivist

Vague and inconclusive? That's the past we know, the life we
lead, the death we dread. Remember Ms Auld-maid when people
used to describe everything quite innocently as modern? Modern
television, modern anything in brown Bakelite, modern washing
machine. Ultra-brite, ultra-modern. Then came Modernity and à
la mode and Modernism to make it all seem rather dated, cheap
and cheerful, the post-war era, you know . . . And now we're
post-modern, we've got beyond ourselves perhaps (or whatever
else it might mean). But the post-modern, this new time beyond
time, merely revisits the modern in an ironic kind of way and the
trouble is, no-one knows what comes after what comes after. We
haven't the language, the mental apparatus to perceive the next

big step, so we're tapdancing backwards like Groucho Marx in reverse to the safety of the golden oldie-time.

But – dang me corduroy britches – the manuscript is bally interesting! I saw right away when it landed on my desk, having come to me by a fabulously circuitous route via the Housing Department, Chief Exec's, Public Relations and the Barrack Street Museum, that something could be done with it. It's untitled, but it's a sort of Portrait of a Dundonian as a Young Artist-type of narrative. As you know, I deal more usually with prehistory finds or artefacts handed in from centuries earlier but these few scruffy pages seemed – seem – as fresh as courtroom evidence. It's only two decades ago, yet already there seems to be little I can pin down as incontrovertible fact, *enimvero*. Even fictionalised fact. But really, how can anything ever be proved? Under this city lies a city under a city of lies, a city. Every human settlement, I remember good old Prof. Weiser saying, is a vast graveyard built upon the dead of ages past. Grave upon grave upon grave. Self under self, a pile of selves I stand, threaded on time. Literally true of course. Under every car park, every super-market. Take the Bell Street car park, which overlooks the polis-shed and the lecky-hoose, gravestones are still visible there, peed upon daily by winos. And under the Nethergate too, bones, mass graves, pop up in the drains. Some folks never move too far from the deadyards, in case they'll end up without a berth, no knee to sit on, when the pianola stops. Then we're off again, eyeing each other, calculating the ailments, the debilitations, but we always do come back to our six by four. There is a mound for each of us, a green hill far away.

Stella Auld, 43, denoted 'career woman' by men. Okay, I'm enthusiastic about my job. Bloody enthusiastic actually. Okay, I'm utterly between partners at the moment (and frankly couldn't be bothered about relationships after the last one). But there's more to young Stella than the job. A lot more. There's my garden, a bonny work of art in itself, my house at Baldovie Toll and, of course, Fingal. Yup, I've often thought one of my worst ideas is having such a ferocious feline and a bird-table, bird-bath, nut-feeders and pecka-treats in the same garden. Apart from that, there's a jolly pair of otters in the old curling pond and sometimes they stray into my garden. I'm absolutely terrified Fingal might attack them. He has such murderous instincts I cannot curb. I'm an old softie but cruelty to animals makes me literally sick, just even the thought of it. Anyway, I'll be played by Meryl Streep in the movie. She plays characters like me, intelligent, sassy bitches. And she does rather look like me. Well, her nose does. Except she'll play me for money. I play me for a living.

The Meadowside sun filters through ye stained-glass portraits of Graham of Claverhouse and Provost Fletcher on to the faces of our ormulu clock collection. This, between Galleries 4 and 5 is my favourite corridor and I try to walk through it as often as I can during the day. There's something I like about its hushed, sepulchral dimness. Stop. Stop. No-one will read this unless I dramatise. If it's not exciting enough, I'll have to make it up.

Morning, Gertrude.

Morning, Miss Auld.

There. Real conversation. Now, fantasise about having a real life. Wait. Observe the solid bronzed rear of ugly old Queen Vic. Worst statue I've ever seen. No artistic merit. Nothing like the dignity of Dame Judy Dench. None. Zilch. Zip. *Nada. Rien.* Visited Dundee in 1844 for half an hour. Couldn't get out quick enough to Blair Atholl. Passed through the city centre like a blur, holding her nose. Frankly someone should blow it (up). Those marigolds are blooming lovely, fuschias. Gorgeous. Parks Department does well every year. Somebody loves their job. Must mention in the right place. Dear Sir, isn't it blooming lovely . . . yours faithfully, Polly Seabloom, Molly Bigbaroom, Maureen Rigmarole (Miss). I am etc. Always cheers me up. Even if manless. Even until and thereof. But not loveless. I've so much to give. Wd make a gd mother. Silence, bitch! Yir owir auld.

Morning, Miss Auld. Don't forget our meeting at two.
Indeed, no. Highlight of my day. Sarky cow.

See. More conversation. It's easy when you know how. Now where was he when I needed men? Torso-man, six pack, probably brain of mince. Have that boy scrubbed and brought to my tent. Helen. Wonder where she? *Courier* but not *Scotsman*. No. No time to read. Besides, might be follow-up in 'Craigie Column' on missing author. Artist. Gerry. Gerrymanders? Gerrymandias? Suppose he could be a she, Geraldine, unlikely? Must check with galleries, Arts Centre that kind of thing, who knows? Ah, Snickers bar. Yes, indeedy! Giant size, of course. Consolation fare. Manless, phallic substitute? Statistics prove giant size consumed only by rampant manless girlies? Bet could. Anything with. What is wrong with me today? Brain all over the place. Back to work? Sit or walk? Nice sunny. But might be seen, alone, aloof, alack, sad harpy. Eat Snickers in street. Reform, 1832? Yes, but. Discreetly. And discretely? Brownfingers, hide. Tissue. Pigeons underfoot. Danger. Fly up sudden, get me in eyes. Knock specs off, trip, fall, skirt over head. Major embarrassment. No, birdy, that's good, keep on strutting. That fool feeding them. Should be banned. Flying vermin, rats in feathers. It's as if they know you have chocolate. Kick I would if not danger of public exposure. Respected Council Employee Mutilates Pigeon in City Square. Sacked. Ridicule. Manless. Age mentioned. How old? Spinster of this parish. Blood on shoes. Ridiculous bully. Object of derision. *Courier* headlines. Story inside. Bird-slayer. Me. RSPB member. In mitigation. Some kind of goitre on its neck. Ugh. Ugly brute. Phallic fear? Mr Freud again, a cock bird, strutting in the hand. Have him round the neck. A bench, ah, bench! Arrange skirt over knee, solid knee. Indecorous: For All Household Improvements, No Job Too Small. Howkins. No he me sees? He no see me? Me see him no, no. See me he no. Okay, passed. He's past, soon retire. That time funny, hand on knee. What he after, hardly a pass? Lonely, desperate, more like. Odd, though, always phoning after that little things for a week or two no real reason maybe fancied me impossible not likely uncertain who cares not him fancy too old smelly tweed tobacco, belly. Ugh! These specs need adjusting. Maybe should get less severe. These new plastic penny-rounders. Eye-test. Eyes worsening. Change of image, brighten up, only 43. Time yet. Time for hockey, come along girls. Knees together. And so in. Sunshine behind. Office, manuscript. Letters, phone. Meeting. Two. Hour, twenty minutes yet.

Oh, Miss Auld!
Yes, Gertrude?

Blinks, spectacles slipping down severe sharp nose, flaxen blonde wisps of hair catching the light from the window behind her. The nerve centre of this place. Ageless and truly magnificent. In control of all, but now embarrassed.

There was a message for you, Miss Auld, but . . . I'm afraid . . . she frowns. It vas most odd, and I vas not able to take full details for you. Ver you expecting a ring?

Well, Gertrude, you never know. I live in hope.

Her frown deepens. Anyvay, it vas a foreign voice, very heavy accent, rather formal you know, a Russian gentleman perhaps. I have his name, it vas a Mr . . . she glances down at her telephone log . . . Michael Bak . . . Baktyne or Backton. I'm afraid I can only guess at the spellings. He vas calling from a long vay avay and he vas very faint. He said it vas something about a dialogue and there vas somethings about a carnival . . . and he said he had a . . . (it sounds silly) . . . but I think he said he had a polyphone. Does that ring any bells for you?

Perhaps he was wanting information about our Vikings Exhibition? He couldn't have been Norwegian?

But his polyphone it couldn't have been vorkink properly because he just got fainter and faded avay so I had to put the phone down. He has not ring back.

Thank you, Gertrude, don't worry. He probably will, if it's anything important. We're always open.

There, that wasn't too difficult, was it?

II Inbestigatio

I DON'T THINK I HAVE to tell you that readers want a novel to be one thing: complete and discrete, a linear narrative unity, its simple/single message clear and unambiguous. And it may indeed jolly well look like one thing. You can, after all, slap it down on the breakfast table. Commit murder with it by hitting loved one over unprepared bonce. And it *is* one thing in the sense that it's a manuscript, an object, an artefact, a weapon. It can be fastened together and put in an envelope, but when you start to look closely at it you see that it is many things and it is nothing. It contradicts itself, is ambiguous, contains errors and inaccuracies. Some of the research upon which it is based might be superficial, even downright inaccurate. Has to be read and reread many many times before it even begins to gain a sense of unity and, even then, that unity is just in the one mind and is probably incommunicable in the sense in which it was originally intended. And that's assuming there's no deliberate intention to mislead. This ms presents other problems. It's a set of stories – a collage of second-rate urban myths – embedded inside a story, and the story of it is something else. It's fragmented, there's no clear narrative, no feeling for the characters (such as they are), except perhaps Lester Logan. It's not so much a novel as simply a text, a literary game. A text which moves from hammerbeams to corbelling, from interior to exterior, from half-light to radiance, from north to south. But there is absolutely no suspension of disbelief. As for Gerry himself, one could reflect upon how much love he must have lost to write so badly, but it's ironic that the ms itself should seem to end, assuming this was the end and that there's not more which has been lost or removed, with awareness of the problem of the evidence. Very much my field, of course. If I can't prove any of it is factual then it would be entirely useless as far as I'm concerned – of no value as social history.

It's good to get out and about, to walk the city on a working day, even if it is raining. As it is, miserably drizzling. Swish, swoosh – the onomatopoeia of car tyres, can't you just hear it? Luckily, I've got my blue nylon cagoule and my red beret, and, wisely, the flat suede brogues. As I hurry across the roundabout to Lochee Road, I see the whitewash of the renovated castle half-shrouded among its ring of trees. Posh business offices now. Cannons lunge out of a parapet, erect and mouthing silent blanks of wet air at the Dundee Survival Group nightshelter below and me, hurrying by. That was a metaphor. How was it for you? *Kiss my ass for a bottle of Four Crown, me darlin.* Dundee's forgotten park, Dudhope, does anyone ever go there? Doesn't look like the kind of place I would. Dank, drear. Not very sure about these little streets off Polepark, since they knocked some tenements down. Dung em ding dang doon in Dundee toon. Those whale's tooth sculptures covered in red graffiti again, tut-tut. Poor Ally Smart's public art. A mistake putting Oor Wullie images on them. Half-whales are ladies but now gendered masculine. Oor Wullie, your wullie, abody's wullie. Do they get pleasure out of it? Kicking and stabbing at everything, scratching, scoring, graffiti-ing. Very irritating. Little oiks. The only way to make their mark on the world. Aerosol spray. Like dogs on lampposts. Now, there's the Council man, I'll bet. Fifties, neat, grey suit, wax jacket, umbrella. The box-file gives him away. Nothing wrong with his eyesight. He's managed to sidestep that large mound of coiled yellow dogturd.

Miss Auld?

You're Mr Walker, Surveyors Department?

Indeed. May I suggest we sit in the car? I'm not sure precisely what you want me to show you.

Good heavens! What does he have in mind? Prevaricate. Well, but I'm actually . . . I'm absolutely . . . that is . . . too wet . . .

That's okay. Let me open . . .

Well, if you're absolutely sure. I'll just nip this off first. Cagoule surgically removed without knocking off specs. There. Stripped for action.

Now, Miss Auld . . . or is it Mrs?

Oh, goodness, call me Stella please.

Of course. Now, Miss . . . Stella . . . all I've been told is that you want to see the site of Pole Street and that it's something to do with an old manuscript found in the area.

Not quite. It wasn't actually found here but I am trying to locate the author who did actually live here about 1975. We're trying to evaluate the ms from a social history point of view. I don't know the actual number in Pole Street but it must have been jolly close to the Lochee Road junction.

Ah. Now, if you could just take an end of this map . . . This was produced by the old Dundee Corporation and it dates back to the 1960s but there wasn't any development in the area until the early 1980s when most of the tenements at the top of Polepark, around Ramsay Street and Fyffe Street were demolished.

Hmn. I see. So Pole Street was rather small? From reading the manuscript, I had imagined it rather bigger. The author describes it, let me see, let me see, as stepping up the hill and speaks about pudding-stone and its being very flaky.

Mr Walker wiped the condensation off the windscreen with a leather rag. Then he opened the window a few inches, and coughed. Pudding-stone is right. Most of the houses are pudding-stone, which is partly why they have had to be demolished, but Pole Street was a cut-through from Polepark to Lawrence Street and it had only two tenements in it. The only street in the area that steps up a hill in any way is Benvie Road itself.

The only house numbers I actually have, Mr Walker, are numbers 20 and 22 Pole Street and some tenants' names.

Not possible. Pole Street itself was demolished in 1942 but the numbers only went to 4.

1942? Demolished? Oh, dear, but the author of the manuscript is writing in 1975. He talks about having a view of the whole street stepping up the hill, all the washing in the

103

backgreens. The flats also had outside toilets on the stair. There were, apparently, three floors in his block.

As I say, Miss . . . Stella, it sounds more like Benvie Road. That was an area of cheap flats in the 1970s. Some were actually condemned property, which meant that the rents were very low. Might this person have been the type to be attracted to low rent flats?

Very much so. Were they Council properties then?

Oh no. Some . . . less salubrious private landlords moved in and bought up whole blocks, then sub-let them on fixed yearly contracts. As far as I know the demolition orders were never proceeded with, so the landlords did well out of the deal. There were a number of different landlords. But there's a chap at the shop on the corner of Cleghorn Street and Benvie Road. I think he had a few flats and might still have. He's a decent bloke and he'd probably know who the other landlords were.

Thank you, that's jolly helpful, I'll speak to him but first I wonder if I could have a look at the site.

Well, if you really think . . . I have a key for that wooden door. That lets us on to the site. It's a former car-repair workshop. But there's honestly nothing to see, just bare earth. They haven't started the foundations yet.

And he's right, young Stella. We clamber out of the car and there actually is nothing to see, merely a hole in the ground, with little pieces of brick, stumps of wood and some sodden scraps of paper. A prepared bed for the growing of new buildings. Who knows what moulders underneath. Prof. Weiser again. History the study of the graveyard. *Sepulchretum.*

So this actually was Pole Street?

As I say, it's been derelict since the war. There was a bit of a delay with permissions for new housing. Several applications came and went but developers lost interest in brownfield sites like these. Wanted to build on greenfield sites: you know, clean, unused land in the green belt on the periphery. Cheaper to develop. There's little we can do.

My meeting with Mr Arshad of the Corner Shop in Cleghorn Street further convinced me that the Pole Street of Gerry's manuscript is based on Benvie Road. But numbers 20 and 22 Benvie Road are private flats and I could not get access. Mr Arshad gave me some names of the previous landlords. I'll try them later – if they're still in business. Wonder why Gerry felt the need to disguise the street name? It's almost as if he's tried to make it difficult for the reader. Anyway, I can catch a 26 Douglas bus from here, the corner that always reminds me of the old Rep, and just a little bit down the hill, into the lee of the candy-coloured multi's. Oh, goody, a bus is coming. Timed that nicely.

How much is it actually to the top of Craigie Avenue, driver?

Echty p.

Eighty p?

Na, pit it in thi slot love, here. *Here.*

Wow, jolly embarrassing, in front of a bus-load of faces staring at me. Awkward sod. It's been so long since I've been on a bus. Eighty p. Silly auld Stella should have taken the car from Wellgate car park. Especially since it's raining. Nice though just sitting letting the driver take the strain. Drehvir Dundee dialect word. Dreh vir. Called me love. Just couldn't see the slot, specs all misted. Love slot.

A wee hurl through Meadowside. One's place of toil and up along the Viccy Road. Relax all muscles, let eyes close. Maybe I'll have more luck with Dean Avenue or Strips of Craigie Road. Stand, Stella, stand up, rapidly approaching Eastern Necropolis. Walk, lurch, grab, hold on. Those magnificent gates, triple-arched Gothic. Gates to nowhere, except oblivion, and, look, a prepared grave, mound of wet clean-looking soil, wooden battens and tarpaulin. No sign of Gerry peeing though. All that's missing is the main character, the plantee. Descend, also get off. You'd think they'd have no more space. Thank god it's not me, not this time. Now, Dean Avenue first, I think, pass East Haddon Road. Bet they get envelopes wrongly addressed. East Haddock Road? East Hardon? Well-trimmed hedges, to within an inch of their leaves. Next right and down the hill.

Number 22 is the one with the grass needing to be cut. Ring bell. *Sonnez la cloche.* Not in? No? Wait. Shapes moving behind whorled glass. Slowly, slowly. Opens.

Mrs Mochan? *Zimmerfrau.*

Eh, that's me mehsel. Sour-face, downturned mouth, smell of cabbage. Ji wahnt?

I'm Miss Auld. Did you get my letter?

Le'ur? Wut le'ur?

Fae thi Cooncul!

Oh eh, fae thi Cooncul. Ehv hud a le'ur.

I just want a wee chat . . .

Oh eh. Mon in.

We begin a slow progression down the hall. Only sound is clicking of zimmer and sound of rubber stopper on lino. At the doorway of living room, Mrs Mochan halts and waggles her frame to indicate I should go in.

Watna cuppa tea? Eh'll mak ya cuppa tea. Hi – yir no eftir meh money ur yiz, hen? Coz eh've nae money till thi moarnz moarn till eh clect meh penshun.

No tea thanks. How long have you lived in this house?

Eh? Eh canna mak yiz oot. Meh hearin aid's broke. Yull need ti speak up, lass. Eh canna hear yiz.

Mony year yi bided here?

Oh meh goad. There's nae need ti shout. Ehm an ald wumman but ehv stull meh lugs. Eh've bided here fehv year.

Five years?

Eh, fehv year. Fae meh lad dehd.

And before that how long?

Eh, wut, lassie?

And before that?

Afore meh man dehd? Saxteen, no, eh tell a leh, seevin'een year, hen, afore meh man dehd.

Twenty-two years in this house?

Seeven'een, lass. Eh bided seevin'een year wi meh man. Ah, they wiz brah years, lass. He wiz a brah fellae but eh've nae fehmlay, there's jist me mehsel.

D'yi mind o thi bag thit wiz fund in thi attic?

Eh. Wiz me fund it, lass. Eh wis reddin-up the attic. Ehd nae ehdea wut it wiz. Pippers an that, ken. So eh wis eftir throwin um awa but meh neebur, Mrs Branty, she's a weeda same as me, she says, tae hud on ti thi pippers, she says. They micht belang sumdee. So eh gied thum tae hur an she brung them tae thi lehbray, ken.

They were written by a boy called Gerry. Do you mind o him?

Nut. Eh nehvir kend thi laddie.

There was a family, Gerry's mother, his stepfather Ronald Bennet and his brother Philip, who used to work in Brown's.

Aw eh. Eh ken Broon's ahriyt, the big store in thi Heh Street but eh huv nae ehdea aboot thi fehmlay. Eh've lived here twin'ay-twa year yi ken, lass. Twin'ay-twa.

How did it get into your attic?

Eh huv nae blinkin ehdea, lass, nae ehdea at a.

Well, thanks for your time. Is Mrs Branty in just now?

Eh'm sorry, wut yiz sayin, lass?

Mrs Branty is she in?

Eh, well she should be. Shiz no gettin oot cause o her ehs. Huz thi cataracts, ken. She's doon fur thi operation, lass.

Mrs Branty wasn't in. Or maybe she also was rather deaf. Walk up Strips of Craigie Road. Pre-fabs here, before they widened the Greendykes Road but the number where Gerry's mother lived in 1975, number 2, seems not to exist now. The evens seem to start at number 4. Funny. Of course, there's the danger that Gerry might have altered the name of the street, just as he seems to have done with Pole Street. This is becoming detective fiction. But it was this street anyway. Better get back to the office, wasted enough time on this already today. Throat sore from shouting into the ear of Mrs Mochan. Why do they wear hearing aids that don't work? Very frustrating. Nice to be called lass though. Choccy? Ah, Dairy Milk. Yum yum.

Must free up some time tonight for my doctorate. I'm losing touch with it.

Eighty p in the love slot.

III Lunam et cantus amoris

I T JOLLY WELL COMES as a shock to realise that the author of the ms, Gerry Whoever – if Gerry is even his name – is a contemporary of mine. Assuming that he was 20 or thereabouts in 1975, then we were – or are – about the same age. But Gerry was far more socially involved. At 20, I was terminally shy. Anorak girl with zits and long greasy mouse-coloured hair. I'd hardly been to any discos. My set of friends at Edinburgh Uni were too intellectual and we all spent far too much time swotting for our degrees. In a way, I feel I missed out, should have been a bit wilder, lived a little more. It wasn't that I was a frump, at least I don't think so. Maybe you do. I had boyfriends, but they weren't usually wild types. David, Adrian, Jeremy. Jeremy was a bit of a catch. Even now he makes me think . . . whoa there! Most of my girlfriends thought I was in serious danger with him. A medical student. Rather out of the normal run for me. Met him at the Sports Union Open Day after we'd won our hockey match against Strathclyde 2nds. God knows what he was doing there. But all that is well in the past, I suppose, for me. Haven't seen any of the old crowd since the twenty-year reunion. Twenty years. Blimey! Quite a few changes. Rather sad really. Most of the others well partnered, most husbanded, and breeding – even Sally Mill, for god's sake, whose teeth looked even worse than when she was a student. Asked Stephen from Barrack Street to accompany me but he cried off at the last minute. Typical male. A better offer, he said. Or did I imagine that part?

Anyway, to work. I've gone through the ms and made a list of clues to check. For example, the pubs mentioned, the old Tav and Willie Frew's in Hawkhill are long since demolished. The Scout is now Slattery's. Mennies, or to give it its proper name, the Speedwell Tavern in Perth Road, is still in business as is the Three Barrels in Strathmartine Road and Laings in Roseangle but none affords any sort of useful clue to the people in the stories. I can vaguely remember the old Tavern, now the site of the University Sports Centre, and the original Willie Frew's, just a few doors further up near the school playground, all demolished to make way for the ring road. Willie Frew's I remember used to have the worst pub toilet in Dundee. And there was only one, shared by both sexes. You had to get a girlfriend to guard the door in case some man tried to come in. It was usually in a disgusting state too.

The 3J's in Reform Street I also remember, although I was never in there. I remember the Rector, E. R. Skinner, or was it Neddy Sibbald (it was certainly one of those Rectum), solemnly declaring at prayers that it was out of bounds. Seemingly it was the epicentre of a set of drug-takers and despoilers of virgins. It was widely known of course that there were spies all over the city centre who would report any person in a school blazer seen around the town during class times, particularly in the redlight vicinity of the 3J's. Old Boys and Old Girls. *Pro Bonum Schola*. You needed special permission in triplicate and the approving word of God Herself to go out of the gates. Except at lunchtimes. Yet the city centre was so tantalisingly close. Some of the boys in my class used to take off their ties and put ski-anoraks on over their blazers then spend their lunchtimes in the Hansom Cab. Or playing snooker in the YM in Ward Road or go down to the Arcade under the Caird Hall. The rest scuffed about in the pebbles playing footie with a tennis ball. We girls just gossiped on the steps, watching the boys, or wandered around the shops. Don't think I ever kissed a boy until I was 20. Odd thought. Even then it was with the lights off. Not once at school. And I didn't taste alcohol till I was 18. Bit of a goody-goody, I suppose, but I don't regret it. Didn't want to upset my parents, being an only child.

I have very vague memories of Frank Russell's bookshop when it was in the basement just up the Nethergate a bit from where Blackwell's bookshop is now. The Park Chipshop in Arbroath Road is still there but since the redevelopment of Victoria Road, Scott's secondhand bookshop has gone. I remember it, opposite where the Steps Theatre is now. It was demolished recently, about 1990, when the Victoria Cinema was pulled down. I can vaguely remember the Central Bar but the Terra Nova is long gone. I was never inside either.

Patullo's Seed Potato warehouse at the Camperdown dock has gone, which is a pity as that might have been more fruitful with regard to the whereabouts of Atholl Graham. On the other hand, I spoke to Fiona Small, the Senior Personnel Officer at NCR Kingsway West, but, after checking her list of employees, present and previous, she could find no record of a Ronald Bennet, of 2 Strips of Craigie Road. Hugh Dickson's pawnshop in the Hilltown did apparently exist at the time Gerry is writing. The father, W. G. Dickson, had a pawnbroker's at Westport from the mid-1950s to the 1960s and around the mid-1970s, the son opened a small pawnbroker's in a private ground-floor flat. The traditional three brass balls hung outside on the Hilltown but the small shop was entered from a side door in the tenement close. When the son committed suicide the business was terminated.

I've yet to approach Brown's Department Store. I'd prefer to hold off until I have Gerry – and Philip's – surname. Must remember to ask about the two Donnas there as well. *Prima Donna* and *Donna Secundus*. The Bridal Assistant and the Exhibitionist. It's a wonder they didn't find out about Gerry's two-timing. The Tivoli, a rather seedy X-film cinema in Bonnybank Road, was pulled down years ago. Another long-shot would be Holman's the Ship Repairers in Penzance and Mr Cameron in the Jobcentre there. It's rather long ago, but you never know. And of course, I could write to Spalding & Dougall, publishers, London, to attempt to track down Lester Logan. His mother's flat was in the Hilltown area and it might have been a Council property so that's another and more likely possibility.

Maybe Tayside Police can corroborate the story about the

Cortachy Castle burglary and the name Craig Stewart. I'll get on to Stewart Ross at Tayside Police Information Office.

But what really intrigues me is the reference to a redheaded High School girl called Rachel, who became an actress. Assuming it's not her real name, I might have known her from school. I've racked my brains to think who it could be. But then she only plays a minor role in this and if she's in London now it might be difficult to contact her. The names given in full in Gerry's ms are Scott Walker, Rab Stewart, Stewart Mouncey, Innes Thompson, Stephen Walsh, Alec Robinson, Billy Forbes, Tony Woods and Mike Ward. Also Eliza Craigie-Aitchison – that's surely a rather famous and easily-traceable name – if it's real?

It's hard to know where to start. Gerry has constructed a fictional Dundee from factual elements as if to deny that it is – or that any of it is – fiction. Yet he fictionalised Benvie Road as Pole Street. It's going to be difficult to separate the real Dundee in which he was writing as a real Dundonian from the fictional personae he created and the fictional city-stage that really existed only in his mind.

A tall, bearded man in a green and yellow tweed suit was shaking hands with Johnathan Weeder in his office, when I entered.

Nice timing, Stella, Johnathan said, appreciatively. This is Professor Bill Garden. Stella Auld. We shook hands. He had a firm grip and, I noticed, somewhat irrelevently, his bushy eyebrows were like a glacier on its side. His eyes, piercing blue, somewhat devastated my impression of him as an old man.

Stella is our prehistory expert.

Hardly expert, I demurred.

Very pleased to know you, Stella, said the Professor, and I detected a transatlantic twang. He was slow to release my hand and I had a little tingle which I wouldn't even admit to myself. There was something Abraham Lincolnish about him. Then again, he reminded me strongly of J. P. Donleavy. Austerity, mature skinniness. Married though, wedding ring.

Stella, I'm just telling John here that I'm working with Robin Turner at the House of Dun Neolithic Barrows dig.

I liked the way he was focusing on me, as if he knew that he and I were historians while Johnathan was a mere administrator.

I don't know if that's in your remit, Stella, The Neolithic Age, but it's proving mighty interesting.

I gave him my second-best smile. Well of course . . . in the local paper just yesterday . . .

There has been quite considerable press interest, said Johnathan. And of course, it's so near to us. What's the particular aspect that's brought you over the water, all the way from Harvard, Professor?

Sheer chance, John, just sheer chance. I was scheduled to attend a few conferences in the south but had a few days spare so I came up to see Robin – he's an old buddy. It seems Robin was routinely cataloguing a series of Bronze Age mounds when he realised that one of the mounds was considerably older. It had been modified as a later burial site. So, instead of dating from 1800 BC, he found it was a Neolithic round cairn which might date from 3500 BC, which makes it some of the oldest material finds anywhere in the UK.

I felt my enthusiasm rising. Can you imagine, Johnathan? I mean this would be by far the oldest site in Tayside. A site of national importance, indeed, those dates would jolly well put it in contention to be older than Skara Brae or Maes Howe, which of course are older than Stonehenge.

Johnathan was looking worried. Stella, isn't this Ron Howkin's patch? I mean if we are to request the loan of artefacts?

Oh well Johnathan, yes, if it comes to it, but you're way ahead of me. Let's establish contact with the team first to find out first hand what they've got. Perhaps Professor Garden . . .?

Bill . . . Bill . . . please. Um, as I figure it, the importance of the find is in terms of the overlap of your Stone Age, Beaker and Bronze Ages. The concept of earlier structures modified but still in use by later groups, proving continuity rather than outright change.

That's always the difficult part of any dig.

You're right, Stella. Absolutely right. That's why Robin's taking it slow.

The Professor and I were sparking now, but Johnathan felt aggrieved at being left out. So he had to interrupt, pompously. It's as if he's terrified of enthusiasm.

We'd certainly hope that Dundee, as the nearest big city, could get some of the riches of this dun. No question about it, he declaimed. We're always looking to expand our prehistory section of the museum, which, if I say it myself, is particularly excellent and always draws the schools back. There's nothing like having genuine artefacts to give plenty of hands-on experiences to visitors. It's also important to compete for all new finds with Montrose Museum, which is improving itself – though of course, Bill, no-one would ever admit to competitiveness. We're all dear colleagues after all.

You don't have to tell me, Garden grinned. The pressure's the same in the academic community. Senior staff must keep up their publications record. But I'm sure we could come to some arrangement between us, and Robin, over the findings. And then he very deliberately and out of sight of Johnathan, winked at me. He was sending him up. I had to stifle my laugh as a cough.

Let's adjourn to the café, Johnathan suggested. It is, after all, nearly lunchtime. You will be my guest, Professor?

Oh, sure? I'd love to join you both for a bite.

I could not be certain I had seen the suspicion of a wince at the corners of Johnathan's mouth, for it was replaced almost as soon as it appeared by a professional blandness which was its more usual expression.

The conversation widened to other subjects and I found myself explaining my Ph.D. work. Bill, I'm doing a part-time Ph.D. at St Andrew's University, and my subject, The Celtic Mormaers of Angus, covers the relationship between the Mormaers or High Stewards and the 'Scottish' kings, from the early eighth to the tenth century. It's an area of intense debate, though I always expect it to bore everyone to tears. I rarely get a chance to talk about it.

I think most colleagues of mine would be highly interested in revisionist work on the Picts.

Well, that's very kind of you to say . . .

That's what I'm always telling Stella, Johnathan interrupted,

113

which wasn't exactly true, to say the least. Now, if you'll excuse me, I'll see if I can find Ron Howkins. He'd be interested to meet the Professor.

Sure, Bill nodded and turned to me. Stella, the Picts are still big in prehistory, especially in the States, just because they're so shrouded in mystique. Correct me if I'm wrong, Stella, but the date when they first appeared as a race and their disappearance around . . . around . . .

Around the late ninth century . . .

Yeah, complete mystery. And then there's the mystery of their dealings and integration with the Scots of Ireland to fight those Vikings and how they came to be totally assimilated after that king whose name always escapes me . . .?

Kenneth MacAlpin.

The very same. And even their name, what they called themselves. Unless any new work on the subject has solved that problem? I guess I'm not really up to speed on the Picts. But what is the area you're covering in your work?

Ah. Well, the Celtic Mormaers of Angus is a localised study so I'm particularly looking at the question of how much the Angus sub-regulus family is also the premier royal family of the whole of the Pictish domain, both north and south.

I looked over but he merely nodded.

I'm also considering the question of whether the Pictish heirarchy of Oenghus I and his brothers derived from the Eoghanacht of Magh Gerginn, of Munster, and of course I have to cover ongoing debates about the levels of Norman and Anglo-Saxon influences upon the old Celtic aristocracy. The work also considers political and geographical differences between the earliest Pictish province in this area which was named Circinn, its renaming as Fortrenn in the seventh century and in the next, by its present name, Angus.

Why, that's fascinating. So your paper sort of covers the development of Pictishness in one little area? So what was the name they first used to call themselves?

The earliest vernacular sources show that the first name they used was *Cruithni*. But even that's hotly debated.

How do you spell that?

I'll write it down for you. Can I borrow your napkin? There. And it's pronounced exactly as it looks, croothnoi.

Fascinating. Picts was the Roman name, of course, painted people . . .

Yes. But there's also the sense of the word that simply means 'our enemies'. What's really interesting though, Bill, is the changing perceptions, the overview, about the Picts and pro-to-Pictishness. I mean, were they only a minority, an upper class? What were the differences, linguistic or cultural, if any, between the majority of the people in this area with the Celtic, Gaelic-speaking Scots? The suggestion is that there were very few differences which was why integration was latterly so successful. Maybe the ease of assimilation proves the similarity of languages, both certainly Celtic in origin. But you see, Bill, some historians are very fond of the idea of the Picts as a national and racial entity, and have maximised Pictishness to include the total society descending from the earliest known Bronze Age residents in the area and claimed that this single and united nation, the Picts, ruled most of Scotland for a thousand years, for all of the first ten centuries.

What do you think yourself? What's your gut instinct?

It's seductive, unfortunately, much is still speculation. What my doctorate needs is a good dollop of solid field data, from recent excavations of some of the South Angus sites, but I can't see me getting as much as a sniff of permission to take time off for it. Far less approval from the requisite authorities.

I can certainly relate to that problem, Stella. I've been there. But maybe you should speak to Johnathan or Jonathan's super-iors? I'm sure there could be funding, research grants . . . for such an important piece of work. Maybe I could rake the ashes a little when I'm back at Harvard?

I'd be obliged if you wouldn't, Professor, not just at the moment, thanks all the same. I have my reasons and it's all rather political. I want to get a bit further on with my doctorate before I take any big steps.

Certainly, but if I can be of any assistance later . . .

You two look as if you're hatching a conspiracy, Johnathan said breezily. Now Stella, you mustn't monopolise our visitor. Professor, I'd like you to meet Ron Howkins, he's my colleague who deals with acquisitions and lendings.

If you'll excuse me, Bill, I said, that's my cue. I stood up and we shook hands again. Very nice meeting you, Professor.

And you. Later?

It was well into the evening before I could free my head from all worries about work and my Ph.D. and the horrible sense of time flashing by, chances missed. He hadn't rung. I had thought he might. I thought he might have got my home number and rung me about dinner. As a result I hadn't eaten anything just in case.

Tapping . . . Fingal! Poor soul. Come in. I'd forgotten about you. Poor wee soul you're all cold. Aw . . .

Nothing on the box. *Morse* on tomorrow night, must endeavour to watch. I think I'll just listen to some good music. I rarely relax to good music these days. And I should do more reading for pleasure. Long time since I read a book cover to cover just for the fun of it, fiction I mean. Mostly just skim and scan, for work. Forget . . . forget the doctorate. Yes. Put on CD. Nilsson. Yes, yes, a little touch of Schmilsson in the night. Soothing. It's so difficult nowadays I find to switch off completely what passes for my mind. Stress, tension, anxiety. Why? Everything going well. *Sleepyhands are creeping to the end of the clock.* Pick out a book to read. Further stress – difficulty of making decision. *Rhythms of the river on the side of the boat.* First one I see. No, perhaps not. *Rocka-bye my baby.* This one? This? A. L. Kennedy, *So I Am Glad* everyone's raved about. *Sleepytime is nigh.* Used to know her, went to the High School, lot younger than me though. Very successful. *Ragtime lullaby.* No, too neurotic, angst-ridden, want something less . . . something soporific. Trollope? Joanna or Anthony. Certainly fits the bill but no, should read something better. Poetry? Herbert, local genius. Oxford now. Forked Tongue. Yes. Get into it. First, coffee, biscuit perhaps? Plump up cushions. *I wonder who's kissing.* No, Fingal, nothing for you, you've food left. *Her now.*

116

Food here, look. *Wonder who's showing.* Stupid mog. Didn't mean that. *Her how.* No, sorry, Fing.

Looks like rain out. *Who's looking into her eyes.*

Sit.

Read. *Te-ll-ing lies.*

Pictish Whispers. Page 17. What are the serrations down the tongue, stitchings in the tissue of the language, half-forgotten graftings of two strains of rose, like a border between nations that may tear . . . *Oh I wonder . . .*

Or watch the video? *Who's buying the wine?* Phone. Could it be? Yes? No.

Mrs Auld, my name is Mandy and I'm not trying to sell anything. I'm conducting a market research survey on behalf of Living Kitchens. I'm not trying to sell anything but . . .

Oh. My husband died yesterday. I'm awaiting a call from the funeral director. I thought this was it.

Works every time. Living Kitchens? What next? Lively furniture? Excitable toilets?

Read. The act of translation is always with us, touching us like love . . .

Help, I'm nodding off. *As time goes by.* It's only nine o'clock. *On that you can rely.* Hardly keep my eyes open. *No matter what the future brings.* Must be my exciting lifestyle. *To bed. Moonlight and lovesongs.*

But that's not the end of it, my busy, busy mind, always ferreting in the unconscious, or is it subconscious, Jungian collective, something. Anyway. And I'm drifting or travelling but not in the car, not walking, somehow edging forwards, with my eyes leading and I'm in the familiar place, yes I know where I am, through the tall trees, the hushed and silent and shocked place where no female goes alone so late at night, dark, but I'm not scared. It's the familiar place and although I'm almost naked, I'm protected by the power of the Mormaers in their sacred place. *Kingaltenyne,* presided over by the calm bride of the white combs. These deep wooded dells, oaks and elms and sycamores and Douglas firs in the moonlight and everything frosted. My feet without shoes but somehow gliding safely over the wet

117

rutted soil, the nettles and brambles, up the slope to the stone ring, the square bastions hanging over the lip of the knoll. Into the circle, the rustle of rabbits. Stand in the narrow entrance place, facing the holly that has rooted itself in the circle, seventy feet in diameter, of ponderous blocks. In the distance I hear the flat notes of the horn, the carnyx. They are hunting the wild boar. I am become Bride, the beautiful, the sisterly, the aid-woman, the foster-mother, I preside over fire, over art, over all beauty, here in my chapel. And I feel the cold wetness of old stone as I sit upon the outer walls and relive these earlier times in the hush and sepulchral sway of trees and soft murmuring of the burn in the dell and the furtive scrapings of wild creatures, the rush of long ago voices of those I knew, the laughter and songs of companion-ship that will never come again here and yet I know that I'm awake and weeping. Oh, goodness me.

And sometime later in my bed at Baldovie Toll, barely two miles away on the same dark night, I awake and feel the wetness of my cheeks and the fierce sense of loss that we can never know. And yet my feet are jolly sore from the rough ground and my ankles are scratched and I'm actually entirely naked.

IV St Bride's Ring

A FEW DAYS LATER, prompted by curiosity, I revisited St Bride's Ring at Kingennie. It's a key site for my doctoral work and funnily enough, it's also one of the least known, whose precise history is more or less unrecorded. I don't think these two facts are unrelated. I think of it as my site, but it's more than just a site to me, it's my House of Peace, my Blawearie and I'm pleased to say that I've never seen anyone else there.

It's a stone ring, seventy feet in diameter, whose walls are seven feet thick and it sits on the rim of a small knoll in a deep wooded dell, entirely invisible from the small B road which passes through the trees between the grounds of Kingennie House (which contains a medieval chapel visited by Mary Queen of Scots) and a long-disused and overgrown quarry which is the source of the Monifieth burn. It's an ancient ring-fort, a sacred place, whose period is impossible to determine but certainly it was in use by the Picts at an early stage. An important defensive structure to the Mormaers of the Angus area, it lay on the edges of a vast forest extending on all sides, the habitat of boar and wolf. There is a religious connection with Bride or Brigit, unless of course, this is a historical error for Brude, last King of the Northern Picts, who defeated Kenneth MacAlpin's Scots at Pitalpin, near Liff Hospital. I'd dearly like to excavate it, but it lies on private land.

The first thing I want to do, and this might sound pretty odd, is to see if my nightdress is there. Of course I knew it couldn't be

119

but the fact was I'd been dreaming of the place regularly for the last few months, not every night of course, but often enough to make me wonder if I should see somebody about it. Not that the dreams were unpleasant and they are more or less always the same. I simply seem to visit the place at night and there's some kind of regression into the past, not very extensive but there's a peculiar visual intensity about the whole thing as if there's a kind of obvious message that I'm missing.

Drive off the road up a rutted sidetrack that leads to South Kingennie farm and park in the ditch at the wide bend with the farm just in view. You find the narrow track that leads into the wood and takes you down through the mulched leaves and dry soil to a dry gulch which follows the curve round the bottom of the knoll beneath the gigantic trees. It's very secluded and peaceful with bees and the occasional scramble of pigeons from their treetop nests. No other sounds penetrate the copse. You are alone as you climb the steep soft slope towards the looming grey-green buttresses of the rocks. It's so soft and springy underfoot you can't help but wonder if it's hollow underneath.

It wasn't until I breasted the rim of the knoll that I saw it. First one, then more. White things in the rowans and the holly bush and the smaller trees that surround the stone circle. White things that seem to flutter like large butterflies held aloft on twigs and as I got nearer I felt my skin prickle although I knew I was alone. The only person in the twentieth century anywhere in the vicinity was me. I went up to the white things and saw that they were tied to twigs, little strips of cloth like pale flowers by some sad maiden cherished. I looked around. I could hardly believe it. There must have been a dozen, maybe a score, like tapers burning through the night of time. I felt violated. Who had been in my sacred place? Who else had come here and done this? What was the significance . . . although I knew that it was a form of propitiation, an ancient folk custom. The berries of the rowan were blood-red, brighter than red, intense and yet somehow sinister among the foliage. Was I even now being watched? My skin is crawling as if there are maggots under my clothes. Get a grip, Stella, there's no-one here. But of course there is, there always is

120

and in this place there remains a kind of supernatural essence. That's not very historical, I know, but there it is. And at least I've solved the mystery of the missing nightdress.

Further shocks: I can hardly believe what's in the *Courier* today. Another fascinating shaggy-dog story, this time about a camp dating from the Mesolithic period, radio-carbon-dated to approx. 9,500 years old, found at Fife Ness near Crail. The oldest site ever found in Scotland with the exception of the island of Rum. Far older than House of Dun! These hunter-fishers were living right at the end of the last Ice Age, alongside the retreating glaciers. These are the earliest people known in Scotland. Flint fragments, charcoal and burnt hazelnuts found in pits. It's jolly wonderful, amazing. I feel like singing. First, the Neolithic barrows, now this. Instead of moving forward at the moment, Scotland seems to be going back in time. Our dead massively outnumber the living. We're a nation of museums, we've treasures of the past galore to cover our lack of an illustrious present. We're obsessed with what was, where we've been, because we're embarrassed about where we are.

The Ayebeens: it's aye been done this wey afore, we durstna change it noo.

The Hauders-doon: we must lower the expectations of the Scottish people, Uncle Thomas, if we're to keep Scotland truly British.

The Dinna-kens: nae use asking me, lassie, ye'll hae to speak tae ma man. He tells me whit wey tae vote. Ah kin aye depend on him.

And sundry arselickers and their couthy, canty wee dance of the editorials wi' the glottal stops in a' the best places! Kenneth MacTraitor's Tartan Tumshies wearing the motley of the fool in Grannie's Heilan Hame here in the lowlands o' cholesterol. When did we first get constipated with this parochial disease? Oh, Stellas both, young Stella and Stella auld, I prescribe one cup of black coffee and bedrest . . . we're almost self-governing, honest! Or we could meditate dourly like Donald; um, er um, er um, errum . . .

121

Prehistory Section
Dundee Museums
McManus Centre
Dundee

Dear Johnathan,

Anonymous Dundee Manuscript

I' ve had a minor coup. After exhaustive investigation
of the electoral roll for Polepark and Benvie Road,
I finally came upon a Grimes at number 13 but this was
in 1978 not 1975 and there was no 'Gerald' concurrent
among the tenants then. I' ve been informed there were
two flats on the ground floor and three on each of
the first, second and third floors. The tenants' names
are simply listed for the address and are on the roll in
no particular order. There certainly were some dubious
names in number 13 in 1978: *Aindreas MacAlbainn*,
presumably half-Greek, half-Gael? And what should one
make of an aristocratic name like Alan James Duncan
Hope-Bourne in such a location where the rent was only
£1.50 per week? Not counting the married men living
with their wives, there are five male names, Allan,
Carrol, Gibson, Louch and Scott. There are also
three female names, Hazel Lacey, Maureen Dear and
Wendy Dolan at the same address. I' m convinced one of
these must be the High School girl, Rachel, who went on
to become an actress. Of course, this is highly
speculative. I must contact the High School Bursar.

So it' s beginning to look as if Gerry fictionalised
the year as well as the location and I' m now considering
the possibility that he lived in Benvie Road and that
the novel takes place between 1975 and 1978. It' s possible
it was indeed started in 1975. But the deeper I delve, the

less certain I can be. Maybe Gerry is one of the listed
tenants for 13 Benvie Road in 1978, maybe not. At the
time, the flats were semi-derelict properties it seems
and there was a floating population of tenants and
sub-tenants who came and went with great frequency.

The most alarming thing about my discovery is that it
puts the period of the novel beyond the punk watershed.
Although punk rock did not reach Dundee until 1977, when
it did, it changed everything overnight. But this
seismic change is certainly not reflected in the ms.
I wonder why.

In conclusion, I think it unlikely that we will be able
to use the manuscript or its author, if found, in our
new corporate PR campaign, 'Dundee Out Loud'. While these
are, in theory, voices from Dundee's past (and in fact,
some of the content consists almost entirely of
dialogue recorded apparently verbatim), there are just
too many seamy elements which might subvert the positive
image we wish to put across and which might not sit
well with our investment strategy. More importantly,
I have to say that much of the content is rather less
than desirable. These are, in the main, rather squalid
stories full of unlikely events, drug-taking,
criminality and petty characters who are shiftless
nobodies and instantly forgettable. Is this the image
we wish our city to project?

We can discuss this in greater detail next week at
our meeting in the President Mandela Centre.

Yours sincerely,

Stella

Stella Auld
Documentary Resources Archivist

The President Nelson Mandela Neighbourhood Resources Centre. Or the lehbray as it's still known by some Dundonians, who're not quite on board our corporate restructuring apperceptive programme. The letter buys me some time because I've become absorbed by newspaper stories about Aberdeen University Geology Department's research at Rhynie, in Aberdeenshire. It seems it's the best-preserved site on earth where primitive life first appeared, in the form of thermophilic bacteria which can withstand temperatures above boiling point and very acid conditions as existed in the hot springs on earth 400 million years ago. So they're drilling a hole 200 metres down into the rock to find samples of the bacteria. If they can find it, they'll be able to try to trace it on Mars. I suppose if it could survive 400 million years in Rhynie, it could survive anything! But when does mineral become biological, and can these bacterium be legally defined as the first Scots?

I've been dipping into the Portrait of a Dundonian again and notice that I've previously overlooked the wee history lesson in the first chapter and the baloney about Agricola being a reasonable man. Even Tacitus never claimed that, Gerry. And as for the great victory at Mons Graupius, well, the only 'proof' is in Tactitus' eulogy for his father-in-law (note: not uncle, Gerry) in 'filial piety'. But Tacitus knows how to avoid unpalatable facts, *suaviter in modo*. In none of his works is there a single reference to a Roman defeat. As we now know, the eight years of Agricola's command were a *disaster*, culminating in a heavy *defeat* at Mons Graupius, fought near Ardoch in Gleneagles, in late summer, 83. A hundred miles from Bennachie and the Moray Coast, Gerry, but then Tacitus thought Ireland was next door to Spain. Far from being outnumbered by Calgacus' 27,000 Caledonians, Agricola commanded a total of 63,300 with at least 55,000 deployed in the field. His total losses were very heavy, with more than 360 Roman officers perishing on the field or in the retreat that followed it. He was harried all the way to the other side of the Gulf of Bodotria (the Forth), since the Caledonians rejected his plea for a truce and remained in triumphant possession of the battleground. Defeat was undoubtedly the reason he was recalled as soon the bad news reached the emperor. So why have generations been fed the lie of a magnificent Roman victory?

But over now to Dundee's own Jim Spence for a sports update.

Well, it's been pretty generally a dismal season for the Latin lads, Brian. Too many home draws and then that heavy away defeat. The Legates must have been jumping in the Tiber in rage. Not that there was anything wrong with Agricola's starting line-up. In the front line, he had Ardoch, Strageath, Bertha, Inchtuthill and Cardean, the centres were Dalgincross, Findoch and Carpow. In the back line there was Grassy Walls and Lintrose with Kirkbuddo in goal and Oathlaw on the bench. Not a line-up to sniff at Brian, drawn from throughout the European Leagues, but it's understood team boss, Agricola – known locally hereabouts as The Farmer – will be standing down next season with a return to the Italian League likely.

Time methinks for a long hot·lazy bath. First put cat out of house. Like so. Out. Then run hot and cold. Herbal salts. Too hot. More cold. Steamed mirrors. Find I can think clearest in a hot bath. Womblike. Unless I start to fall asleep. Makes me reflective. The 'truth' of Gerry's schoolboy knowledge about Mons Graupius. Every bit as true as these stories of his from Dundee in the 1970s and 1960s. For perhaps the only truth about the past is not that there is no truth; no single identified picture, but that there is *no past*. Understand? We live in the now and there is no definite link between all these moments of nowness that we previously inhabited. I can see that Gerry's earnest desire – and he's certainly earnest – to chronicle the stories of his friends and to place himself centrally in the stories as a character fails because he is trying a technique which replaces the linear narrative of classic realist fiction with a jumble of disconnected oral tales. I'm sure you'll agree. It seems that he is obsessed by the ancient Celtic fixation with 'truth', of 'true stories' or the events or urban myths which he has heard about. He wants to describe them in a manner which puts them beyond mere fiction, into incontestable folk-myth. Thus he makes no

125

attempt to build up characters or situations other than through the pattern of voices recalling from a void events which even they have trouble in recalling precisely. They briefly retell therefore what has only ever been hearsay, gossip or rumour.

It really is most beautifully hot. *Très chaud*, Claude. I feel no pressure upon my bod, no physical insistence, no demands, no sensations, except for this deliciously cold drop drip dropping from the tap, condensation-dulled chrome, upon the ball of my right toe.

You have to laugh though because a lot of our knowledge of 'Scotland' prior to written records in the tenth century comes from Tacitus, who does exactly the same thing as Gerry! His Life of Agricola was written to be declaimed, whereas Gerry's ms is the declaimed put into writing! The oblique view, out of 'filial piety'. Except Gerry calls his oblique view 'drink-summoned eulogies'. Stories of Dundonians. Stories of Caledonians. Each person is a story, an anecdote. Each life is a sentence. Oh, why should we believe any of it?

This heat is making sweat prickle on my scalp all around my hairline, trickle under my hair, face, cheeks, point of chin. Wonderful, exude those toxins, girl!

All time is telescoped by problems of evidence. Mind you, soon we'll be in a position where evidence will be irrelevant. We'll all be universally aware of everything at the same moment. What was it Marshall McLuhan used to call the final phase of the extension of mankind? Sexist as that sounds, if not embarrassingly Freudian too. If I remember my semiotics lectures, we will, then, ah . . . live mythically and integrally but no longer continue to think (as we still do) in the old, fragmented space and time patterns of the pre-electronic age. Trouble is, we'll no longer be able to concern ourselves with the precise nuances of *meaning* since we'll be more interested in the global effect of the *content*. In fact, with action-reaction almost simultaneous in every human individual, there will have to be a new definition – a Spinozistic definition – of the self. Our exclusivity is what makes us individual but at this point in our mental evolution, we'll all be fully inclusive all of the time, so our selves will no longer be individual but multiple. It's the logic of the advance in technological simulation of consciousness, and I can't see what we can do to stop it. Benedict de Spinoza's greatest dream becomes reality! Ineluctably, my dear hominid.

Pass the pumice backscratcher, young Stell, there's a dear.

Ta, taus, tava, me auld star.

Ah, yon's the very place, ducks, atween the blades!

Yes, yes, 'tis where to resolve the tension. No need to get a man in. The regiments may stand down. One does one's own. Scrit. Scrat. Scrape.

Yes, Gerry's ms is as oblique as the Life of Agricola. Only covers the minor details, the superficial, the unimportant. From Tacitus, we got finicky details of status and prestige, the plotting against Agricola in Rome, the corruption of the Domitian court, from Gerry, we learn what people wore and what they listened to and the minor events of their lives. We get none of the major news of the day, they're both documents of trivial detail. Mind you, many Dundonians probably think Agricola is a flavoured fizzy drink.

Wrapped in my white towelling robe, I open the patio doors and call for the cat. I feel the dew or frost falling through the still night air. It's pitch black, but the slight moisture shines and glistens in the stray light oozing out past me into the dark. The stars are out, millions, zillions, trillions, quadrillions of them. Just as Gerry described from the Eastern Necropolis in 1975. Were they shining here too, in the thousand year *reich* of the Picts? Did weatherbeaten faces look upwards in contentment from this very spot? Little faces in nameless places looking up to distant suns. What's really changed? We still don't know. We do not know.

V Duplus

I'M UNDER A hairdryer in a salon in the Murraygate when I should be examining written artefacts in the office or trying to summarise the key aims of my doctorate in advance of my supervisory meeting next month.

Ah, fiddlesticks! I'm on flexi-time and it's nice just sitting here and letting the landscapes of *Homes and Gardens* roll across my eyeballs and, I don't mind admitting, I've got a treasonably large Fruit and Nut on the table in front of me, hidden in the pages of *Marie Claire*. Ages since I've read a woman's magazine, whatever that might be supposed to mean.

SEX – ARE WOMEN GETTING TOO MUCH?
EASY STEPS TO GORGEOUS BREASTS!
ENGAGED FOR THIRTY YEARS – WHY WON'T HE MARRY ME?
I LOST EIGHT BABIES THEN I CHANGED MY HAIR!

I'm a bit giggly. I feel vaguely naughty. I feel like a schoolgirl. (Well, you'll have to wait, you impatient dyke! Ho, ho, ho.)

We're nearly ready now. Another five minutes, Mrs Auld?

Are we really? The royal wee. And this lassie thinks I'm married. She probably thinks I look married. It's just normal wear and tear, hen. A hard life.

It's awfully pleasant to be pampered.

Good. Right, Mrs Auld. Let's have a look. There we are. Gosh! Not bad . . .

128

It *does* look nice, don't you think, Mrs Auld? You suit your hair up like this. Perhaps you should have it done more often, rather than just for your special evening.

She's right. I can hardly recognise myself. Glamorous or what? And I've a new dress as well. Except I can't do anything about my legs. Hockeyplayer's legs. Shaving them won't make them shapely. Only problem is I've no date, no special evening. This whole charade is purely a defensive reaction to *her* – the Other Woman.

First I knew about her was when Ron Howkins entered with a sheepish look. Followed by the sheep in question. In lamb's clothing; short mini skirt, legs from here to Bell Street finished off in clumpy shoes with four-inch heels and shiny black hair halfway down her back. In neat little jacket. Well cut. About 22 but the first thing I saw, you saw, we saw, they saw, was her *legs*, smooth, golden, long, only an ounce or two from skinny. I hated her absolutely then, especially when Ron . . .

Miss Martin, I'd like you to meet our Documentary Resources Archivist, Stella Auld. Stella – this is Jill Martin, she's going to be your double for the next few weeks. He grinned slyly. What I mean is, she's – Jill – is taking some months off before her training course starts, and is joining us for work experience.

She simpered down at me and I felt the irresistible desire to claw her eyes out. Instead I smiled uncertainly up from my desk. I see.

Naturally we thought of you, Howkins prattled on, pompously, as Miss Martin rearranged her legs, with so much new material coming in . . . fast-moving . . . the cutting edge . . . the acknowledged requirement for another member of staff since John Barnet retired. I hope you can keep her busy. He beamed at her. It's of no value to you if you're not kept busy.

I immediately thought of that long-postponed and much dreaded task of computer-logging the entire collection, and grinned broadly. I felt much better after that nasty thought. How would Miss Legs 98 bear up under that dusty task?

I'm sure I can devise a programme of work that will give you a flavour . . . I said, after Ron had reluctantly left, sidling out with a last squint at her legs. Take this desk and hang your jacket here.

Please try to keep your legs out of my sight. They make me sick, so wear a boiler-suit tomorrow and all the time you are in my office. Or dungarees, preferably the kind with leather knee-pads. If that's impossible may I suggest double amputation? And I fled on the pretext of personal business, wishing I had really said these nasty things. Aren't we gals bitchy?

I just knew that by the time I got back to the office, she'd have them all in there, admiring her. The jannies, Ron Howkins, the Curator, the local press, Councillors, all the randy males in the immediate vicinity of Dundee. Cramming in for a peek, slavering, like one-eyed mushrooms prospering in the dark.

Actually she was alone and I soon found that she wasn't like that. She complimented me on my hair and then made me a cup of coffee. In fact, we went for lunch together. She told me men gave her a hard time. She wasn't making a pun. Actually I don't think she'd know a pun if she was offered one on a sideplate. She was rather earnest and, by the early afternoon, annoyingly con-spiratorial, but it was a conspiracy in which I was the older confidant, the sister, even auntie or mother, in *loco parentis*. Some of her conversation about nightclubs and boys was a thorough mystery to me but she didn't seem to be aware of it. A funny thing happened. I began to like her. She had no side to her, she was completely and utterly transparent. I could under-stand her, and although I envied her her looks, could see that they weren't an unmitigated advantage. Probably the reason I found her easy to get on with was her surrender of the intellectual high-ground. As long as I'm not challenged in that sphere, I can relax and . . . well, patronise, pleasantly of course.

Ron stopped me in the corridor. How is your new protégé working out?

Oh she's fine. We're getting along.

I thought so. She's rather . . . I mean . . .

I knew what he meant but I waited, cruelly . . . rather what?

Well, she's very young.

Young? Oh yes. She's 22.

I meant rather . . . you know . . . keen.

Is she? I wouldn't know.

I mean keen on getting *experience*.

Really? She's pretty . . . inexperienced, then? I wouldn't know. I haven't read her cv. I leave that to you men.

To you men? Poor Ron looked baffled. But he still wouldn't leave it. Men? You think she's . . . she's . . .

Needing experience? Yes. *Desperately.*

Gosh. I never thought. I wouldn't. I mean. Lovely girl, he gushed.

And only 22.

Yes. Only 22. When I was that age . . .

Yes. I'm sure you would. I left him there, gasping, panting, hoist with his own pornographic thoughts.

I became the centre of gossip about Jill. All the males could think of when they saw me, was her, and so they chatted to me about her, hoping to hear some sexy titbit they could use to inflate their secret fantasies. I began to manipulate their image of her by subtly, very subtly, implying that I had learned, in confidence, of all kinds of sexual salaciousness involving Jill. This drove them mad. They wanted to know but none could blatantly ask. It was a game of hints and whispers. Poor Jill. They fantasised about her when it was all men together. Frankly I'm glad she was her and not me.

I began to manipulate her too, subtly, very subtly suggesting dress improvements, longer skirts, a more mature, more author-itative look. She was quite amenable to these suggestions and I found her willingness rather flattering. I was like a big sister to her. Oh yes, I would say. *Of course*, I mean, wouldn't *you*? Surely you *would*?

I kept her busy too, and give her her due, she didn't demur, she got on with the job. In this way, she would hold the fort and I was freed up to do fieldwork. By the second week, I hardly needed to go into the office. She didn't complain. (I didn't know – the little cow didn't tell me – that she was being debriefed regularly by the Curator, in his office, after hours. Of that, more anon.)

It's so fascinating, she said, when I told her about the manu-script. He sort of reminds me of my dad. Except my dad isn't an artist. He used to wear bell-bottom flares though and I suppose he'd like that kind of music. Somebody must know something about Gerry or Lester Logan. It's like a ghost story and you're hunting for clues.

The phone rang. Jill was quick to take the call. Hello, Documentary Resources Department. I couldn't help smiling. She was being so obliging and suddenly she had upgraded us to a department. I left her to it.

It was a miserable day, rain oozing unseen out of louring grey cloudcover. An oppressive stillness that was already early evening. Once you get across the Claypots roundabout with its thirty-seven sets of traffic lights and pass the ends of Balunie Avenue and Balunie Drive, then cross the Dighty, you're into the country, almost. Give or take the odd tyre factory and industrial estate or two. Baldovie Toll has the feel of the country though, and once you turn left into the small section of old road opposite the old curling pond, you're home. I pull in between the two large trees across the brick driveway and park side on to the gable end. The cat appears twining its tail around the trellis post at the front door. Oh you, Fingal. What're you up to?

The first thing I do when I get home in the daylight, which isn't that often, is make myself a mug of coffee and sink into the sofa in the conservatory. Worth every penny, the Victorian-style conservatory and I usually drift off into a doze as the evening sun gilds the western sky and filters through the trees of next door's garden. We're a little community here at Baldovie Toll, just four cottages and we keep ourselves to ourselves. It's an enclave, a wee corner of the country perched on the rim of the city. Then I'll wake up and make a wood fire in the lounge and switch on Radio Four in the kitchen and begin to cook myself something. I have a sedentary life, comfortable, hermetic, manless.

Often I'll fall asleep in front of the crackling fire and it'll be very late when I shuffle off to bed. Then I'll put out all the lights and drift off watching the inexorable advance of red digital numerals on my bedside clock-radio, listening to the bongs of Big Ben that give me such reassurance. I think that's because of the time I worked in London. Who'd think that such a familiar sound repeated nightly over years could hypnotise . . . if that's what it does. There's an emotional trigger there somewhere. Then the *Shipping Forecast.* I find that oh so acutely soporific, the mantra-like enunciation of these strange off-shore areas in the sensible shoes BBC accent while I'm tucked up cosy, knees at my breasts.

And now the area forecasts for the next twenty-four hours. The voice pleasantly modulated, dry and eminently reassuring. Winding down the day. I'm half-asleep already. *Sea area Viking, south-westerly becoming variable four or five.* Because it's dark I can concentrate on the sounds and meanings of the words coming through the hundreds of miles of wet air to me. *Drizzle at first. Moderate, with fog patches becoming clear.* All I can imagine, wee fishing boats swelling on the rough tides way out there in the dark sea, shuddering in twenty-foot swells. On evil nights, the wind rattling my lead-paned windows after the central heating has switched off, I can thrill to the idea of the radio waves linking us, me and my imaginary skipper in *Malin, Hebrides, Rockall and Faroes.* I love the canting rhythm and lunging assonance of the names *South Utsire, Dogger, Fisher, German Bight and Biscay. Lundy, Shannon, Finisterre, west or south-west three or four increasing five or six. Rain light to heavy, prolonged.* It's poetry of the soul telling us we're still alive and lucky to be tucked up cosy. Somehow I don't feel so alone, feel part of a great mass of sleeping humanity in the dark streets, crescents, lanes and avenues, entire sleeping suburbs. It's as if I'm hovering above it all, like God, looking down benignly from a dizzy height on street-lights, rain falling on cities, continents. From thinking of myself alone, I've expanded to think globally of humanity altogether facing the dark in our different same human ways and places united species.

And now we leave you with 'Sailing By', gently undulating, rippling golden swells of lullaby sleeping another chorus in a broader key diminishing repeating plangent leaving distant echo distant seagulls wash of sleepy tides and repeat endlesslesslessly.

VI Fulbus

JILL MARTIN BEGAN to prove herself a useful assistant and we
soon became inseparable as the pressure mounted upon me
to locate the author of the mysterious manuscript. The Curator
was a prominent member of the new Council PR campaign
'Dundee Out Loud', based on voices from the city's past. Despite
the misgivings of Johnathan Weeder, Ron Howkins and myself
that Gerry's was not an altogether appropriate Dundee voice for
the purposes of the campaign, the Curator had already blabbed
about its existence at a senior-level meeting in City Square. Even
though he'd not had as much as a glimpse of the ms. Nothing less
was wanted now but that Gerry should be disinterred to stand
with them in the full glare of TV lights and cameras to hype the
city to major investors.

Jill was looking unnaturally pleased with herself that morning.
Her hair was tied back sensibly and she was wearing black silk
trousers and a magenta cardigan. I soon discovered that she had
worked some magic with the address of Mrs Logan. Seems she'd
spent the previous evening haunting the Hilltown area, knocking
on doors.

Didn't take me an hour to find someone who remembered
Mrs Logan and her son, Lester, she said. Only those are not the
real names.

Well, that's jolly good. But how do you know it's the right
family?

She handed me a mug of coffee, perfectly made, exactly as I

134

like it. Because the lady who remembered them knew that she had gone to a residential home and I phoned up and checked. It was still quite early so I got a fiend (sic) to drive me to the home and I spoke to her.

Jill was fairly smirking now so I knew what to expect.

Very nice old lady. Just like my grannie. So I've got Lester's address, or should I say Stephen's. His real name is Stephen Brack and he lives at Bridgend of Cardean, in Angus, just north of Meigle. But I haven't rung him because I presume you'll want to do that.

Proper little Sherlock. Well done. Yes, I'll follow that up. I'd better ring him straight away.

I did. A middle-aged male voice, an eminently sensible male voice with gravitas and assurance answered after a short while. I explained the situation. There was an added warmth in his considered reply but far less than I'd expected.

Oh yes, certainly. It'd be far better if you could make the trip out here since my car is presently out of commission. Would you be able to find us, or do I need to give you directions? It's really the back of beyond, so perhaps I'd better . . .

Jill was agog. So what's he like?

I don't know.

You don't know? I mean is he full of stories like in the manuscript . . . What does he sound like? Is he dead hip?

I won't know till I see him. This afternoon.

This afternoon? Can I come?

'Fraid not. I saw the disappointment on her absurdly young face. I need you to get on with the logging-in. We must make progress on that. Still, you've done awfully well. I'll give you all the details when I get back.

Before I set out, I made a second photocopy of the manuscript, thinking that I might leave it with Lester/Stephen if he was amenable in order to get his help to locate some of the other people mentioned in the text.

It was a pleasant run out to Meigle. I took the B954 at Birkhill. Some lines of an old folksong rattled loose in my head; *for their hats were o the birk . . . that grows not in ony ditch or seugh but at the gates o paradise that birk grew fair eneuch* . . . The road was almost empty, except for a couple of tractors which I had to follow laboriously down through the Glack of Newtyle. Then the long straight, the sharp corner at the Belmont Arms. Meigle. I followed the instructions, turning right then right again into a tiny road that led down into trees at the bridge of Cardean. I caught a glimpse of water through the trees below. And just there I saw the wooden sign 'Finlags' and turned off left on to a tiny rutted track in deep woods with the smell of fresh water. I drove for perhaps a hundred yards until it seemed I would be in the river, but there, in an idyllic seclusion, entirely concealed from all prying eyes, was a small pretty cottage. If you didn't know it was there you'd never find it, truly, as Stephen had said, the back of beyond. I parked on a gravel area, watched by two silent and canny collies and stepped out of the car. I could hear music from the house, loud, classical, possibly Beethoven. Pink pillar roses and yellow *kerria* twined around a wooden trellis beside a pair of green wellies at the open front door. There was a brass logo above the nameplate but I could not decipher the Latin, which might anyway have been Gaelic.

I knocked and a voice inside shouted come in.

The hall and indeed the whole house had a kind of peaceful cottage-in-the-woods-feel, a brackenish smell and was rather gloomy, in deep shade. Everything was subterranean, green, pine-smelling. I almost expected the armchairs to be mossed over or the wallpaper to be of leaves. But Lester Logan or Stephen Brack was real enough. He was, as I had expected, about 50, and his hair was greying at the temples although it was still thick and luxuriant. His handshake was deliberately firm.

You didn't have any difficulty in coming over? Most visitors seem to get lost along the way. We chose it because it's so out-of-this world, peaceful. We're never bothered here. We never see any real people from one year to the next. Anyway, you're here now, so why don't we go through to the parlour?

He led the way into a room at the side of the house which barely benefited from a dim natural light that filtered through a thick green mass of foliage. Everything in the room was in a shade of brown. The textile covering of the armchair he ushered me to felt damp.

My wife, Fay, is out at the moment, collecting mushrooms for tea. You like mushrooms?

Yes, I said, reluctantly. But I wasn't intending to take up much of your time. Just a few questions then I'll be off.

Nonsense. You must stay for tea. My wife's mushroom soup is out of this world. But we'll have coffee as soon as she gets back. Which won't be long.

Really, he was nothing like I had expected. I could see him but dimly across the small room, the poor light illuminating only the profile of his face. Clean-shaven and somehow now sunken in as if the previously round smoothness of his face had suffered in a vacuum. Somehow, with his burgundy velvet waistcoat, cream cravat and baggy black trousers, he looked entirely unlike the portrait presented by Gerry. A different person. And yet, I told myself, it was more than twenty years ago.

I coughed to clear my throat. So, um, we have this manuscript, this fictional text written by someone called Gerry in the mid-seventies and we're trying to trace him.

You'll have a job, Brack said, smiling.

Why's that?

Well, I haven't seen him for years. I've no idea where he is.

What was his surname?

He shrugged, arms out to the sides, palms uppermost. Jeepers, you know, I don't think I ever knew that. Not that we were all that close, just sort-of occasional mates, part of the crowd. I think it was Mcsomething. McAllister? McAllan? I think he went to Craigie High. I didn't know him at school, though, because I went to the Johnnies, St John's Secondary. I think we probably knew each other through the 3J's and pubs like the Scout, the Tav, Willie Frew's and Mennies.

So you weren't that close? The manuscript gives the impression you were.

Ho-ho, does it? Well, we spent some time together before he went away on his travels. Didn't see him much after that.

But you did see him after he went to Spain?

137

Is that where he went? Yes, I think so. In the pub, once or twice. Not for years and years.

There were some sounds in the hall and a woman entered quietly.

My wife, said Brack, jumping to his feet. Fay.

She really was extraordinarily beautiful, translucent, petite, pale with a paleness almost luminous but what struck me first and most forcibly was the sense of the familiar. I knew her! She was familiar to me. In a mere flicker of eyelids I felt recognition flooding over me. Of course! She was . . . the spitting image of Jill Martin! They could have been twins. I must have been gaping. Her hair was thick, black, long and shiny, all the more striking against the delicate china-pale skin.

Do you know each other? Brack asked quizzically.

No, but. But she – Fay – looks very like someone I know.

Happens all the time, Brack said. People are always saying that. Aren't they, dear?

Fay just smiled and, with a swirl of her long dark coat and skirt, turned to make the coffee. Don't mind Stephen, she said softly, he's so full of enthusiasms. He's got loads of stories, but fortunately none of them are true. She pulled off her black gloves. How do you like your coffee?

Now, where were we? Brack inquired as we resumed our seats in the gloomy parlour.

Gerry's manuscript. I have a copy here and I'd welcome your thoughts on it, if you have time to look it over.

I'd love to. It looks quite short. He weighed it upon his palm. How many words in it?

I don't know. About a hundred pages. Is that short?

Oh, yes, most of my manuscripts are longer. Average about 75,000 words. My published books . . . well, vary in length.

Cramp in Strange Places?

Sorry?

Isn't that the title of your book? Published by Spalding & Dougall?

Good grief . . . Spalding & Dougall . . . I once sent them a script but it was rejected, and that wasn't the title. That was a long time ago. Since then I've published six books, non-fiction, but I've got loads of novels tucked away here unpublished. Trouble is, publishers don't know their arses from their kneecaps these days.

That sounds familiar.

Brack looked puzzled. Does it? Anyway, Spalding & Dougall went bust that's how sharp they were. Now, I'm not saying it was because they failed to publish my manuscript . . . He tapped the photocopied ms. So what is this like? I'd no idea old Gerry'd written something. Course he always said he would . . . but I never saw anything he wrote. He picked up the first page and read. Hey, Lester Logan – is this supposed to be me? *Smoky shadows lingered across his sunbrowned face . . . cobwebbed spaces under his eyes . . . star of David medallion . . .* ho-ho, yes, I *did* wear one of those. But didn't everyone. Lester Logan, he repeated, savouring the syllables. I quite like it – I might use it as a pseudonym. Hey! I'm not buying *this*. Waiting *for Alec Stewart to offer him a Woodbine*. It was always the other way round, that skinflint never offered anyone a fag yet! But . . . the description is fairly accurate. The old Hawkhill Tavern, those were the days. Yes, we hung around there a lot. Yes, you know, I'd rather like to read this. It'd be like looking back at a diary. Not that I've got a diary. I hardly ever talk about the old days. Fay doesn't like it. Doesn't like to hear about my other women.

Do you see any of your friends of those days?

Not often. We rarely go into old *Taodunum* these days. Then my eyesight is quite poor. I have to wear my specs. Sometimes I think I see someone I recognise, but I can never really be certain. The other week I saw someone that might've been Phinny but I just wasn't sure, so I didn't go up to him. We all look different these days anyway. Maybe none of the old crowd would recognise me now. It's amazing what time does to you – loss of teeth, hair, a bit of a belly. Mind you, I don't think I look too bad considering. How old would you say I am, Stella?

Oh, that's . . . I'm not very good at ages, but I know you must be in your . . . late forties.

Ho-ho. I'm 52. I was an end-of-the-war baby.

Really? Well, back to this. Gerry's book is about the end of his relationship with a girl called Wanda. Who went off with a guy called Kenneth Syme.

Wanda? I remember Wanda. She was a gorgeous babe. But she didn't go off with someone called Syme. Way I remember it, Gerry packed her in and then regretted it. She started going out with a guy called Ian Wayward-Small, but that was long after. He'd a band, I remember, called The Villains. Load a crap. He looked like . . . well he was as ugly as . . . Mick Jagger. He'd an E-type jag too, show-off red, it was. That's it. He was an E-type Jagger. Bit of a wanker. Sorry.

That's alright.

Did he tell you about Hogmanay, what . . . in 1977, I think. Gerry and me had been at the cider, the real stuff, Merrydown you know, before we even went out, I think we'd also had a bottle of Advocaat. In my maw's house, on the Hilltown. Then we went round all the pubs and got blootered. But Gerry came over all nostalgic for Wanda. He had this present you see, he'd bought her, a wee radio in the shape of a coke can, and he wanted to deliver it. So after the pubs closed and we'd been to the City Square for the usual carry-on, kissing loads of birds, and, I seem to remember puking up a few times, well, we set off to find Wanda. We were really loaded. We called at the place where she used to live but these friends of hers said no, she was at Ian's place and that was really just around the corner in the Cleggie, Cleghorn Street. So we trooped round there. Well, Gerry went up the stairs to the flat and knocked on the door. Seems it was answered by Wayward-Small in his dressing gown. Is Wanda here? Gerry asks. Yes. Well, Gerry didn't know what to do. So he tamely hands in the prezzie. Could you give her this, from Gerry, he says. Then he comes back down the stairs, but on the way down, he's bawling. Weeping his eyes out. Also he bashes his watch on the wall. So when I see him on the pavement, it seems to me there's been a fight. Well, I don't know what came over me. I'm not the violent type, as Gerry would tell you. But I belted up the stair and when Wayward-Small opened the door, I let him have it. I booted him around the room and broke a chair on his head and

140

busted his fingers (he was a guitarist) and during the mayhem, I saw Wanda in the altogether in the other room, but of course, I didn't tell Gerry this, he was bad enough already. So we ended up sleeping it off in his pad in Benvie Road.

So Benvie Road was where he lived?

Yes, number 15, or was it 17? A right dump. So next day, Gerry was at his mum's and all the family were there, his grannie, his uncle, aunts, etc. Having the turkey dinner when the polis called. Took Gerry outside to sit in the car, in full view of the neighbours. Anyway they tried to get Gerry to give evidence against me. Told him I had a long record for violence, which is a load of guff, but Gerry told them it was him who had done the job on Wayward-Small and of course Wanda was *his* girlfriend, so they had to believe it. So there was no evidence either way and the case never came to court. But the funny thing was, and this is hilarious, Stella, that the story got about, except that Wayward-Small . . . imagine having that monicker, I mean it's not good advertising, is it? Eohw, I sey, cheps, my name's Small, Small by name, small by nature, haw, haw haw . . . Where was I?

The funny thing.

Fay entered with mugs of coffee. Is Stephen boring you to death with his stories of the old days?

No. It's interesting.

You don't take sugar?

Perfect. Thank you.

Thank you, darling. Yes, the funny thing was that Wayward-Small was two-timing Wanda anyway. It was widely known that his girlfriend, Sophie, was in South Africa, so the story developed that I'd been having an affair with her – with Sophie – and had given him a good belting because he'd been mistreating her. Wanda's name wasn't even mentioned. She took it very badly, actually. In order to get revenge on Small, who dumped her when Sophie came back from her trip, she started to go out with his best mate. Funny kind of revenge. Actually, I think she'd had some kind of mini-breakdown. Anyway, he, a well-known artist by the way, Jake Sultana (which must have really irked Gerry), dumped her too, within a couple of months. I never saw her after

141

that. Seems Wayward-Small was known for using the same technique with girls, he always picked up babes who were just finishing with other guys, or who were going with his mates – vulnerable ones. He was a flash bugger and an ugly bugger, but somehow babes like, or liked, that kind of approach, the treat 'em mean, keep 'em keen kind of thing. Never did that myself of course. And I don't regret what I did to him.

So can you make any suggestions as to where I might start to look for Gerry?

As I said, he wasn't really one of the old crowd, the real old crowd from the sixties. I didn't know him till the early or even mid-seventies. I kind of dropped out of the scene about then. The best times were much earlier. The early sixties when I was a kid. Everything was new then, there wasn't the cynical, exploitative thing. People did their own thing at first but then it became kind of a uniform and everyone was doing it. We were in at the start. We were the first in Dundee. It was exciting and new. The bands were great. It was fantastic being a teenager then.

You played in a band then?

Well, yeah, but it was just a school thing. Nothing anybody'd want to remember. Everybody was in a band, it was just the thing you did. Course we'd no real intruments, just a cheap guitar and a homemade stand-up bass and some washing boards and a piece of wood to play them with. We'd drums made out of tea-chests. The Bluebeats we called ourselves. We played in Andy Blyth's bedroom. He went on to play in the Staccato 5. Andy, Tam Berry, Gordie Stewart, Ronnie Vettraino, Pete Poland. Pete was Dundee's Jerry Lee Lewis. He's a great saxophonist, you must have seen him around town, burly, wee hip beard, quiff, leather jacket? Great guy. We all used to hang around at the Monkey parade at the Palais on a Sunday. Do you know that you weren't allowed to stand still? See, they didn't have an entertainments licence, so we all had to keep moving, around and around. It was crazy. They had people employed just to keep you moving. Then there were the Twisting marathons a little later. Some of the Dundee bands from that time nearly made it, the Hudson Hi-Four – they worked in Hamburg with the Beatles – and of course everybody knew Robbie McIntosh, later of the Average White Band. He went to the same school as me. Lived in Kincardine Street – it's long ago knocked down – in the Blue Mountains, off Hawkhill. He was poisoned you know, in LA by a guy called Kenneth Moss. Robbie's legal guardians still live in the Ferry.

It all came bubbling out like an overdue confession. It was too much. Can I use your toilet? I stood up abruptly.

Sure, first left.

After I'd washed my hands I went into the kitchen. Fay was preparing vegetables. Exhausting, isn't he? she smiled.

Well, he's certainly full of stories. Very animated.

Yes, he never gets the chance to tell them, so when someone like you comes along, it all comes out in a great burst and it's pretty overwhelming.

When did you meet him?

Oh, we've been married about ten years. We met in the bookshop where I was working in Edinburgh. I'm originally from Dundee though.

Stephen was reading the manuscript when I returned. He looked up and grinned. I don't remember a party like this where someone fired a gun. But I know who Rab is – and he's rather like this. It's the sort of thing he would do.

So the novel is based on genuine incidents?

Probably, but the names are mostly changed. It's fiction but it's based on things that did happen. The story here is not nearly outrageous enough, not nearly as incredible as the actual truth.

You've never written about those days yourself?

Na. No-one'd want to read it. It's all in the past. I tried of course, but I soon found that the only way I could get books published was to write about things and places that people wanted to read about. I've published books on antique barometers, on old churches in Kent, on the game of *pétanque*, on Scottish regiments (that sold well, and went into four different language editions), on silver buttons and buckled shoes. It's a living, although it's hardly James Joyce.

Is that what you wanted to be?

Oh, yeah, a great literary novelist. Dundee's never had one you

143

know. Oh, it's had some successful writers. Chic – a good friend of mine till his recent death – that's Charles MacHardy, he was a good writer. Also played a mean piano, a real jazz buff. And Rosamunde Pilcher out at Invergowrie. Of course there have been various jute-saga-vendors, purveyors of great puddings of cliché and conventional romance set in what the publishers claim to be the authentic Dundee, as if we're a one-genre town. Oh, but there were a few of us, Stella, complete unknowns. We used to go to the writing class at the Uni. Carl MacDougall's. Now he was a *mensch*. I think Billy Connolly got his best jokes from Carl. But no-one ever published our novels and sometimes I think maybe they never will.

VII Uxor

I DID ENJOY THE mushroom soup, wonderfully restorative. Fay seemed pleased. I had a second bowl. There's three kinds of mushroom in it, she said, all picked today from the wood. There's wild allum, wild garlic and essence of chestnut. That's my own idea.

Fay has an imaginative sense of cuisine, Stephen smiled wryly. I leave her to it, she hasn't poisoned me yet. Would you like some bread before the next course, it's homemade wholemeal?

I followed Fay into the tiny kitchen carrying the used plates.

I was wondering, she said, when you first saw me, you looked astonished. Who is it that I look like?

You're the absolute double of the girl that works with me. You wouldn't happen to have a twin sister?

I'm an only child and both my parents are dead.

Oh dear, I'm sorry . . .

No problem. It all happened very long ago. But what is her name? I felt myself being regarded by her green, seagreen eyes, all the greener for being set in such a wan face, upturned, shining under the bare kitchen bulb.

Her name is Jill, Jill Martin. She's 22.

Fay turned away, disappointedly. I don't know her. Could you take the wine through to Stephen?

Certainly. *This* is an unusual object, I said, inspecting an exquisite brass implement, what do you use it for?

Oh that? I use it to drain cooking oil. It's a tundish.

A what?

A tundish, a sort of funnel. Stephen bought it for me at an

antique shop in Dublin when we were on our honeymoon. It used to belong to some famous priest.

Later, we went out for a walk to clear our heads as Brack put it. There was a spare pair of wellies for me. Wellies were certainly needed. We walked down through the sopping-wet birch and rowan trees which were spectacularly covered in thick lime-coloured lichen, that made the low-lying wood, set on boggy tussocks, seem like a spectral winter graveyard. We came suddenly to the banks of the river, silent and glassy, that surged between submerged trees. I noticed water welling up over my boots and with alarm realised I had almost stepped off soggy land into deep water. I stepped back hastily and almost collided with Brack.

Careful. It's deep there.

Thanks for telling me, I said sarcastically.

There wasn't much bird-life despite his claim of kingfisher, dipper and heron. We stepped over to the dry trunk of a felled tree which thrust out into turgid waters, muddy with the previous day's heavy rain. I half-sat, half-leaned against the crumbly bark.

If Gerry's manuscript has a predominant theme, I began, if I can turn the subject back to that, it's probably the idea of nostalgia, of something lost. He's haunted by his sense of loss. Seems he felt that he had missed out on the sixties and wanted to make his own adventures.

Yeah, well, I can imagine that, Brack said, hoisting himself up on to the trunk nearer the mighty uprooted boss of the tree, solid with earthed roots, which had been bent over by some great wind and plucked neatly from the ground like a scab plucked off the skin. There were always loads of stories about things we'd done, the great times and the not-so-great times. Gerry didn't really say much, just listened. I wouldn't have guessed it was bugging him. I just thought he was a quiet guy. God, it's twenty years, I can barely remember him.

Being around Stephen, Fay said, you more or less have to be quiet. Can't get a word in edgeways.

Thank you, darling! But what am I supposed to do? I like to tell stories. Things interest me and I write – or make – stories about them. What's wrong with that?

146

Nothing at all, I said, observing a large white polythene sheet trapped and entwined by the surging waters around the limb of the tree halfway across the river. It eddied and fretted this way and that diving under and above the surface like a massive salmon but it clung to its twig and almost but never quite parted from it.

It's just that Gerry's novel – if it is a novel – is mainly made up of stories other people told him, with a small commentary about how bad it made him feel to be the listener and never the story-teller. There's almost nothing about him in the ms. Well, obviously, which is why I've had so much difficulty tracking down anything real in it. Like for example the real you.

Brack laughed. There is only one me.

I heard Fay snort some comment I didn't quite catch.

But I can't really see, said Brack, why you're bothering so much. I mean – you're not going to publish it, are you?

Well, we might. If we could get his permission.

Really? Why not publish some of *my* stuff instead? I'd give you my permission right now. Get the stories direct from the story-teller instead of secondhand.

But I'm not a literary critic. I'm dealing with the manuscript as an artefact that's come to me – as a documentary resource. It's the story behind the manuscript I'm interested in, not the actual details of the contents as literature, or whatever.

Pity. Sounds like a thin excuse, mind you. So what happens next?

If you'd care to read the ms, we could meet again and discuss your reaction to it. See if anything comes out of it.

That's a bit anthropological. Still, it might be an interesting read. I could read it tonight. Wouldn't take me long.

We'd reached an area of little hills about eight to ten feet high amid piles of dead twigs which were slowly mutating into bramble cities. There were many clumps of moss and spongy lichen was everywhere. Again I was alarmed by water seeping up over the arch of my wellies.

This is a kind of fairy glade, Brack said. These are called, in Scots, tullochs, or fairy mounds, sort of enchanted tummocks or tussocks. Funny, there's three words for you all sounding similar

147

and more or less meaning the same thing though I can't think of an exact English meaning.

Tumuli, I said without thinking. Of course, that's Latin.

Exactly, Brack replied, as if I'd just proved his point. But *tumuli* has the sense of something buried underneath, something you'd have to dig up to find. Whereas tullochs don't have that sort of . . . archaeological implication. They themselves are enchanted, there's nothing sort of . . . inside them.

Barrows, said Fay following behind. That's an English word.

Yes, said Brack, but that's even more archaeological. In fact it's an actual archaeological term.

I thought for a moment. I don't really follow . . . what point are you trying to make?

Simply that the Scots language veers more to the metaphysical. That the Scots are more mystically aware. The language has more inherent potential.

I see, I said. Funny. Gerry makes a broadly-similar point somewhere in the manuscript. Of course it's a howling generalisation.

Of course. What isn't?

Change the subject, said Fay. This is where I get some of my best mushrooms. She pointed with forefinger protruding from her black woollen gloves. Over there in the shade of that large oak.

I've always wanted to try those magic mushrooms, I surprised myself by saying. The ones that make you hallucinate.

You've never tried them? Fay seemed surprised. You should. I could give you some to try. Just enough for yourself.

How would I take them? What are the risks?

Risks? Not much, if you're sensible. Just swallow some with a cup of coffee. About forty to start with. Never take more than about a hundred at one time.

Seems a lot . . .

They're very small. And they're dried. I know people who're into eating fly agaric. Now they're really strong.

Aren't they poisonous?

Stephen nodded vigorously. Sure are. Kill you stone dead.

Fay shrugged. It's like anything. If you're careful, it's okay.

The trick is to get ones that are beyond the potent period. The Picts, you know, used to drink the urine of the few animals that could eat it.

Charming!

True, though, said Brack. Ambrosia of the gods and nectar, were, according to Robert Graves, anyway, hallucinatory fungi. People have been tripping out on the stuff for thousands of years. Of course, now it's illegal – it didn't used to be – to eat it. Still not illegal to pick it of course. Makes me angry. We let people have guns and knives made by people to kill other people but we make laws to stop people taking natural substances that grow free in the wild.

I changed the subject. These are funny little hills. I wonder how they came about.

I don't know, but I bet this land has never been under cultivation. I suspect this whole area was forest and perhaps these mounds were formed over decaying tree stumps.

That sounds quite likely.

There is – as you'll know, Stella – lots of evidence of settlements of all ages in this area, Iron Age, Pictish, Roman, it's all here. Not that it means much.

Not mean much? How do you mean?

Brack lifted a branch from across our path. Well, it's evidence – but of what? I mean, here at Bridgend of Cardean – which should be renamed by the way, Bridgehead of Cardean, since this was the outer edge of the Roman Empire . . . well, here especially, we're in a position to see that history is just a series of myths.

Well of course, that's what history largely is, take it from me.

In other words, Stella, history is what historians get paid to do, what they write. Like a series of fatuous fashion statements:

In the Iron Age, most people were wearing wool.
The first reference to a Mormaer of Angus is 938.
Groovy chicks wear tie-dyed kaftans and plastic beads.

And absolutely the worst thing about it, Brack said emphatically, kicking the mossed stump of a tree with the toes of his wellington boot, is the claim that it has *validity*. That history is a sort of science of ultimate truth. That there is some kind of continuity, progress, an upward journey. When the only real truth is of disconnectedness of individual from individual, how separate we all are from even our closest relations. All going through time apart absolutely.

I can see you're a sceptic.

At the end of the day, that's what we all are. We have to be. Cause it's all just stories, disembodied voices, rumours, gossip, shaggy-dog tales. I and you and each of us can only tell what's true by our individual feelings, by a sort of psychic resonance within us.

Oh come on, there's radio-carbon dating . . . a whole methodology out there that can prove . . .

Brack was ahead of me on the narrow track and as he pushed aside a thick screen of low, lichened trees, I only caught the word . . . *manipulations.*

On the drive back to Dundee, with my headlights full on for most of the way with the very occasional exception of oncoming lights which forced me to dip, I thought that my thoughts were running loose and treacherous in my head. I felt lost somehow as if I was coming apart in some way, as if some certainties had collapsed internally, as if my vital organs had turned to mush and my body had begun rotting from the inside. I wondered if I was coming down with something. I've always conceived myself, as you know, to be two Stellas. Or at least two. I'm Stella Auld, devious and Scotchly cynical, and I'm young Stella, the way I was or the way I like to remember myself in early womanhood, optimistic, altruistic, a citizen of world culture, seeking the good in everyone. But the weight of who I now am, what I am becoming, gets ever heavier with each passing day and now young Stella barely peeps out from the gathering adiposity and the hardening carapace of bitter experience and the knowledge of personal defeat, personal failure and personal mediocrity.

But each of these *personae* tries to deny the existence of the other. It must. For if Stella Auld should blink awake and catch an addled glimpse of the other she would be glimpsing the truth of how defeated, pessimistic and thwarted she has become. And if young Stella should gain a flashing insight into what she will ineluctably become, she will be miserable in extremis. How to go on? It's the common thought of both, and it links them, impossibly, in stasis. A stasis of shifting perceptions but a stasis that is, above all, doomed. Oh, I (Stellas both) can intellectualise about it, because I let it remain as something I can consider without letting myself be overtly affected by it. But my life lacks the full reality of itself. I live as if behind a veil. Like one among a tableau of beautiful melancholy women in romantic raiment glimpsed from the battlements at dusk, full of psychic possibilities. Except the romantic raiment will turn out to be an industrial strength canvas shroud which chafes the skin just as soon as the nearly-dead begin to walk.

I find myself considering, once again, as I race along that straight piece of road before the bends below Birkhill, that odd tussocky area by the river at Bridgend of Cardean where Brack and his wife led me earlier in the afternoon. Those tullochs could be a site of ancient sepulture. Come to think of it, it must be very close to the site of the most northerly of the Romans' permanent camps. The frontiers of empire. Must study some maps in the archive. It might be an unmarked area of ancient graves. I recall the legend of the fairy hill, into which a mortal is enticed, returning no older to find a world that has atrophied. I've always been fascinated by the idea of what is beneath, behind or beyond. As a girl always peering round corners to see what I could catch in the act. At such times I find myself considering myself considering, watching, observing myself acutely. I'm wondering now about my vivid dreams of Kingennie. That nonsense about the nightdress. When I had simply forgotten – or wilfully disremembered – that I had given it away to the charity shop in Brook Street. Driving in early one morning I had stopped and left it in a bag of other old clothes outside their door. But do I really remember doing that? And what of my exhaustion the next morning, my muddy feet, the scratches and bruises on my shins? The garden. My own garden. Sleepwalking, sort of.

I'm a long way from myself as I watch myself return home.

VIII 𝔉ília

THE OLD CERTAINTIES continue to dissolve in front of me. There's some kind of process in train that I'm no longer able to control, that it seems I must merely observe as best I can. For example, I spent much time today trying to find certain books I felt I required, but failed to find them. Later, I found I could not remember quite why I had felt I required them in the first place. Then I forgot to go into work. It was half past ten in the morning before I realised I wasn't where I should be. For some reason I'd been thinking it was Saturday. It was as if I'd been drugged, or was under some spell. I phoned and phoned but Jill wasn't in the office. Gertrude on reception said she was in, somewhere, but could never quite locate her. Then it was lunchtime and I discovered that Fingal had been sick behind the sofa so I had to clean it up. Then I remembered that I was supposed to ring Stephen Brack, so I did, but the phone rang and rang, unanswered. I must have had a bit of a doze then because the next thing I remember the doorbell was ringing. It was Jill. She'd come by taxi. It was about five o'clock.

I had a bit of trouble finding you. Your phone seems to be out of order.

Is it? Well come in. I went to check the phone and found it was off the hook. I'm afraid I just . . . I . . . couldn't face it today, I said. I tried ringing in but Gertrude could never find you.

I got the message. Anyway, how're you?

I'm still a bit dopy, excuse me, I was having a doze. Anything important happen today?

152

Not a lot. Howkins was in and out all day. Letching as usual. His tongue practically hanging out.

As long as that's all that was hanging out.

I never intend to get near enough to find out.

Good girl. Come and have a glass of wine. D'you prefer red or white?

Oh, Stell, I'm not really a wine kind of person. You choose. You're the boss. Oh, this is a really lovely place you live in. Much better than my grotty flat. The taxi driver kept asking me for directions. He'd no idea. He had to switch the meter off. We were all up by the old Ballumbie Hotel and way round at the back of Whitfield. But I remembered it was beside the Michelin factory.

Well it's easier to find than Bridgend of Cardean anyway. Here – this is a medium white, you'll like it. Later, I'll make us something to eat.

I don't want to put you to any bother . . .

I'm very pleased to have you here. Would you like a wee tour before it gets dark?

Oh yes. And I'd like to meet your cat.

I showed her around the garden and into the greenhouse and she admired the small rockery, whose primulas were already in bloom like yellow butterflies.

You must spend a lot of time working in the garden.

Not really. I potter about. Mostly, I come back from work and fall asleep in the conservatory. It gets very warm in there with the sun shining in.

I'd love to have a place with a garden like this and a conservatory.

Then Fingal dropped by to say hello. It was odd. For some reason he took an instant dislike to Jill, bristling and arching. He recoiled and remained defiant, hunched into the wall.

Maybe he smelt some rival cat on me, Jill suggested.

He hasn't been himself for some days, but I've never seen him quite like this.

After his initial display, there was something of a transformation and Fingal calmed down, even managed a little soft purring, under Jill's ministrations.

153

We seem to be friends now. I'm glad.

We sat in the deep armchairs in the Victorian-style conservatory watching the evening sun slowly sinking over Hawick Drive.

This is nice wine, fruity.

Fruity yourself!

Jill spluttered over herself. Don't make me laugh!

I'll get you a cloth, I said. Strange to say, I found that my earlier *ennui* had dissipated. Truth was, I jolly well enjoyed her company. I'd found a soulmate of sorts. We'd become quite close quite quickly. I suppose I was flattered that she got on with me, the boss, and didn't find me too square. But there was perhaps more to it than that. She was filial, like the daughter I'd never had, never would have. She was like a younger me, me the way I used to be.

Later, we blethered in the kitchen/dinette while I made a large, spicy chilli-con-carne.

I like to put loads of garlic in it. That alright with you?

You're the boss. I don't mind. What's in this paperbag, some sort of dried mushrooms?

Um. Yes, I got those from Stephen Brack's wife, Fay. She's what you might call a wise woman – wise in the ways of nature, you know, herbal lore and natural medicaments. An alternative kind of person.

If I didn't know better, Stell, I'd say these were the kind of magic mushrooms I've heard my dad talk about that used to give people hallucinations. Hippies used to take them.

Oh no, no, these are different, my goodness, they're for . . . um, women's troubles. I quickly changed the subject. So your dad was a bit of a hippy then?

Oh yeah! In his younger days. You should see his photos. He went to a lot of rock festivals, Stonehenge and that. He's always going on about it. He looked awful. He had this kind of straggly beard and long thick hair. Mind you, he doesn't look much better now. Of course he isn't my *real* dad.

Oh? What, did your mother marry again?

No. I was adopted as a baby. They told me when I was eighteen. Up till then I believed they were my real parents. It was a bit of a shock, but they've brought me up and as I've never known who my real parents were, it doesn't really matter. As far as I'm concerned, they are my mum and dad and nothing can change that. Can I have some more wine? It's really neat.

Hold out your glass.

Sort of green, isn't it, pale? She held it up to the dying twilight. Yet it's also sort of golden, pink. Stella, I sometimes wonder if maybe this is why I'm so interested in making a career working with history and archaeology – you know, to find out what happened before – where we all came from. Our origins and ancestors and that.

I lost my own parents you know. I mean, they're both dead, I found myself saying which is funny as I never talk about it to anybody. I felt I could, with Jill.

She looked up at me, almost childlike, from the rim of her glass. No. How come? Oh, maybe you don't want to talk about it?

It's alright. It was ten years ago. They were on holiday in Spain. They hired a car and it went off a sharp bend on a steep mountain road. They were killed outright.

An accident?

Oh yes, no other vehicle was involved. I went to look at the place where it happened. In the Pyrenees. They're buried there, in a local cemetery. I couldn't face having them brought home, all that palaver. We had a small family ceremony at our local church then I went over to supervise the burial.

You've no brothers or sisters?

None. Anyway, have some more wine. Let's change the subject.

Okay, so how did you get on at Bridgend of Cardean with the Bracks?

Quite well. They had me stay for tea. I didn't get home till midnight. Fay made me mushroom soup. It was weird.

That's a funny kind of name, Fay? I've never heard of anyone called Fay before.

Ah, she's nice, you'd like her. Stephen is a bit enthusiastic though. Would talk the hind legs off a donkey. According to him,

Gerry wasn't that close a friend to him and he doesn't even remember his surname.

Oh dear. So what happens next?

I've given him the manuscript and I've to call back to see him when he's read it. Should be tonight only I can't get him on the phone. I'll go tomorrow.

I'd like to come with you.

Yes, that's an idea. Which reminds me. You know, Fay looks remarkably like you. It struck me straightaway when I saw her. Of course she's a little older, maybe in her thirties.

How odd. I must have a read of the manuscript myself, if I may.

Of course. My copy is in my desk drawer. As long as you put it back.

I was thinking, Stell, if we can locate Gerry and he's willing we could set up an exhibition, based on Dundee in the sixties and seventies, get some photographs of the city – what it was like at the time, invite people to submit their own photographs and stories and get some of the people in the novel to turn up at an event when they could talk about what it was like. We could make a big thing of it, the clothes, the clubs, the music and local bands, what d'you think?

Well, I'd read it first if I were you, it's not really that kind of thing. It's pretty squalid and frankly I wonder if it gives the right kind of tone. Some of it is pretentious, some is poorly-written, some deals with drug-taking and the glorification of . . . minor criminality and loose morality. Maybe it's just not the kind of thing that would show Dundee in a good light. You'll see what I mean when you read it.

Maybe it could be edited?

Censorship? I doubt if the author would go along with that idea. Now, why not open another bottle of wine, here's the opener.

I'm getting a little tiddly.

You'll feel better when you eat. What did Ron Howkins have to say by the way?

He was looking for you, something about some transfer of

Pictish artefacts to Angus Council. Said he'd catch you tomorrow.

He'll be lucky. Old Ron. You know he tried it on with me once. A while ago now. Funny sort of thing. I was in his office standing beside him. He was sitting down. Next thing he's put his hand out and put it around my thigh. I couldn't believe it was happening.

My god! The perv . . .

Actually, I don't think he actually knew what he was doing. We were concentrating on something and he kept talking while it was going on. Sort of lifted my leg up a bit, then he took his hand away and neither of us said anything. I was too embarrassed to mention it.

If he tried that with me, I'd sock him in the balls.

It was a strange thing. I really don't think he knew what he was doing.

Sexual harassment all the same. Even though there were no witnesses.

People would say I was making it up. They'd say I was just repressed, frustrated, a frump. It'd ruin my career prospects.

You have to stand up for yourself. Anyway you're not a frump. I think you're very attractive.

Hardly! Still it's nice of you to say.

Honestly, you're not bad at all for your age.

Now look – you've made me spill wine all over myself. For my age! Thanks a lot.

What I mean is, you're very . . . elegant. You just need a little jazzing up maybe. Some younger clothes. Shorter skirts . . .

Oh thank you! Mutton dressed as lamb you mean.

You're not too old to be going out on the town. If you want to meet a man that is. You should come out with me and my mates some night. It'd be a giggle.

No thank you, my boogie-ing days are long gone, thank goodness. I prefer a quiet drink of wine and a nice meal, preferably at my own fireside.

But you've got to get out now and then.

Well, now and then I do, madam. I'm not absolutely gone to

157

seed you know. Mind you, I must say I can't remember the last time I went out with a man.

See.

It was probably Stephen Blinshall. He works at the Barrack Street Museum. We were just friends though. Completely platonic.

So when was the last time you had a shag?

Jill! Don't be so rude.

Sorry. Must be the wine. I'm getting a bit squiffy. Anyway I've given up on men myself. Just fumbly pigs.

Fumbly pigs?

I mean fingering . . . you know, hands all over you. I never meet the right kind . . . Snogging's alright but they get upset if you won't go home with them the first night.

You *are* getting a bit tiddly. We'd better eat – and no more *vino veritas* for you for a while, young lady. Have some orange juice instead.

Oh no, Stell, now I've got the hiccups.

IX Refutatio

I SEEMED TO BE okay next morning and set off early for Bridgend of Cardean, picking up Jill on the way. I'd got up full of resolutions and one of them was to finish with Gerry's damned manuscript one way or another today and get on with some serious work on my doctorate. Jill was brightly enthusiastic as we left the city behind.

It's lovely out here. I love the country, she said as we took the sharp bend out of Birkhill.

Do you indeed? I hope it's not too wet underfoot. I forgot to tell you to bring your wellies.

I don't have any wellies. I've got walking boots though. I could have brought them.

It'll be alright.

You phoned him then – Brack?

Oh yes. He's full of it. Sounds as if he's ready to talk our heads off. I brought my dictaphone. If it gets too much we'll switch it on and leave him in a room with it.

You're naughty! I bet he's really nice. What's this place? Auchterhouse?

The rest of it is up the hill there. It has it's own hill. Used to be a hospital up there too. It's a nice walk on a good day. Nice view.

I never really come out this way.

You should.

Not much else was said until we turned off the road into the trees at Bridgend of Cardean. I was in a funny mood, feeling lightheaded, irresponsible. I think at the time I put it down to slight hunger pains and the pleasure of being out of the office.

I couldn't have found this place on my own, Jill said, as we cruised through the shade of the overhanging trees.

Stephen Brack was waiting for us in front of the house. He wore a thick old sweater, much patched, of an indeterminate greyish green colour and green wellies. He came over and supervised my parking. For the first time I realised how hairy he was. He'd hairs growing out of his nostrils and ears and dark fur on the back of his neck and wrists.

Hey. Nice to see you again. I've been reading the thing you left with me. Gerry's book. What a hoot.

My name's Jill Martin, Jill said, stepping out of the car and shaking hands. I watched Brack's face closely but there were no unusual indications that he found a startling resemblance in her to his wife. I suspected that he would be flirty with her, as he wasn't with me, and I was right, his hand going into the small of her back to usher her inside the house. I trailed in behind, poefaced (sic). We seated ourselves in the stagnant shadow of the brown lounge.

Where's Fay? I inquired. Will she be joining us?

Na. She's out. She might be back later. So where do we start?

We've brought a dictaphone, Jill said, helpfully.

I had to interrupt to forestall an imminent outpouring from Stephen Brack. Yes, but we're not interested in the *minutia* of the manuscript, really, just any information you can give us which might help to trace Gerry and any other of the real people mentioned in it.

Well, I've been thinking and I think the surname was McAllister. The self-description he gives of himself is accurate. I didn't really know Wanda but the description of her seems correct too as far as it goes. I don't know if she was a teacher and, as I told you already, the circumstances of the relationship with Kenneth Syme are pure fiction. What surprised me, Stella, was that my mother is described accurately in it.

I've met your mother, Jill said. That was how we traced you.

Brack turned to her. Have you? From the nursing home? And

160

she gave you . . .? She didn't mention it. Anyway, other things that ring a bell. The mural. I remember that, also the Brigitte Bardot poster. That was originally mine, you know. I wish I knew what had happened to it. The story about the grandfather clock at Rab's party. True. Yes, Coke is true and the stories about Phinny are true. I'm sure he's still living in Dundee. Try the Pitfour Street area. I haven't seen him in years.

Brack then became rather animated and jumped to his feet. Haven't seen Craig for years either. Thank goodness. Don't want too, either. *Don't* give him my address if you see him. He's the kind of guy to bear a grudge.

We won't, Jill grinned. Although we're hardly likely to come across him.

As for Dangerous, Jim Carroll, Atholl Graham, Alec Swan – these are all real people and probably still live somewhere in Dundee. Big Bob, I suppose, is based on Bob Erskine. Eddie Lambert moved away yonks ago. Tony Woods. He'll be easy to find. It's true that he was rejected by the Foreign Legion but whether it was really because of his eyesight, I couldn't say. I can vaguely remember someone like Belair Billy living in Benvie Road but he wasn't in my immediate social circle if you know what I mean.

I don't think he was in anyone's social circle, I said.

Brack laughed. Yeah, very non-U. The only thing I remember about him was the time he was rooting in the bins at the bottom of the outside stairs. See, we were sitting in Gerry's flat on the ground floor blethering when we heard muttering and shuffling noises. Looked out and there was that no-hoper, Belair . . . going through the bins. The way the light was shining in, we could only see him in silhouette. It was like something out of a Chaplin movie. He had these baggy pants and a long black coat he'd probably stolen from somewhere. He must have seen something he really liked in one of the bins because he reached in lower and lower and all we heard was grunting. Anyway, he got in so far he toppled over and his feet came up into the air. There he was wobbling about inside the bin which is tottering about with his feet sticking up in the air which is blue with curses. After a couple of seconds the bin went right over and Billy was freed. It was hilarious. At least, it was at the time. Ach, you had to see it. Benvie Road was a hell of a place in the winter. Very cold. Too cold to use the outside lavvy. We used to . . . some people used to . . . well, defecate on to newspaper and roll it up and put it in the bins because the loos had iced up. One time one time someone threw it over the plettie towards the bins area and a whole team of cats swooped on to it.

That's *gross*, Jill complained, delightedly.

Yeah. The cats must have thought it was a fresh fish-supper.

Disgusting!

To return to Gerry, Stephen. You said you thought you'd seen him in Dundee after his travels.

I think so. Years and years ago. In the Tay Bridge Bar, I think, around about Christmas time. He was a bit thinner, hair was shorter too. He was very tanned. But I didn't speak to him, not really. He was with other people. I think I only spoke to him in the bog.

The bog?

Oh, the toilet . . . when we both went . . . If I remember he was rather strange. Said he was not living in Dundee because somebody, or some people or something was after him, or he was in debt . . . or something like that. I just accepted it at the time. It was pretty usual. I've no idea when it was though. Early eighties? Mid-eighties? Couldn't say.

And he didn't mention anything about a manuscript to you then? Jill asked.

Nope. Hey – another thing. I notice he swiped some of my ideas in his fifth chapter. Yeah, the idea of the list of mundane objects as symbols of decay. He stole that from me. Kind of sticks out, doesn't it? It's too pretentious for the rest of the book. The idea that he's drowning in dross cultural values. It comes from one of my books. He nicked it! The rotter. No doubt about it. It doesn't work in his text. Probably doesn't work in mine either. And as for the idea that I worked in the War Office. Well, can you imagine it? And the frankly libelous tale about me with the girl at the party and the doorknob . . . But the burglary at Cortachy

162

Castle is true enough. As far as I know. Innes got five years for it. The Ginsberg story is completely true by the way. It was the start of my criminal career. It was funny actually because when I got taken into the cells I met loads of other guys who were in there for dope offences. Like Eddie Lambert. He's a great artist by the way, makes a right packet now, has his own studio. He's done really well. Yep, anyway, *then* Eddie was in Perth for possession and contempt of court. Stood up in the dock dressed only in a tattie sack with Unemployed painted all over it in red paint. Gave the judge a right load of abuse and caused a lot of bother. Wee Billy Forbes, now, he was another guy who got into a load of trouble. One time he arrived at my door and dived straight into my toilet. Had a load of acid on blotting paper up his jackzie in a condom. Smuggled it over from Amsterdam. Poor Billy's dead now of course. Died at 19. Accidental overdose. Mind you, you couldn't really say that Billy just *died*. There was nothing passive about it. He charged headlong out of life at full speed. He was a great guy. So was Alec Robinson. Killed on his motorbike not far from here, near Newtyle. Doing the ton no-hands, no-feet, crazy bastard. And Scoop too, quite recently. I had a drink with the guy a month ago. He only found out he'd cancer two weeks before he died. Tragic. You could not meet a nicer guy. And Mike Ward, only 41, died just this year.

Yes, but what do you think happened to Gerry? Jill asked, rather impatiently.

I don't think he's still in Dundee. Mind you, it's been so long, I might not recognise him now anyway.

Did your wife know him? Jill asked.

Not as far as I know. Fay was living in Edinburgh when I met her. That was about ten years ago. She was brought up in Dundee though. Left the city in the mid-seventies when she was about sixteen.

I was hoping to meet her, Jill said. Stella says she looks rather like me.

Really? I don't think so. Well, perhaps, now I look at you. Of course, you're a lot younger. Actually you know now I can see a bit of a resemblance come to think of it. It's a pity she's out.

What did you think of the manuscript's ending? I asked. How it just fades out? I wondered if something had happened to him . . . or if he'd had some kind of breakdown . . . but if you saw him in the 1980s, he must have been alright.

Yeah, it's a funny kind of ending. Something to do with some female. I think probably the ending bit of it is just lost. I don't think it's meant to be enigmatic. That's merely our interpretation. I have to say, all due respect to Gerry – an old friend – that the manuscript, to me, at least, really isn't worth all the time and effort we're putting into it. It's hardly some lost masterpiece and it doesn't really sort of shine a light into a fascinating but overlooked period of Dundee life. You could hardly say that. I mean the sixties and seventies are barely history. There's loads of people still around who could tell you far better what life was really like then in Dundee. Me, for instance.

Maybe, but we've spent some time trying to locate the people in Gerry's manuscript and we've not been able to trace a single one. Not to actually speak to. Except you.

Yeah, that's because they were young people and most have probably moved away.

But some must still be around. People leave traces, don't just disappear off the face of the earth.

I don't agree with you there, Brack said. People disappear all the time. Sometimes I feel as if I'm just overwhelmed by ghosts. In *spiritus sancti*. Even people I talked to only days ago could have died in the meantime. Some mornings I can't get out of bed because of the weight of dead souls sitting on my chest.

That sounds like a good excuse! said Jill, glancing at me. I'll have to try it.

Oh no, you won't!

But I'm serious, Stephen said. The long dead live for all eternity in our ears. Singing voices from the grave forced to perform every time you switch on a radio or record player. I mean, listening, you can't tell if a person is alive or dead, can you? Many of my best mates are dead, but the memory of them is still part of my everyday experience. It's like Harry Lime said. How many of the little dots could you afford to lose? It only matters when the dots are closely involved with you. Then it's personal.

No-one completely and absolutely disappears, Stephen.

True, they continue to exist in people's memories. Question is whether the memories are genuine or fake. Take for example Skeets Boliver, the Dundee superband of the seventies. Gerry mentioned one of their singles that had to be renamed . . .

Oh yes, something about a brickhouse door?

Ho-ho. That was the *polite* version. But Gerry doesn't mention that their biggest song was 'Peddie Street'. Now, I remember seeing them doing it on some TV programme. It was on a Sunday I think, one of those early evening trendy religious programmes. We were in the Tav and suddenly there it was, there they were, singing the song with actual footage of Peddie Street. I couldn't believe it. It was so astonishing. But no-one else was bothered and, in fact, the barman changed channels. It was like an act of treachery.

And the point is?

Well, the song was about Peddie Street and the old days, cause Mike Marra, who wrote the song was around then but some stupid London record producer got the title wrong and so it came out as 'Pity Street'. Which meant nothing at all to anybody. But the point is that for those like me who were around at the time, we remember what it was about but most people would go by the evidence, which is otherwise, d'y'see? So it comes down to whether you believe in your instincts and your memory or in history, the recorded evidence.

Interesting story, and I can see why it matters . . .

But *can* you? This manuscript of Gerry's is partly fake, partly genuine. It seems to me by the way that that's what it's really about. Memory. Recalling and forgetting. Holding on and letting go. Gerry's past and the pasts of the people he knew. He felt trapped in our past through the stories that interested him and so he set out to write his own version and now it's all that's left of what he knew and believed, so how can it be proved or disproved?

X Calamitas

S TEPHEN BRACK HAD refuted most of the substance of the manuscript and had not been able to give me further clues about its author, so, on the following afternoon, I wrote what I intended to be my final briefing report – my final Dear John letter – on the manuscript.

Prehistory Section
Dundee Museums
McManus Centre
Dundee

Dear Johnathan,

Anonymous Dundee Manuscript

I have re-interviewed Stephen Brack and pursued with the Education Department and the Housing Division the name Gerald McAllister and its variants, yet have once again drawn a blank.

I therefore feel enough time has been devoted to the manuscript and propose to curtail our researches for the time being.

You have my earlier misgivings as to the literary quality
of the content.

I hope you will agree this is our only sensible course
of action in the circumstances.

Yours sincerely,

Stella

Stella Auld
Documentary Resources Archivist

I slipped the top copy into a Council grid envelope, popped it
into the internal mail and filed the manuscript, pages of notes and
the *Courier* clippings into a box-file. Goodbye Gerry McAllister –
or whatever your name is. *Sic transit gloria mundi.* When Jill
came back, I had resumed work on the artefacts catalogue which
was to be the Dundee Council contribution to the national
archive at the new Pictish Centre at Aberlemno.

I've just put away all the stuff about the manuscript, I told Jill
as she came in the door. Time to get on with other things.

Aw, that's a pity, she said, sitting down and brushing her hair.
I was just getting interested in it. Can I still take it home to
read?

I'd prefer if you didn't. Our main priority is to get all this stuff
on to the database. First, I must nip out for a sandwich. Want
anything while I'm out?

I don't suppose you could post this for me. It's a present for my
nan.

If it means you'll get on with the cataloguing.

I'll make a start.

Good girl.

I stood in the busy post office at Ward Road letting my mind
drift. My eyes had gone a little out of focus. I was in a queue, half-
attending to the TV monitor adverts, half-listening to the conversations around me, letting it wash over and around me.

Dundee Out Loud. Voices from the City's Past. Interspersed with voices from the city's present. On the loudspeaker:

Cashier number nine, please (tense, male, Scots) *Cashier number four, please* (matronly female) *Cashier number two, please* (Dundonian male, abrupt, possibly uncouth) *Cashier number four, please* (pleasant warmth cut short abruptly) *Cashier number one, please* (this is rather beneath me, pal, so hurry up, will you) *Cashier number nine, please* (it's Bill Paterson . . . yes, it is, it's me, I'm here in Dundee) *Cashier number four please* (voice of experience and sympathy, Hannah Gordon/Moira Gamble?) *Cashier number two, please* (*did* he say please?) *Cashier number one* . . . Someone poking me from behind . . . *please.*

An old lady. Her prim mouth says: On yi go, hen, thir's ane lad free . . .

I wish there was, hen. Thank you.

Cashier number one more polite than his disembodied voice over the loudspeaker suggests. Thank you. But was it *his* voice? Or did they get other people to record the message? Why not just use one voice for all? Of course, a variety of different voices might help to maximise the individuality of the service provided, but what if somebody was off sick or swapped desks with someone else?

One pound eighty first class, ninety-seven second?

First, please. *Is* it his voice? Can't be sure. If someone took over this counter, then might not the voices get mixed up? Was it just coincidence that cashier number one has a male voice? He might not see it that way.

Thank you. Voices in the head. Loudspeaker. What he did not say. Thank you. Change. *Cashier number* . . . *Cashier number* Must drive them daft sitting there all day, voices repeating. In the head. Brainwashing. Maybe they each become the kind of cashier the loudspeaker tells us they are. Like their semiotic label.

When I got back to the office, intending to consume my chicken-salad sandwiches with a cup of coffee, Ron Howkins was sitting in my chair at my desk. Moreover, he was distracting Jill from her work. I was irritated but determined not to show it.

Late lunch? Howkins asked, nodding at my sandwiches. The obvious. He scratched at the back of his scalp.

Is there something?

He stood up and moved away, with a final pat at his increasing baldness. Eh, yes, apart from the pleasure of seeing you ladies, there is. Um, Johnathan Weeder asked me to come down, um, on the matter of the Dundee manuscript. It seems there's been a development and the Curator is keen to pursue it.

A development? I said in my best Lady Bracknell tones.

Mnm. Some photographs of Dundee in the 1960s and 1970s have been donated by a local teacher who is also an amateur photographer and it's been suggested – by me, actually – that we could tie this manuscript of yours and the photos together into an exhibition and event.

Original.

Sorry, what was that, Jill?

Nothing.

But apart from the manuscript you've nothing . . .?

Aha. But this chap Brack seemingly is keen to come along and he has access to some others mentioned in the book. The Curator seems to feel . . .

Well! I plunked down my sandwiches angrily. I've just written to Johnathan wrapping it all up. We've really got more important things to get on with. The new Pictish Centre . . .

I understand. I do. All I can say is the Curator personally asked me to . . . to discuss it with you and to . . . draw it all together. I think I can find enough photos to illustrate some aspects of the manuscript and Brack and his friends will do short talks but the point of the whole thing will be to provide a focus for public participation. To get people to come in with their stories and pictures. Swinging Dundee I was thinking of calling it. And I'm pleased to say the Curator likes my idea.

So, essentially, you're . . . taking over the project?

Howkins had just enough conscience left to allow a slight blush to creep into his cheeks.

Well, Stella, as you know, I don't like to tread on anyone's . . . on your . . . toes, but I hope we can work together on this.

Oh yes. By the way, Ron, how come Brack is involved? Did you contact him?

Howkins went brick red. Oh no, no. I wouldn't have. Of course not. Not without speaking to you first. I know you went to see him. And Jill here. No. He contacted us.

Really? He phoned up? And he didn't ask to speak to me?

Apparently not. Well, I must be getting along. We can chat again after I've spoken to Brack. He's coming to see me tomorrow forenoon. Him and his wife. Speak to you later. Bye. Howkins was out of the room and down the corridor like a rat down a drainpipe.

The double-dealing shit! I hissed as loudly as I dared.

Jill was smiling and shaking her head. Behind your back. But it sounds like Stephen Brack's miffed that we didn't get him more involved.

I'm sure he must have asked for me. Tell you what, Jill, how do you fancy giving him a ring and finding out when he's due here? We can play Howkins at his own game. Ask him to pop up to see me ten minutes before he's due to see Ron.

In this way, I set my plans. In this job you're always looking out for your back and you have to be able to move strategically. Do it to them before it gets done to you. Funny, I've begun to conceive a real dislike for Brack and Gerry et al. Come to think of it I'd never really thought of them as nice people. Hedonists and bores, hearking back to their glory days. Shiftless. None of them with a job worthy of the name. Poncing upon the goodwill of the welfare state and calling it art. Denouncing all workers as cultureless while taking their money to have the idleness to think great thoughts. *All work is merely exercise unless creative* wrote Gerry. Huh! Said with the full weight of knowledge of someone who'd never worked in his life. He had some nerve!

These were some of my thoughts as I turned into my little brick driveway. Usually Fingal arrives to supervise my unloading, but tonight, no Fingal. He still hadn't arrived by the time I'd made my tea and settled in front of the telly. He's pretty much a homeloving cat. It wasn't like him to miss out on some fresh lambs' liver. It was still waiting for him in his bowl at the back door as it began to get dark. He hadn't returned by the time I went to bed and I lay listening for the cat flap until I fell asleep.

170

Next morning the food hadn't been touched. I was really worried but I had no option except to leave for work as usual. I'd be thinking about the furry one all day.

Things didn't go as planned. Not at all. It was a *fiasco*. Jill did intercept the Bracks in the vestibule and was bringing them up to my office when Howkins with Weeder in tow suddenly ambushed them. I heard the voices and came out into the corridor. We all trooped down to Howkins' palatial office overlooking the rose gardens and the *Courier* building. In the ensuing discussion I was only able to insert a few misgivings into the proceedings but the enthusiasm of the others was such that I was actually described as being overtly negative. *Me*! Worst of all, though, was that Jill, whom I had thought to be my pretty homunculus, my creature, sided with Howkins and the others. Once back in my office, I turned on her.

What do you think you were *doing*? I expected you to back me up.

She pouted. Why? I don't agree with you. It's a good idea, and if you remember it's the same idea that I had, when I came to your house, on Wednesday evening.

You made me look small – in front of those men.

No, I didn't. This is about a good idea for an event. It's not about your ego.

My ego! How *dare* you . . .

She shrugged her shoulders and tossed her hair. Look, Stella, we're friends and you're my boss . . . but that doesn't mean I've to agree with everything you say. This event is going to take place. Everyone else is up for it. So we should be in there, getting our share of the work and the credit.

But what about our cataloguing? That's the real work as far as we, professionally, are concerned. That's what being Documentary Resources Archivist is all about. The Pictish Centre is the newest development in Ancient History for years. They – Howkins and the others – are only interested in scoring some minor PR points for Dundee and their own careers. They're not really interested in anything worth while and long term. In two years' time who'll remember this manuscript and the backstreet

171

nobodies in it? Brack and the others, and their futile petty doings and the trivia of music and fashion blah di blah. Who cares? But in two years the Pictish Centre will have gained an international reputation and be drawing people here from all over the world.

Yeah, but the Swinging Dundee event will interest loads of Dundonians. Maybe hundreds will come forward to share their experiences . . . even though they're not thousands of years old . . . and just ordinary people.

The insubordination had gone too far! Now, look, that's the remit of Arts and Heritage, Jill. For your information, they have a whole department to handle oral history events.

Well, I've been here a month now and . . . . and I've had nothing else exciting to do, she pouted, like a tempestuous teenager.

Oh thanks! No-one said it was to be exciting. Work generally isn't.

There was a sulky silence for a few moments, as I dug out the manuscript and the file from the bottom of the cupboard.

Jill was first to speak. Anyway, Stella, don't Fay and I look alike? Johnathan Weeder noticed it straight off. Even Ron Howkins said so. She's very nice, isn't she? I suppose I'll look like her when I get older. At least I hope I do. She's amazing for her age. We could be sisters.

I took a deep breath, prepared to forget and forgive. Didn't I tell you? I don't suppose you *are* related?

You mean because I'm adopted? I don't know who my real mother is. It's a thought . . .

Brack said Fay used to live in Dundee before she went to Edinburgh. Anyway, look, Jill, I have to nip off home just now. Fingal was out all night.

Oh, the poor old cat. I'll hold the fort here.

Now, don't commit us – or yourself – to too much on the exhibition. Keep us out of it as much as you can – without seeming to do so, if you know what I mean. It really is the remit of Arts and Heritage.

Okay.

I drove home as rapidly as I could, thinking the worst, feeling

172

numb from the events of the morning. Feeling as if I'd been mugged. For months now I've had this suspicion that I'm being conspired against, that things are going on that I don't know about.

Things got much *much* worse. I found Fingal's poor dead body behind the greenhouse. Stretched out, stiff as a plank. He'd been dead since yesterday. The pathetic sight of the bowl of chopped liver at the backdoor made me break down and cry. Fingal had been with me for seven years, my constant companion, my only true friend.

In the afternoon, I buried him in a little ceremony, under the rowan tree that'd been his favourite. I had my tape recorder playing Enya's 'Silent Night' from *Paint the Sky with Stars* and it put tears in my eyes as I laid his little body, inside a Marks & Spencer's green plastic bag into the hole and covered it over with earth. I made a simple wooden cross and wrote on it 'Fingal' and the date in pink lipstick. Later, I'll make a better one. No more cats for me. I have a lot of photos of the good times. Fingal had a happy life. I was good to him. He liked being with me. I had a glass of wine then one or two more and finished the bottle on my own. I couldn't believe I wouldn't ever see him again. I'd no idea how he died. There wasn't a mark on him. I'd worry about that later. Now all I can think about is that never again will I . . . stroke his warm fur behind the ears. Or listen to his happy mesmeric purring on my lap.

I threw out his bowl with the stale chopped liver still in it and stood staring at the neat tins of catfood stacked on the kitchen shelves, which he would never watch me open. But I could sense his presence still around the place. It wasn't a smell, although hairs lingered on the sofa, it was a sort of perception, generally, of the senses. I felt as if he was around the corner and would come if I whistled him. Which is why I never would whistle him, so as not to be disproved, not to be disappointed.

XI 𝔖𝔱 𝔅𝔯𝔦𝔤𝔦𝔡'𝔰 𝔈𝔳𝔢

I KEPT NOTICING THE paperbag of dried mushrooms Fay'd
given me. I kept picking it up throughout the afternoon and
looking inside. I'd poke about at them, sniff them, take them out
on to my palm. They were dry and scrunchy but didn't have any
smell. It was like Alice and those eat-me pills. Could I? Truth to
tell, I felt absolutely rotten enough to do almost anything. And
tomorrow was Sunday anyway so it didn't matter. If I'd been a
little more clued up I'd have noticed at the time that it was also the
first of February. So what? So. St Brigid's Day on the old Celtic
calendar. Maybe that could account for it. Something must.

I'd taken them all, you see, with a cup of black coffee to get rid of
the dry taste. I was trying not to think of the terrible fungicidal
poisons working in me. I was monitoring my heartbeat, slumped on
the sofa but all was well. Maybe they would have no effect at all? I
drew the blinds and waited for what might or might not happen.
What sublime suggestions might emerge, I wondered, from the
ancestral triggers of my psyche, what essences might be revealed,
which places within myself might I choose to visit? Watchful forever,
serene, my spirit at the centre sat in a circle mentally wrapping
around itself. Stella watches Stella the auld watches she young.

And shortly the auld maid arose and shed all her clothes saying
fare'll d'ye well, today. And the thing was, I could see myself
doing this and taking the torch and knowing the batteries were
low and without shoes and without a thought about the reality of
the trip two miles in the dark along a country road and through

174

muddy fields but it was cathartic, a journey made dreamlike by the drug and not caring if I was seen because I was unembarassable, safe within or beyond myself, seeing myself distantly, yet feeling as secure as I've ever felt and noises off were at a low ebb, there was a kind of singing in my ears, an occasional light effect mostly under my eyelids I think. I began to hear in my ear the thundering sound of my heart, the outrush of arteries, the infall of veins, and as I listened it began to slow until I felt myself straining to hear in the prolonged silences between the beats. Each gap was an abyss of perfect peace, of no contact with the body or solid surfaces. My anxiety ceased altogether. I began to develop an acute sense of smell – the night-time instincts. I sat on a stone wall with my bare feet in a pool of yellow light. I saw, or intuited, bats streak across the corners of my vision and heard worms disturb the surface close to my toes. Then I began to see vivid colours. The moon's ironic face, half-turned, a matinee idol, in a sky of mauve stripes, its reflection sideways, a raddled *chanteuse* in a nightclub *boudoir*. I was walking somehow inside my head comfortably inside a padded velvet skull-box, soft and warm. I remember fondling bark of an especially beautiful tree and stumbling a lot. I was unimpeded. I felt no weariness. I was making swift progress to the accustomed place, the familiar track, through the farmyard buildings the heap of discarded rubble the whisper of trees, the soggy squelch of last autumn's leaf mould underfoot and ascending softly happily to the stone circle high among swaying welcoming trees. I had no sense of the borders of the self but was able to touch and feel the sharp lip of the rock slabs of the headland enclosure and feel rain-forged dimples across the face of the entrance stone, and work, fingertip by fingertip, my way over and around. It seemed that I was looking for something. I sought something hidden, buried beneath
something previously visible
something beyond recall, ennervating some sixth sense
something I did not know but knew was there
something residual, atavistic, a possession whose ownership transcended my existence, an essence pre-existing the me of myself. I felt astonished, amazed, and completely calm all

together as I watched myself feel carefully along the wall, probing minute cracks and surfaces, slithering in the soft muddy litter, sinking to my knees, my scrabbling growing more frenzied and desperate. Yet the I who supervised myself was intensely calm and with equanimity observed the ruined fingers making claws to turf out a hollow below stones, digging like a badger in the dim light of the moon. I had no thoughts that were not pertinent to this and all I could think of was this time I am going to do it. The certainty held me transfixed. I was on my knees with my face pressed beneath the lowest stone of the face, at the base of a Douglas fir tree. Leaning deeper in, I could smell some strong scent unknown to me. I felt myself being drawn into some great hollow space, some other existence. I felt only exultation and great joy. I was going to do it. I was going to go in.

It was as if a voice, a sonorous but human voice, *vox humanitas*, was speaking to me, it was gentle and somehow familiar . . . press your fingers deep into the grooved stoneclefts, it seemed to say, where rain has fallen for centuries . . . feel your impact upon the dead . . . feel the vibrations of history at your fingertips. Lay your forehead on this ancient megalith, this holy *reliquiae* that connects us to the beginning of time. Listen deep down into the chained molecules of stoneness for the rhythmic incantations of ancestral blood . . . Oh deep deep is desire far away beneath borne upon the long rhythm of time and its years its years its years of mossy histories . . .

Slipping, sliding out of time, losing my handholds . . . falling? Or falling through time? I could no longer comprehend the voice which was far away behind but I felt movement downwards and in time, new sounds, new noises I couldn't distinguish. I felt myself losing sensibility of time, caught in its crux . . . St Brigid, calm bride of the white combs, I called upon you then to save me timeously . . .

> *stone, stone, cold here, fire-smells*
> *dark, dreadful . . . very very scared*
> *don't know when . . .*

they/we are sat/sitting around in a narrow clammy space lit only by a foul-smelling and crackling fire in a stone kist in the centre of this place dominated by ugly shadows and gutteral noise(s) they/we are talking/have talked and I/we feel overwhelming fear that I/we will be discovered as an intruder, a foreigner I/we am/are dominated by others this me that these others . . . we . . . are of the cumberlachs, fugitive slaves. Looking cautiously in the tight packed, smokeblacked space I/we see faces unshaven and blackened in smoke and shadow. I/we try to study them but my/our eyes are hazy . . . other's eyes . . . the eyes of a stranger. Suddenly there is a fearsome roar and a blinding light as part of the roof, I/we see now is turf, is lifted up and wind and rain and daylight crash into me/us. As my/our eyes adjust I/we soon see the others dressed in coarse wool although I/we only see their lower halves as they climb out of our shelter. Legs fastened in folds of thick wool swing in front of my face as someone clambers out then there is a delay and an unmistakable oath sworn and a strong hand grips me/us and hauls me/us out bodily. I/we am/are smaller than the rest, it seems, a youth, I/we see now as I/we stand amongst them beside the stone quarry. We are slave workers, I/we sense that we are unwilling, coarsened by toil, dumb beasts. I/we see armed kerns standing nearby. I/we see large forests on all sides. The kerns have short hair, some clean-shaven carry rectangular shields with a central boss. One or two have round metal helmets with flanged attachments over their ears. Their swords are short and thick with flared edges. One has metal ornaments on his arms and around his neck. The others seem to defer to him. Despite their weaponry they're rather short and puny. There is further uproar, an armed party is loudly arriving, many spears, many metal helmets, one carries a cloth banner on a pole, all have swords. Then we are running, pellmell through the trees, each for himself, in disorder. I/we find that my/our legs function very well and I/we leave behind me/us the shouts of the soldiers and the grunts of my/our fellows as I/we spring into deeper forest, a shadowed deep greenness of thickets and brambles and rampant sodden rhododendron cathedrals and rowans . . . others run naked screaming in the dawn and looking over my shoulder I/we see distant fire rinsing the bracken catching the brittle twigs yirding the crude thatch but my/our legs are weary and I/we collapse at last under a bush and hear only my/our gasping breath and the beat of my/our own fear. My/our legs ache.

And with these fingers these are my fingers invading at the private places but deep, deep, these fingers, my own leg, so minutely examined these mine the hair follicles, its scandalous bareness, presses deeper into the yielding ooze of mud between the my the toes . . .

Failing to create a spark from these old tombs, these cooling memories, this quietening glade, this slowing of corpuscles in the run of veins leaving you, Stella, lying in the trampled mud, alone, released, relieved, but with a thickening rime of sweat.

Much later I supposed in the abject darkness of the earth's night. Blackness so intense you can't see a hand placed on the end of your nose. Were it not for some stars of friendly disposition and a small sliver of an old sweetiewife moon, you could not have made the weary return journey, the torchlight, before it failed entirely, was paltry, then rancid . . .

What is it? What *is* it? Strange noise. Of metals colliding nearby. Not far. Familiar. It was as if something . . . suddenly connected . . . switched on like thermostats or air conditioners. It was a bell. Yes, *tintinnabulum*. A milkman's bell. The enchantment or trance or stupor was ended. I knew I could go inside. The doors were opened to me. I shivered uncontrollably as I entered in out of the cool dawn air. The mustiness and the foreign smells made my nostrils flare. I was absolutely numb and exhausted beyond all exhaustion.

I ran the shower and stood there on the brink of the falling screen of water, domestic, warmed, civilising water, with no memory, no joy, no anticipation. Then I stepped in and, at last, and in the cold light of dawn, began the brutal business of washing me off myself.

XII Cessio

AFTER I'D SLEPT around the clock, questions began to flood my brain in such profusion that I couldn't think at all. I let the telephone ring and ring. The priority was my sanity, or otherwise. Physically, I felt drained. My whole body ached and was covered in bruises and scratches. I couldn't write it off as merely a bad dream, like the nightdress incident. This time I had actually done what I dreamed I had done. It hadn't been a dream. My fingernails were ruined, my fingers were scabbed sore and blackened. Dried blood oozed from cuts and blisters on my soles and in the mirror I saw that I had a prominent scar on the bridge of my nose. My bedsheets and the duvet were a mess.

The one thing missing was any sense of excitement. I should have been *ecstatic*. Finally, I had made some sort of real connection . . . a sort of vision, brief revelation . . . whatever it was it was much more than I'd ever had before. But there was, instead of excitement, merely a feeling of responsibility. As if I had a duty to conceal what I had seen, to tell no-one. It was weird. The experience itself was too fragmentary to be of great value and, oddly, it was more a matter of smells and a sixth sense of alienness than a real piece of historical experience. There was nothing of language or cultural revelations, more a memory of great fear and the tactile vividness of the action, my flight through the woods, the smell of fire, the sounds of pursuit. It was more snapshot of the sensory than the historical.

It's two days later and I find I'm spending hours in front of old

179

photographs of myself. And peering into the mirror in the bedroom. In pictures I'm with others, or I'm alone elsewhere. I can never quite grasp the *otherness* of seeing myself. I'm always outside the inside of me. Looking in the mirror, I'm trying to trace the effects of time, the weight of each day pressing upon my face, trying to see beyond my eyes. Of course, I can tell you this, try to explain, but I can't do any more for you. You are the third participant and you must do it for yourself. This story is only this story for me, when it's with you, it's your story. I might be in it, but I'm only me in your story just as you can be her in mine.

The Curator was standing in my office and I almost bumped into him as I came in the door. His hand stretched out.

You have a copy of this manuscript?

Certainly. I handed it to him and noted that as he took it his hand was shaking. His face went suddenly pale then and he fell back or sat down abruptly. He flicked the cover over and I saw a tear start at his eyes.

Are you alright? I stammered.

Could you please . . . lock the door?

Certainly.

He flicked over the pages agitatedly, then made as if to rise. He gasped, choked, and just made it across the small office to the waste paper bin where he crouched and vomited.

I stood aghast, completely lost for words. A full minute passed in near silence.

When he could speak, I heard him say: I had . . . forgotten. It was so long ago. He coughed and dabbed at his wet mouth. In an earlier life . . .

And then I knew and yet could not fully believe.

You know, don't you? he queried, looking into my face. I found it rather uncomfortable. I nodded.

Well, I think I do. I think so.

Look, I'll be frank with you. I need your discretion. You work with Jill and . . .

Jill?

The Curator had been standing in my office and I almost bumped into him leaving as I came in the door. I put the manuscript down on Jill's desk.

You're so *young*, Jill. This was written before you were even born.

I thought you had decided it was 1975?

It was started then. Gerry started it in 1975.

Well, that was the year I was born. What a coincidence. I'm as old as this is. She held the thick wad of discoloured pages in her hand, as if weighing it. The fruit of his loins.

I must have paled visibly because she came over. Are you alright, Stella? Gosh, you've gone ever so white. Was it something I said?

No, no, I managed to croak out. I'm alright. Water . . .

Jill would never in her life come as close to real truth as she did then. Of course, I could not tell her. I knew that *absolutely*. It would wreck the lives of Stephen and Fay and Jill's adopted parents, Mr and Mrs Martin, and of course, Jill herself. Who could say what effect it might have on her. But I was greatly affected, I have to confess, by the sight of her standing there with that manuscript in her hand as if weighing it up, testing it's worth and value, when it and she had been conceived by the same man. Linda Scaith, an old schoolfriend

He began to cry. There is nothing more guaranteed to set my teeth on edge than the pathetic sound of a man's crying.

Jill knows more than she should, I said rather harshly.

He looked up. Ah, I see now that you don't understand after all. I've been . . . seeing . . . her, he said through his tears, head in his hands.

Seeing her? Oh, God. I had no idea. What a mix-up.

That's putting it mildly. I don't know what I'm going to do. What can I say to her?

But didn't you have any idea that the manuscript might be familiar to you? Didn't you see the piece about it in the *Courier*?

I was on holiday. I saw memos from Johnathan Weeder and yourself, but I never read – or even saw – the ms. All I was told was that it was a Dundee novel of the 1970s. It just didn't occur to me at all that it might be something I had written. I had forgotten all about it.

As you forgot about Fay? I said quietly.

Oh yes. Well that's hardly my fault. I didn't know at the time she was pregnant. And – there's no guarantee anyway that she – Jill is mine. His face crumpled anew into tears and self-pity.

Of course, I heard that Fay had paid a visit to my mother but by the time I returned to Dundee and learned that, Fay had left the city and it was too late. I suppose Jill *is* mine. I always felt we had a kind of psychic bond from the first. I don't suppose Fay would lie about a thing like that. What am I going to do? I feel such a fool.

Cancelling the 'Swinging Dundee' event might be a start.

Of course. Of course. No question. You were – are – right. Yes. And no-one must be told. I'll have to rely on your complete discretion. It's a very tricky situation.

I'm sure it must be.

now working at the DSS had sent me, as a personal and secret favour, the extract from her birth certificate, which listed her mother and father as Fay Mearns and Gerald McArdle, though the latter was not present at the birth in Dundee Royal Infirmary and is denoted as 'absent'. The only connection the two ever made was on the pages of this manuscript but to prove that, you will need the services of a forensic scientist. I knew that it was best to let sleeping dogs lie. There was no need to dig up bygones. Jill had made her bed and I must let her lie in it, without telling her about the gardener who had prepared that bed and sowed the seed.

I can see you might accuse me of being less than diligent. After all, I had incontrovertible proof of the name of the author of the manuscript. But Jill herself is the only absolute proof and I could not see how to proceed without causing the ruin of her life, and for all that, McArdle might be dead. What was the point? To make my decision easier, there was the continuing squabble over how to organise 'Swinging Dundee'. We'd had a parade of some of Brack's mates from the old days and far from being gallant desperadoes and handsome and witty womanisers, they were a dour and doggy lot, middle aged, undistinguished. A couple of wearied teachers, an accountant, a graphic designer, even a double-glazing salesman. Between them they had the charisma of a smoked haddock.

It was quite easy actually. I simply waited behind until everyone else had gone, until the cleaners were working elsewhere and all the office doors were open, then I made a swift raid on all the copies of the manuscript. There were only three and the original. No-one saw me leave the building. As soon as I got home, I dug a hole in the back garden not far from Fingal's little mound and dropped all of them in and covered it over. It was some time before anyone

Can I . . . rely upon your discretion? My wife . . . you know . . .

Yes. And I daresay Jill wouldn't be too pleased either if the whole thing came out.

Now, Stella, when I said I was seeing her, I don't want you to get the wrong impression. What I meant . . . mean . . . was that I took her out to dinner a couple of times. And a visit to the cinema. Nothing more. All perfectly innocent. I haven't . . . well, I have . . . but only twice. Thank god.

Jill never told me, I said. And I'm rather surprised about it.

I know what you mean. What did such an attractive young woman see in me. Say it. An old fool, well, middle aged anyway. But I'm being frank with you now. I hope you'll understand, holding nothing back, because I believe I can trust you, and because I feel you deserve some sort of an explanation. I'm not now as I was then. I used to be . . . well . . . you've read (or I assume you've read) the ms . . .

I have. And I would never have imagined it was written by you. For a start I was looking for an author named Gerald.

He stood up. It's my middle name. When I was younger, I disliked my Christian name, Frank. I can't remember why. It wasn't a question of using a pseudonym. I conceived the ms as a sort of diary, not as a novel. It was important to me then. As you can probably guess, I had some kind of a breakdown. I just lost my sense of who I was, a crisis of confidence.

Now – I have to go. We could perhaps talk later. I think I'm entitled to collect up all the copies of this. How many are there anyway?

Four, as far as I know.

Could you perhaps collect them for me? I'll be frank with you. I must absolutely rely on your continuing discretion.

Of course, I told him. In the interests mentioned anything about it and then there was uproar. For a day or two. No-one could quite believe what had happened. We searched high and low in the building for days and memos flew back and forth from the Curator to Johnathan, to Ron Howkins and to me. But eventually the whole thing quietened down and the event itself was mothballed.

Everyone got on with other projects and I wasn't sorry. Two weeks later, Ron Howkins was trying to enlist my support for something else.

It's a good idea, Stella, and it's not too far removed from what we were trying to achieve with our 'Swinging Dundee' project. You know, the one that was mysteriously cancelled for no very good reason.

There's nothing wrong with my memory. It was only two weeks ago for goodness sake.

Well, we should work together on this idea. I don't know what the precise problem was with 'Swinging Dundee', but I'm sure we could manage to circumvent any similar problems.

I'll ask Jill if she wants to be involved, but as for me . . .

Howkins looked baffled. Eh, Jill . . .? Who's Jill?

Jill Martin. I smiled. Who else?

Jill Martin? He repeated slowly as if he'd never heard the name.

Jill!

Sorry. I don't know who you mean.

For god's sake, Ron. What's going on? The girl who works here. In this office. With me. Long dark hair, long legs . . .

No-one works in this office except you. Not since John Barnet left.

He gave me an odd look, and walked out. I was so shocked I sat down. What was going on? That afternoon, I left early to avoid the rush-hour traffic. I made myself a coffee and sat, fuming, in the conservatory till Tony arrived home.

What's up? he queried. Not bad news? Not Council reorganisation?

of your wife . . . Jill, and her step-parents and Fay and Stephen Brack, I'll say nothing.

No-one else knows, except you. No-one else could possibly imagine . . .

No. And Jill?

Well, of course, I won't be seeing her again – not in that way. In fact, I can't see her at all. That's to be my punishment of course. To be in the proximity of my daughter without being acknowledged as her father.

Yes. That will be hard for you.

He put out his left hand and grasped the doorknob. Thank you. Thank you for your help and your sympathy. He held out his right hand. I'd like you to understand . . . I feel as if you might . . . If you've read this.

I'd welcome a private discussion on the manuscript. Just to clear up loose ends for my own information, although officially all research on it will end now.

And if you could collect up the copies. It'll need to be done carefully without alerting suspicions. Tact will be needed with Ron Howkins: he's rather keen on the idea of an event.

And already I was conspiring with him. Him? The despoiler of his own daughter. The incestuous philanderer, adulterer, drug-taking waster . . . my boss, the Curator, F. G. McAdam.

Not yet no. Ron bloody Howkins. That's what. He's absolutely the end. I think he's having some kind of a breakdown. I had him in the office today trying to say he's never heard of Jill.

Never heard of her? You mean the girl that works with you? And he . . .?

Yes. Denied even knowing her name. Which is amazing as I've told you how often he letches after her.

From what you told me about her, I'd be letching after her myself.

And you wouldn't ever letch after me, I suppose?

Of course I would. You're my wife. I wouldn't have married you if I hadn't fancied you. You know that. But she – Jill – is only 21, isn't she? I mean, I know how much you'd like to be her, well, be 21 at least.

She's 22. And she is very like me, or me as I used to be. You know, dear, sometimes I think I'm losing my marbles. Weird things are happening to me. Those strange dreams.

Dreams? You mean *the* dream? That's what ten years of marriage does to the sane, I expect, Tony said. Let's stop talking about work. Now look here, wifelet, have you fed Fingal yet?

And so I sat down again with the blinking manuscript and read the damned thing again, skimming and scanning the pages, searching for the clues I'd missed. Lester Logan/Stephen Brack? Well, it was believable. Once a writer, always a writer . . . the exuberance remains. But could he be the author of the manuscript? Are he and Gerry one and the same? Was Gerry his *alterego*? No. Jolly well impossible. Brack had referred to himself as *the story-teller* and Gerry as a *secondhand* retaler. The other factual elements? Set in Benvie Road not Pole Street. True. Gerry's mother and stepfather, various friends, failed relationship with Wanda . . . god knows. Ah here: *Living in Dundee is a game of senses . . . I was trying to remember . . . these encounters . . .*

183

Blondine . . . Ann . . . the two Donnas . . . another girl after a party in a flat in the Blackness Road. Later, I learned she was only 16. Never saw her again and I can't remember her name so she doesn't really count . . . Oh Gerry, how callous that is! In your single-minded journey to Spain or oblivion or mental breakdown to build your sandcastle what a wreck you made. What pact with the devil had you that in this casual throw-away sentence tucked in a hedonist's paragraph, life, born out of Blackness could erupt unheeded? *Not really count?* Because *you* can't remember, it doesn't exist? As you thrashed your way south, dribbling adjectives and verbs, here a noun was conceived from a discarded sentence. If the word is law, or the word is God, or is with God, here it is Jill, daughter of Fay, disowned, unknown, unknowing, abandoned on the margins, between the lines of the stories.

But the existence of this girl Jill – her paternity – and any connection there might be with the Curator will remain a subject of conjecture since I'm sworn to silence. My sanity or the existence of a husband and a living cat and the truth of *everything* I've told you is privileged information which you can only accept or reject. In whole or in part. What you believe depends on your reading of the manuscript. What you remember and understand. You are the third participant, enfranchised to decide and you must involve yourself in the process of decision.

You could, of course, try a short-cut, try to speak direct to the Curator, though I doubt if she will agree to see you. I have extricated myself finally from the project of exploring Gerry's manuscript – have passed that responsibility over to you. I hereby jolly well and absolutely utterly abrogate any involvement. The responsibility is now yours, enjoy. Frankly, it bored me.

Anyway all that was a year ago and I'm long gone. I accepted a full-time doctoral post at St Andrews to complete my paper. I'm well clear of local government and just as well; it's been a time of reorganisation – cutbacks and redundancies. I got out just in time. The Celtic Mormaers of Angus thesis is now nearly complete. It'll make a book. There's a publisher interested. Life is good.

Actually, I'm jolly sorry I'm about to abandon you like this, directionless, gasping for some sense of it all, some meaning linked to time and place. Where's the *Tumulus* you might ask? Not even a bloody hill . . . a damp sandcastle . . . led all the way through these pages for nothing! But it's all around you, your place on the map, your relationship with the dead. Anyway, I'm not leaving you, it's more like you're leaving me. We don't construct these stories, stories construct us, we are the manipulated, the *material*, honed and shaped in the slipstream of time. So Logan and Big Bob, Billy Forbes, Ronald Bennet, all the others we've met and Ron Howkins and Stephen Brack – and me, of course – all tumble in the swirling dark water as others stare in, faces a pink blur, close to the surface, where the sunbeams strike the water *in that mysterious place half-afraid* in the seconds before we fall in face first and drown in our facticity.

And there you have it, my dear friends. All of it is *tumulus*. Each time I take it out – the original copy by the way – I'm astonished at the quantity of dust on it. How quickly dust accumulates on all that does not move! I wish I could say that the manuscript stories are in some way apocryphal. Well, perhaps they are. Perhaps it's like the story of fairy hill, into which a person is enticed, coming out again to find the world had aged, atrophied, but that he/she is no older. When the reader finally puts down the book he/she discovers that it's already well past bedtime. It's not where you've been but what it was like being there.

So. To summarise. I've Dundee under my fingernails but even I cannot tell what occurs in the spaces before silence or who lives under the raindrop or what happens in the cities beneath this one. Perhaps Brack is right. Maybe all we can know is that some people lived before us and we can tell almost nothing about the things that really mattered to them. Perhaps there is no way in. I don't think that I found one, whatever else I might believe of that odd night at Kingennie or however else I might categorise it. And Gerry too is right. On his very first page: *It is words that bury us, words that smother . . . And yet in words, at other times . . . we can wriggle out from under*. Words are the key. They can confirm or

185

confuse. We know they are in there, our ancestors – the voca-
bulary of human experience – *the foul hordes, like dark throngs of*
worms, who wriggle out of narrow fissures in the rock when the sun
is high and the weather grows warm, as St Patrick said to the early
kings of Dalriada, in what he intended as a good strategic joke at
the expense of the Picts.

FINIS

Taodunum, MCMXCIX